Secret Smuggler of the Sea

Amundson / Porter Adventure, Volume 3

Clifford Farris

Published by Desert Coyote Press LLC, 2022.

Also by Clifford Farris

Amundson / Porter Adventure
The New Viking Gold Mine
Secret Smuggler of the Sea

Porter / Amundson Adventure
Agilis Rising Under Sail
Secret Smuggler of the Sea

Watch for more at https://desertcoyotepress.com/.

Table of Contents

To Ann, my long-suffering wife as an author's widow. You can add my dog, Ozzie, for the walks he missed.

ISBN: 978-1-7332512-7-3

Cover design by CBF.
Book design by CBF.
Published and Printed by Desert Coyote Press LLC
Littleton, CO USA
Desertcoyotepress.com
CliffordFarris@Desertcoyotepress.com

Chapter 1—India

" . . . And a white tiger too drunk to fly?" said Bjorn with a wicked mischievous grin as he held up a gin and tonic garnished with a slice of lime, and clinked the ice.

"Dangerously hung over?" said his substantial seafaring companion, Master Porter with a wink and wave of his cigar.

They sat in wicker chairs around an elephant-shaped table. Bjorn studied the serene Explorer Room of the Bengal Club in Calcutta, India. Trophies from every continent or one of the seven seas proclaimed an intrepid hunter's adventure. His gaze explored a giant globe in the center of the room that displayed the latest findings of geography.

"My friend, we have seven oceans and five continents to explore. You at twenty-four and me at twenty-six we have to speed our adventures."

"I'm too busy sailing the clipper brig, *Agilis*, for side adventures."

A matching pair of vertical elephant tasks six feet long framed a painting of brave explorers confronting the world's wildlife. In the center was a spotted leopard lunging from a pedestal, teeth exposed in a silent roar.

The Bengal club overlooked the esplanade with an English elegance that made it the social center of the largest, richest city in India. Polished brass fixtures were equal to those in Windsor Castle, home of Queen Victoria, back in England. Flags of every nation in the British empire decorated one wall. The wood panels gave off the aroma of rich, polished varnish.

"White or orange, I hope to meet a Bengal tiger before I leave India." He frowned at the spots covering the leopard.

Bjorn and Richard looked across the table to the agent of the East India Company. After seventeen years in Calcutta, a man surely knew tigers.

"The Bengal tiger eats anything on four legs and occasionally harvesters on two, so say the natives. Only starving will the beast eat fermented berries and never to inebriation."

"I have a cat story," said Bjorn, holding out his arm marked with a maze of scars. "A cougar jumped me in California until my dog chewed off her tail." Those claws and teeth left these scars to remind me."

"Remind you of what?"

His blue eyes sparkled, "Why am I back in cat country? I never saw a tiger growing up in Norway, and nature's felines resent my intrusion on their hunting grounds."

"Don't worry, B'horny. A Bengal tiger will spit out his first bite of your Norwegian butt."

"Let's forget about my Mexican Spanish friend who couldn't say my honorable name Bjorn in English."

"Okay."

Richard shook his sweaty curly brown hair and looked at the rectangular fan hung from the ceiling. Slow currents of hot air gave an illusion of comfort but cooled nothing, despite the punkah wallah native pulling the cord.

"Should said tiger hunt a Viking, may I suggest a meal named B'horny?"

"They prefer dog-tired prey in the cool breezes of the evening."

"Cool? Calcutta is an open sweat lodge."

Richard explained the Pomo Indian tribe of California made him an honorary member with a sweat lodge ceremony. "I cannot imagine why Christopher Columbus was so anxious to reach Bengal since the Caribbean Lake is superior. He called the Carib peoples Indians while inhabitants of the India subcontinent called themselves Hindustani."

"I call them natives and your point is irrelevant," said the agent in a tone that settled the issue. He yawned and turned to a portrait on the wall. "I am retiring next year to the cool Himalayan foothills. My God, won't 1854 and this heat ever end? Where's the damn monsoon? It is late."

Beads of sweat dripped from Bjorn's scars. Richard's hair was drenched.

The camaraderie of the gin slumped into daydreams while the pendulum in a tall clock tick-tocked the afternoon away. Bjorn imagined he was climbing a snow-covered mountain in Norway, and Richard savored a refreshing wind in his face aboard his brig, *Agilis*. She lay moored in the Hooghly River among a massive fleet of ocean-going vessels waiting to carry the world's commerce from Calcutta.

The agent's British accent interrupted their reverie. "Drunken tigers are unknown, but not elephants. A pachyderm got wild drunk on rice wine and trampled six people to death before the mahout regained control.

Richard said, "Sounds like my command. Worthless sea dogs when they're drunk, present company and gin excepted, but often useful sober." He raised his glass. "I watched a marauding squirrel inebriate itself on a fermented pumpkin back in New England. It couldn't climb two feet without plopping off, giggling and jerking four little legs in the air."

The table chuckled at the image of jerking squirrels.

"The Bengal region is home to a famous local example."

"Of what?"

The mariners listened now fully attentive.

"A troop of monkeys lives within the walls of the opium factory in Ghazipur. They drink the wastewater and get addicted to the traces of opium in it. The junkie monkeys have lived there for generations. Their walking skeletons won't forage for food, but those rascals do love their fix."

Richard Porter pounded the wicker elephant table and knocked three Waterford crystal glasses to the floor where they shattered. "By God, I've had crew members act the same way. I hate addicts!" White-robed servants replaced the gins and tonic before others swept up the shards of hand-cut glass.

Bjorn wrapped his hand the size of a gorilla's around his new glass and pointed his forefinger at Porter, "With due respect, my opinionated companion of countless adventures, I've sailed with more than one tar who chewed a bit of opium and still made a good mate. By the way, Port, you're getting a little hefty around the middle. Maybe you should climb the rigging to see what we do up there."

"Humph."

"No need to argue, gentlemen. Some men embrace fine brandy, others demon rum. I say let each man handle his own behavior. You will agree, I am sure."

Porter sipped from his glass and said, "Vessels of all kinds stretch for miles along the Hooghly River. Is that common?"

The smug agent brushed a fly off his nose and said, "Calcutta is the port from which the Honorable East India Company supplies half the world with goods. I presume your *Agilis* is securely moored, Mr. . . . what was your name? The Hooghly experiences a tidal bore from the Bay of Bengal twice a day. Vessels surge and roll from the sudden lift of six or seven feet during the passage. Springs must be added to the moorings to relieve the tension on the cables."

"I knew you were prosperous, but that is remarkable."

"We need to discuss your cargo for the East India Company, or EIC as we call it. It is June and the southwest monsoon is nigh. The fleet of sails that embarks to Singapore and the China Sea is impressive, and you will be among their number." He left out that pirates infested the route and elevated the seagoing banditry of their ancestors to new levels of savagery.

"The dockworkers will load your shipment to catch these favorable winds. Will you return this winter on the northeast monsoon?"

"I think not," said Bjorn. "I have a lady friend waiting in San Francisco . . ., I hope." His gaze, framed by his long golden hair that emphasized his rugged Viking presence, penetrated the dark mahogany wall panels and crossed the Pacific to the *Rancho Petaluma Adobe* in Sonoma, California. Maria's scarf waving from the balcony two years ago wished him good luck on the ocean abyss.

Absentmindedly returning her gesture from his wicker chair, he sighed, "Wait for me, Maria, I'm coming home."

Porter tapped his foot and mumbled, "Your EIC ignores the damage your opium causes in China. It destroys the people's ambition and frees foreigners to plunder the Celestial Empire."

Disapproval sullied his handsome face that was beginning to show wrinkles of wisdom from seven years at sea. The last three as master brought on several gray hairs, but not enough to make him distinguished.

The agent chose not to hear him. "Your cargo includes the major product from Ghazipur. As legal as Darjeeling tea, it brings profit to Bengal. I am told it eases the misery of the huddled yellow masses of Cathay."

Bjorn and Porter looked at the mounted trophies on the walls that stared back with glass eyes.

Brushing another fly off his finger knuckle, "While waiting on her Majesty's infernal bureaucracy, I propose a game of Fly Loo."

Bjorn said, "Fly what?"

"Each player places a lump of sugar on the table and makes a wager. The first lump to attract a fly wins. It is felicitous to sample tonic water with a tot of gin during the interim"

"I can't handle more in this heat," said Bjorn.

"Waiter! Sugar cubes." The immaculate Indian in gleaming white muslin placed a bowl of cubes on the wicker table in front of the agent, who passed it around.

Bjorn and Porter kissed their lumps for good luck and arranged them with elaborate gambling gestures. The agent placed his precisely with no gesture.

"Gentlemen, your wagers?"

Bjorn pulled a small garnet from his pocket. "I wager this first-class red garnet from the New Viking Gold Mine I once owned."

With a grunt, the agent said, "Passable but a shabby trifle compared to the rubies from Burma."

"I pledge a fine historical sextant that has guided my *Agilis* across the seas of the world."

"Such an instrument lacks value on land, but an itinerant ship captain might be interested."

"Your wager, sir?"

"There are reports of a man-eating tiger roaming the Sundarban region of East Bengal. I wager a tiger hunt from the back of elephants, and guarantee they will be sober."

The Fly Loo contestants struggled to survive on gins and tonic, while the contrary flies walked around Richard's chapped nose, along the scars on Bjorn's muscular arms, and over the agent's gaunt shoulders.

Despite the excitement, the trio nodded off in the stuffy room to the tick-tock of the longcase clock from Thwaites and Reed, East Sussex, England. It marked the passing of the universe one second at a time and sang the Westminster chimes before striking each hour. It was commissioned exclusively for the East India Company of India.

"Loo!" They leaped out of their languor to the agent's shout.

A fly preened its wings on Bjorn's lump.

"Fair and square," said Richard. "I'll give you the sextant when we return to Agilis."

The agent said, "Beyond all doubt. There's a hunt leaving tomorrow for the vicious man-eating white tiger that is terrorizing the farmers."

Porter glanced at Bjorn. "Our honor, I'm sure. White like a ghost?"

"I cannot guarantee the color but that is the report. Our armory will loan you firearms for protection. By the way, your companion waiting in the vestibule has been a good sport and he may join you. I hear rumors he is an exceptional nautical chef."

Richard said, "You mean Maverick Hatfield. He prepares the best mess on the ocean, but how do you know that?"

"It behooves the EIC to know everything."

"Don't forget, I recommended him," said Bjorn.

"Don't forget, I signed him to Agilis."

"He can barbecue a tiger. I guarantee it."

"Calcutta was interesting, but this steamy Sundarban jungle is wild and exotic," Bjorn said to Richard and Maverick.

Bjorn peered into walls of tangled vegetation on the banks to the soft splashes of the oars the boatman made maneuvering their dinghy canoe up the lazy waterway. They glided by fish cages inside rings of vertical logs to prevent floating away. Blue-backed kingfishers and green-feathered pittas flashed their colors overhead from shore to shore. Curious wild boar and macaque monkeys ventured onto the exposed mudflats to view the intrepid first-time hunters.

Bjorn stared back and noted pathways in the dirt, tufts of orange fur on branches, and a range of sounds, origin unknown.

He half-listened to Maverick muttering at the bushes. The happy, lean cook hummed an old folk tune that echoed through Tennessee hollows. Searches for savory herbs were lessons his grandmother knew that worked on jungle plants too. "What tastes do those strange leaves have? I'll flavor my Sundarban-tiger stew if I can grab some." Green leaves were beyond his grasp. Biting insects, he could not stop. Slapping his arms and back, "Wish something would eat these clouds of biting-me bugs"

Their native shikari guide delivered a running commentary from the bow in British English among twisted roots of mangrove trees. "This area is untamed but not to fear because I know the wildlife by their calls. We're in the Sundarbans which are the natural home of the Bengal tiger. There's one now."

All eyes followed his outstretched finger, but only Bjorn's sharp eyes spotted the orange eyes with slits measuring his prey's strength, their strengths. The stripes on the beast blended with the vegetation and no one but the shikari saw the crouched body, the quivering muscles.

"The tiger attacks from behind and prompts cane cutters to wear masks on the back of their heads. It works until the astute tigers learn the trick and resume mauling the workers."

Bjorn swatted biting bugs as the boat approached the village of basic huts and drifted to a stop against a bamboo jetty. A handwritten sign with a crude drawing of a crouching tiger welcomed hunters.

The party stepped into the outpost deep in the Sundarbans. The shikari conversed briefly with the elder, Abdul Bari.

Abdul greeted them. "I am glad you have come, and we implore your help. A rogue tiger mauled my brother five days ago. My son, at twelve years old, banged pots with the villagers to drive the beast away, but it bit my brother bad." He smiled at his son and said, "You did the best you could."

"I was safe surrounded by many men," said the boy with sad bravado, "but I failed."

"Welcome to our humble settlement. You must be hungry and thirsty after your trip. I have refreshments for you while the village prepares your hunt." He motioned to his wife. "The best for our guests." She fetched a platter filled with fruits and dried fish followed by a teen-aged girl carrying a pitcher of an unknown fermented beverage and cups. She served each guest, starting with the blond Viking descendant.

A wide smile, tiny waist, large eyes framing, "I'm in love," said Bjorn.

"Down boy. No, you're not in love."

Seated on stumps around a central stump, the others served themselves while Abdul organized their expedition.

Abdul motioned for help to unload four enormous guns, a mound of pistols, ammunition, and powder from the dinghy, which rose several inches in the river. Three elephants tethered to trees around a clearing watched with bored interest. They had seen these activities before.

Richard winked at Maverick and snuck up behind Bjorn. With his best imitation of the roar of an attacking tiger, he dug his fingers into the tense shoulders over the scars and roared in his ear. Feeling like prey from experience, Bjorn shot his arms into the air, swung around, and knocked his assailant to the ground. Richard, who was putting on pounds from Maverick's dinners, lay breathless for a few moments.

Bjorn shook himself and said, "Never again, Port. I won't be gentle next time." Richard and Maverick bent over laughing.

Maverick was speechless, but not the guide. "No make monkey tricks, esteemed sahibs. Hunting predators that hunt you is serious work."

Abdul called the hunting party to the trailhead leaving the village and pointed to the biggest animal footprint anyone had seen.

"The man-eater has been here, see."

Crowding around the impression in the dirt, Bjorn spread his fingers and aligned his foot with the impression, "Nine inches across. Chasing prey because the claws extend beyond the pads."

"Bears grow big paws in Tennessee but this beats them by a country mile."

A beetle tumbled into the footprint and Maverick raised his foot to stomp it. In an instant, the mahout restrained the raised foot. "Sahib, deep apologies, but life is sacred. It makes bad karma to kill a life, even an insect. You do not eat them, do you?"

"Never in a thousand years will I eat bugs," said Maverick. The mere thought caused his stomach to flip. "Poor starving people might catch grasshoppers, but thank God I'm not them. Give me a good old beefsteak."

The idea of a steak horrified the Hindu mahout who said, "Our sacred cows are holy. We never kill to eat. You must not either."

Bjorn was too busy carrying the little beetle to safety to join the fuss about sacred cows versus beefsteak. He empathized with underdogs, even those with shiny green built-in armor. He also liked beef.

Karma aside, the size of the print terrified the village as they chattered in Bengali.

"Here is our target," said the shikari impatient to start. He said the tiger was resting, and they had a favorable chance for a shot if they hurried. He led them to the circle of gray swaying elephant trunks.

Bjorn looked up . . . and up . . . and up. "Holy mackerel, my bucking bull in the rodeo was big but these beasts are colossal. Do we ride them?"

Richard said, "Sure you want to? You flew off that bull in front of Maria with the shortest time on record. I can't imagine she was concerned about your condition."

"I'll ride if you please keep your hands off my scars." The fake lion and cook laughed all over again, and the guide frowned.

"Quiet!"

Maverick looked at the three lumbering animals and said, "Them's the biggest brutes I've seen. It needs a forest fire and my secret sauce to barbecue one."

"Watch your language. This dry season before the monsoon makes a jungle wildfire dangerous to animals and people."

"What's that cage on his back?" said Bjorn.

"A howdah."

"How do you get in? No ladder," pointing at the elephant's back.

The mahout explained. "Please to mount on the right where she can see you because she will attack from the left or behind. When she is happy, she flaps her ears and sways the trunk and tail. The trunk examines you for food, but it tickles. If they stare at you with their trunk in their mouth, they feel threatened; do not approach."

Bjorn thought, I still can't climb the damn thing.

"When the animal bends the leg into a step, mount and swing a foot over the shoulder. Dismount the same way."

The shikari shouted to the mahouts, "Please to help these hunters."

The lead mahout tapped the elephant's right side upon which she dutifully bent her right front leg into a step. The mahout motioned for Richard to mount and pull himself into the howdah. Bjorn took the next one.

It was Maverick's turn except the elephant smelled food on his clothes and boosted him by his crotch straight up to the howdah. Richard and Bjorn laughed at the final swat that pushed him to his embarrassment. Maverick studied the swamp on the other side of the elephant. They could not tell if the elephant laughed along with them, but she seemed to enjoy her trick.

The guide handed a rifle to each hunter along with two howdah pistols, the large-caliber handguns with double barrels.

Putting his hands to his mouth like a megaphone, Bjorn hollered, "Here kitty, kitty. Come to papa."

A whispered explosion wracked the shikari. "Quiet! Ignorant white devil." He put his finger to his lips and motioned Bjorn to shut the hell up in Hindustani body language. Torrents of curses in Hindi and Bengali went over Bjorn's head, which was probably a good thing.

The expedition of great white hunters lurched into their first tiger hunt.

Footprints of all kinds assured they were following a natural pathway. Humid pungent odors of fungus, dying plants, insects, flowers on vines, and animal droppings marked the way away from the settlement.

"Striped tigers swim from island to island to hunt deer, wild pigs, macaques, and a honey gatherer now and then." Bjorn soaked up every word of the shikari's explanation.

The stalking squad searched for orange eyes weighing the odds of a successful attack. Negative if the prey was alert.

The lead mahout cautioned that elephants knew their height with the howdah but not riders. He warned them to watch for overhead branches.

Bjorn the tallest pulled his head down a notch or two. A branch that cleared him would clear the others with room to spare.

Relishing his role as the resident expert, the shikari explained that man-eaters hid in sugarcane and waited to pounce on weak victims. "The attack explodes in a streak of orange and black stripes from nowhere and is over." The mahouts studied the trail for the spore to back up the sharp eye of the shikari.

Bjorn watched the guide with calm courage through wary blue eyes. He remembered the cougar assault and thanked his dog for chewing off its tail to save his life. No dogs ran through the legs of the elephants.

Turning backward on the lead animal, their guide whispered to the tiger hunters, "Even in mid-afternoon, the stripes are hard to see in the grass and impossible in the dark. But you can be certain the teeth and claws are always sharp, day or night, dusk or dawn. The men refuse to work or leave the village. If we have a successful hunt, Abdul Bari will turn the pelt into a prized rug."

Bjorn loaded his borrowed rifle with gunpowder and bullets. Richard did the same and said to Bjorn, "It is rare for the master of a small brig to join a tiger hunt, and unknown for a passenger. You are lucky and double for you, Maverick. The"

Sighting along the barrel, Bjorn said, "Look at the length of this gun. It would bring down an elephant." He paused a moment and patted the shoulder of the beast under him. "Sorry about that. We're still friends, aren't we? This is our grandest adventure ever, eh Port."

The falcon eyes of the shikari scanned every bush, vine, mangrove, and dense undergrowth to listen for the sounds of a stalking tiger, but their heavy breathing and that of the elephants obstructed any faint noises. He watched overhead for a circle of crows hovering over a fresh kill.

"This is fun."

"A new adventure for sure."

The guide offered a last bit of advice." If one of us gets separated, he should break the branches of trees on the side in the direction he goes. Leave the broken parts hanging at turning points or creeks so a search party will know his route."

Stuffy warm air filled with body odor, while naturally sweet plants attracted insects and pollinators, and flying bugs turned to sour grit between their teeth.

"We do this every month," said the shikari. "I hope you are enjoying yourselves."

"Completely."

"For sure."

"Where does the ganga grow?"

The elephants dragged the riders under slippery leaves, rough vines, cracked branches and squeezed through a stand of bamboo. The shikari said the striped beast they were stalking was the angry soul of an ancient tribal leader protesting the destruction of the jungle.

Bjorn mumbled under his breath, foolish superstitions.

"Quiet and do not mock beliefs, they can be right. These sinuous animals are ghosts of Aleya living in this delta of the Ganges. Our folklore identifies her as the spirit that lures people into the swamps and drowns them. I warn you, do not chase those floating blue lights in the trees. Aleya's ghost floats above the marshy waters but vanishes when you approach. You die and your spirit becomes the next Aleya."

The procession covered several miles at a measured pace. Sleepiness befogged the mariners as initial excitement faded to boredom under the relentless barrage of insects in muggy monotony.

Caws of crows were the first sign of activity. Their presence warned of a kill, likely guarded by the killer protecting its meal. Underfoot, the spacing of cat tracks showed a leisurely walking pace that led toward the crows with drag marks between two rows of giant alternating footprints.

Bjorn said, "Interesting how animals get along unless they eat each other, but they never hate."

Fresh mixed tracks brought the caravan to a stop. A handgun and a half-smoked chillum pipe of cannabis lay inside the depression of a huge cat print, but they were too late. Nearby lay the half-eaten carcass of Abdul's brother.

Sobbing, the shikari said, "Jungle wisdom is, 'Never wake a sleeping tiger. You do not want to be in its eye.' I say the tiger wants to not be in my eye. It sleeps nearby." He sighed, "Coveted parts of the carcass will follow the opium road to China."

Richard said, "How big do they get?"

"Six hundred pounds. Tigers are rare and valuable because their organs, blood, and bone are much sought after in traditional medicine. Whiskers make the users bulletproof and powdered bones soothe their aches and pains. Rich people from Tokyo to Moscow pay thousands of dollars for a pelt. All parts are powerful, including tiger penis soup to make a lover viral."

Bjorn said, "I am the beast of the bed without tiger dick soup."

Richard said, "I don't doubt it, B'horny. You earned that name somewhere."

"Go to hell. I treat the ladies with respect, in contrast to certain others who abandoned them."

"What are you talking about?"

A hungry streak in orange and black stripes leaped to the rump of Bjorn's elephant and clamped its teeth and claws with a vengeance. Sharp daggers of pain jabbed into the beast's guts. Trunk in mouth, it hunched like an earthquake. The wounded elephant stretched her trunk to bellow anguish and twisted to beat the stripped claws away. The effort ripped the straps securing the howdah to her back and pitched it to the bare ground. On impact, the once beautiful construction collapsed in a pile of splinters. The tiger sprang over the back to attack the mahout, a smaller bite-sized target. She lacerated his arm with sharp fangs that he held up in defense and knocked him into the vegetation.

The guide said, "Strange that the cat released him. They usually carry away their kill to eat."

Riding the howdah down, Maverick landed first and cushioned Bjorn's fall. A loaded elephant gun bounced on them but did not discharge. Bjorn scrambled to his feet and grabbed the elephant gun that worked on tigers as well as larger targets. With his blue eyes and long arms, he aimed. One blast stopped the ferocious animal in mid-bite at the elephant's shoulder, and it collapsed its way to death.

Running up, the shikari said, "Good shot, sahib. Are you all right?"

Richard jumped from his perch on the next animal to help the fallen hunters sprawled on the pile of splinters. "Are you hurt?"

"Better'n falling from a yardarm to the deck planks. Dirt is softer than wood, a little."

Seeing that Bjorn was uninjured, he said, "You wanted to see a tiger before we left India. Here's your chance, close and personal."

"I didn't expect that close."

Maverick was another story. He moaned and could not stand up. Bjorn helped him to his feet. After several quivering deep breaths, he rubbed the back of his neck, smoothed his light brown hair, and said, "I'm fine. Let's go." Bjorn patted his shoulder, "Hang in there partner."

The shikari commented indifferently the mahout can live with one arm. Maybe work elephants in the field, but no longer could guide a hunt.

They rested while the two healthy mahouts took the bleeding, terrified mount, and injured mahout back to the village. Returning with a replacement elephant, they searched the area from their howdahs.

The hunters discovered a lifeless orange and black stripped carcass in the deep grass. "She was in terrible pain from a mass of porcupine quills embedded in the arm and pad of her right leg," said the shikari.

Maverick shuddered because he hated porcupines from painful experiences.

"Nine-inch quills struck a bone and doubled back out. See where she chewed the emerging points to the base and tried to extract them with her teeth."

He poked at the flesh that was soapy and dark yellow under the skin. She must have moaned when she walked, but we couldn't hear the soft sounds over our heavy breathing."

The debilitated paw meant the cat could not hunt normal prey and was forced to search for easier meals. Off to the side, the Hindu mahouts made peace with their karmas.

No action of a human was pardoned. He always submitted to the fruits of his actions, good and bad. God accepted everyone with their flaws, but a man could be reincarnated or cursed as his karma dictated. The mahouts were prepared.

The tiger was orange and black.

Five days before the hunt, the duo of Master Richard Porter strutting on deck and Bjorn standing in the rigging watched the Bay of Bengal divide around *Agilis* and rejoin in the wake.

Porter, using the customary last name onboard instead of Richard, read his well-worn sextant and said, "Twenty-two degrees thirty minutes north and the logbook has us eighty-eight degrees west. That muddy water ahead must be the Hooghly River. We are in India, my friend."

"I see it. Mates tell me high tide launches a tidal bore up the river at six knots. It capsizes small boats extending upstream a hundred miles to Calcutta."

Bjorn clamored down the ratlines to the deck, "I'm halfway around the world in India? Can you believe it?"

"The East India Company in London gave me secret instructions to load an undefined cargo from Ghazipur, situated inland up the Hooghly and Ganges Rivers. I have to contact their governor in Calcutta for approval. The laws of India make our presence upstream highly illegal."

"What's in Ghazipur?

"A delivery destined for Canton, China."

Bjorn did not inquire further because he knew Asia was the theater of strange endeavors better left unsaid and unknown.

Porter said, "You're the sharpest lookout on board. Even though you are a passenger, please watch for the Bengal Pilot Service brig. Nearby, we'll find a lightvessel at sea, what a lighthouse is on land. Look for a red stripe on the side with Pilot Ridge in white letters. It has a forty-four-foot mast with a ball at the head and flashes a light you can see twelve miles away.

"Ship ahoy. Pilot Ridge, two points to starboard." *Agilis* approached and lowered her sails to wait.

A shouted stream of profanity rising from a rowboat furiously splashing toward them announced the river pilot. Regulations and common sense required a guide up the treacherous Hooghly amongst the bars, shoals, bends, and tidal bore to Calcutta and he was it.

Such a stream of blasphemous obscenities poured from the gentleman's mouth that Bjorn could hardly understand him. By ignoring three out of four foul words and interpreting the thick Cockney accent of the rest, he might have said, "The Hooghly is known . . . to be one of the most dangerous rivers in the world . . . curves and bends, very strong current, and bars, parts of the river you cannot cross at ebb tide. The . . . soundings change two . . . feet between tides with . . . silt scoured from the Himalayas. Swiftest . . .

current in straights is middle of the stream, but . . . curved portions . . . outer edge. . . . water is deepest."

Agilis dropped anchor near Calcutta a dumbfounded day and a half later and paid off the profane pilot with relief.

Outlasting protests from the port authority about the irregular destination and bureaucratic wrangling within the EIC bureaucracy, Porter received a reluctant waiver to visit Ghazipur at his own risk.

Their new native pilot was polite and knowledgeable.

Maverick took a break from the stifling galley to stand at the railing and enjoy the plains of Uttar Pradesh state bordering the Hoogley River on the way to the Ganges. Endless fields of white poppy flowers painted the hills to the horizon. Wafts of air brought a sweet, powdery floral fragrance that was new to the cook. The calm directions of the native river pilot gave him confidence they would arrive in Ghazipur, even with the squalls passing over the land and the shifting river bottom.

He plied the pilot with extra tidbits from the pantry in thanks for his diligence.

A slap on the shoulder startled him when Bjorn dropped from the ratlines, "How goes it?"

"I've slaved all day to feed you hungry bastards. I can't imagine why."

"You love us."

"Like hell."

Bjorn said Maverick was lucky he delayed their departure from San Francisco to wait for him. "You are quite the cook for a new jack-tar."

"It's over a year and I'm as seasoned as anybody, but don't call me good. It's a losing battle to hash out salt beef into something fit for human consumption. When the stove pitches from side to side and there are no spices for flavor you get crap."

"I praised you a wonderful chef to get you signed. Since we partnered in the New Viking Gold Mine, we have to stick together. Your barbecued wild hog was a crowd-pleaser."

"It was my secret sauce."

"The marketplace in Ghazipur, if we ever get there, has every seasoning, herb, zest, clove, pepper, and extract known to the world of mess sergeants."

"Now you're talking." Maverick rubbed his hands together at the culinary delights his galley could turn out.

"You're limping sideways. Leg sore from that fall in the howdah?"

"I stumbled on a rough spot in the deck this morning." He hung his head and mumbled, giving the pot a belligerent stir.

"I watched the swabbies holystone the slime from the planks this very morning. That cannonball with your name on it molests you still, it seems."

"I don't shirk my duties from a minor leg ache."

"Show me where it hit."

Maverick raised his pants to reveal the scar from his leg broken last year by a flying cannonball fired off Charleston, South Carolina.

"Look at that. Porter wasn't the best doctor. Your leg bone mended off-center and inflames your muscles."

Bjorn squeezed the leg. "That hurt?"

"Holy shit man, take it easy." Maverick gripped the rungs of the ladder with white knuckles, took several deep breaths, and said, "I am . . . just . . . fine."

"The master might have laudanum to dull the pain."

"Laudanum! That's opium in alcohol and I won't touch that stuff. I needs a clear head at the stove, but I'd appreciate a bit of willow bark tea like my mother used to give me."

"Porter's my friend. Let's go."

"I prefer the spice market."

"You need relief."

"I won't go. I am fine."

Bjorn dragged the cook by his greasy shirt to the cabin. "You're coming with me."

Stumbling to the cabin door, Maverick favored his left leg, but Bjorn chose to not notice. Knock, knock. A deep rumbling voice roared from the other side, "What is it?"

"Can you spare a moment?"

With an audible sigh, the voice said, "Come in."

Looking up from a crowded desk, Porter said, "What's your problem?"

"Our mess sergeant feeds us well, considering our meager shipboard provisions."

"My pleasure," said Maverick as he lowered his head. The uniform behind the desk and the pain in his leg broke his concentration. "I tripped down the ladder and hurt my leg, sir. Mr. Bjorn said you might have willow bark to ease the pain."

Porter stared at him. He remembered the attack in Charleston and the cannonball that broke Maverick's leg. Was it possible his repair of the fracture was unsuccessful? He doubted it.

From his chest of remedies, he poured powdered willow bark into a bottle. "Make a tea and come back in the morning if it still hurts. I'm withholding laudanum because it is habit-forming."

"Thank you, sir."

Back on deck, Bjorn said, "That will help, but we will search for something stronger in the spice bazaar if we ever reach Ghazipur."

"I hope so."

Chapter 2—Ghazipur Greed

Torrents of river rage in unknown languages spewed from junks and fishing boats when *Agilis* bullied them aside to enter the confluence of the Hooghly River and the Ganges. The helmsman turned to port and entered the channel of the Ganges toward Ghazipur.

Eleven exhausting days marked the struggle upstream. The hull frequently scraped bottom as the brig picked her way among the river hazards and traffic. One hundred degrees Fahrenheit was the reading on the mercury thermometer outside the cabin, and heat waves undulated over fields of white poppy blossoms that perfumed the air with a faint, earthy, almost acrid scent. The anchor dropped at the hillside lined with steps where the pilot pointed.

Holding his arms wide, "Welcome to Ghazipur." He explained the Ganges revealed the steps in the dry season before the floods of the monsoon inundated them.

The mariners stared up the ghat steps to the town. There might have been twenty-five levels but the mariners couldn't see around the raised public platforms, smaller platforms near the river for Brahmins, or the mass of Hindus taking ritual baths. The top was dominated by multicolored shrines and temples filled with believers.

Porter said he was occupied with business for several days, and the officers were free to explore the wonders of Ghazipur. "Return by nightfall for your safety. Strange temporal and spiritual forces roam the streets after dark, and there are rumors of ghosts, vampires, thieves, and common wicked men. About women, cleanliness is next to loveliness. Take a good piss afterward to wash out strange diseases."

He did not expect his crew to jump ship into the poverty of India, or risk being shanghaied by another ship.

1

As the anchor splashed to the river bottom, a swarm of empty lighterboats surrounded the hull hoping to offload trade goods from England. Porter went ashore in the lead boat.

Invited into another boat by an anxious paddler, Maverick, Mate Jones and the passenger scanned the waterfront with anticipation.

They leaped from the boat onto the stone ghat steps that were crowded with worshipers taking their sacred absolutions in the Ganges. A cremation service was underway at the far end. In front of the temples mobbed a cluster of chattering urchins who competed for their attention. One stepped forward, "Welcome to Ghazipur."

The Agilis Three stepped onto the soil of India for the first time.

The cacophony of kids erupted around the bewildered sailors. "I am the best guide in Ghazipur." Three others screamed, "Me! Me! Pick me!" So many tugged at the sailors' arms they could barely move.

"Get off of me," said Jones.

"Leave me alone," said Maverick, as he shook the web of little hands loose. "I don't like India."

Jones shook his head and pointed at the biggest boy, "You."

Other urchins jumped up and down, "Pick me. He cheat on you."

He grabbed his chosen arm and shooed away the rest like flies. "Show us Ghazipur."

The selected guide screamed in Hindi, and the mob melted away. He bowed with a smile and said, "At your service, sahib. What to see first?"

Maverick said, "The market."

Jones said, "Souvenir shop."

"Is better the festival, Kumbh Mela. We celebrate in streets today."

Bjorn said, "I'm with you."

The tents and shops lining the streets were their first experience in the mysterious lands of the far east.

The fragrance of the flowers, the enticing scent of freshly baked naan bread, the loud bargaining of customers and vendors, the piles of fruit, the shops selling everything, and the hoards of people marking the entrance to the bazaar were only the beginning.

"Good choices, but you must see the tomb of Viceroy Cornwallis first. My teacher said Lord Cornwallis surrendered to General George Washington somewhere on the other side of the world and came to India to bring peace."

"I didn't know he hid halfway around the world," said Bjorn.

Their guide motioned the trio to follow. Approaching the tomb, they encountered a lofty dome supported by twelve columns rising from a circular platform. The square structure of white marble in the center of the platform bore the bust of Lord Charles Cornwallis. A plaque with a Hindu and Muslim in mourning was carved above an epitaph in English. An opposite plaque showed a European and a native soldier paying homage in Urdu. The circular iron railing around the tomb was beautifully fabricated with spears, bows & arrows, swords, and inverted cannons."

Returning to the chaos of the streets, Bjorn said, "My God, India smells worse than a sailor a block away, and I am one." Jones agreed.

It was true that India had more smells, delicious and noxious, than any other country on earth. They came from street animals and dung, the high and ever-growing mountain of refuse at the edge of town, and street vendors. Others were odors from the sheer number and density of people and a myriad of markets filled with yummy cooking food, and rotting garbage behind.

Bjorn asked their guide about the rumored monkeys overrunning the opium factory. He said it was true and he could show them, but Jones and Maverick were more interested in the marketplace.

"I want the spice shop?" said Maverick.

"Kumbah Mela better, festival in street. People come from far, priests, soldiers, Arabs, and Persians. For sure horse traders from Bukhara, Kabul, and Turkistan to trade. Much fun.

"Do they sell spices?"

A few days after the tiger hunt, Richard met the EIC shipping agent in Ghazipur, with Bjorn along for moral support. Over a cup of Darjeeling tea, the ex-great-tiger-hunter related the details of his pursuit, with only a few embellishments here and there. "Riding that elephant stretched muscles I never knew about and everything hurts." The agent laughed. Bjorn shrugged and worked his shoulders to ease his soreness from the hunt and fall.

The conclave sat under a canopy with the EIC agent and a local elder. Humidity and heat encircled them like a cocoon while humming insects infiltrated the lazy conversation.

Richard said, "Never have I seen such an expanse of flowers. I expected a variety of crops on these small farms."

"I thought we'd see rice and sugarcane with a little wheat for the farmer to feed his family," said the moral support.

The town elder in excellent English said, "Esteemed guests, permit me to explain. Prosperity has come to the Ghazipur district owing to Khas. The seeds heal inflammation, strengthen the heart, and treat insomnia. They soothe the tired muscles of our workers after a long day cutting slits in the seedpods. I can offer a sample for your sore bodies?"

"Slit the pods?" said Richard.

"Good question. We collect the sap that drips out of slitted pods from which we manufacture medicine in the factory."

"What medicine is that?"

"The East India Company calls it opium. It is popular in China, but not so much in India outside of Ayurvedic practitioners."

Bjorn said, "I took my clothes to a Chinese laundry in Sacramento, but never entered the opium den underneath."

"This product has transformed the Uttar Pradesh state. I am planning a three-day wedding for my daughter with the money I save."

"Really?"

The elder said with pride, "The Ghazipur Opium Factory produces the best opium in the world. My brother is the general manager and will allow a visit if you are interested." The agent had never seen the factory and said he was glad for the chance as well.

"We would be honored."

The elder sent a messenger to make the arrangements.

Drowsy in the heat, Bjorn and Richard savored their pipes of tobacco and the Indians their ganja, the local name for cannabis. The agent said, "Did you know Bengal means 'Bhang Land' or cannabis land? Ganja is the more common name in our state of Uttar Pradesh."

Richard handed him the sealed letter from the EIC headquarters in London. "For your eyes only, sir"

With a grunt and shake of his head, the local shipping agent said, "You are directed to deliver thirty-four chests to his eminence, the prefect of the Taiping Heavenly Kingdom in Zhaoqing, China." Clearing his throat and tapping the table, "It is most irregular to bypass the auction house in Calcutta and customs in Canton. Are you aware of the danger?"

"That is my understanding. My vessel has a reputation for speed and maneuverability. She is not a large brig and was able to navigate the Ganges River to Ghazipur with ease, whereas larger ships cannot clear the bars and shoals during the dry season. Only my *Agilis* can ascend the Xi river to Zhaoqing and deliver the cargo directly to the prefect."

"Splendid, if you say so. I will pull the chests from our warehouse this afternoon."

"Chests?"

"Oh yes. We find a compact wooden box weighing ten stone, about one hundred and forty pounds, is convenient for international transport. The EIC demands the strongest chests and finest opium we manufacture. Buried in her Majesty's stifling paperwork is the form that makes you personally responsible for their safe delivery. Ears of spies listen everywhere, in the walls, on the waterfront, and in the river-borne sampans."

His Chinese eminence, Xu Guangjin, is overwhelmed by the Imperial government in Beijing and the Taiping rebellion in the south. We help where we can, and you are a key link. Many spies report to him, even thousands of miles away."

The local elder agreed, "The conversion of our farms from rice, wheat, and cotton to the profitable poppy has improved the state of the native leaders. Many purchase a cow for milk, as recommended by the practitioners of Ayurveda, and chickens for the pot."

He passed the letter back to Porter. "Our business is finished."

Hearing the clap of his hands, a servant brought a pitcher of gin and tonic, chilled with ice brought from Nepal, two hundred miles north. They swapped stories through the afternoon and celebrated their good fortune to collaborate in business, while the workmen gathered the chests. The magnates of opium stretched their legs during an afternoon stroll through Ghazipur.

After a moment of silence at the Lord Cornwallis mausoleum, the urchin guide with an endless stream of chatter steered Bjorn, Maverick, and Jones up and down the exotic streets of Ghazipur.

It was afternoon when they emerged near the central fish market. Wooden bait-and-tackle shops with disintegrating roofs and broken signs rose on either side of narrow streets lined with wholesalers of dried fish.

Throngs of people and crisscrossing tent poles filled the already-busy streets with intense preparations for the Kumba Mela Hindu pilgrimage held every twelve years.

Rounding a corner, they barged into a discussion among Master of *Agilis* and agent of the EIC accompanied by an unknown person.

"Look who's here. Where might this cohort of matelots be going?"

Opportunistic in the ways of hustle, the urchin guide envisioned a bigger fee and opening his arms wide, invited them to explore Ghazipur together. The unknown man introduced himself as the elder of the town. He winked at the group and said, "I suggest we follow our escort. Young man, lead us to the factory?"

The escort puffed his chest out, "Follow me."

They strolled to a walled complex on the banks of the Ganges. It covered fifty-one acres and sprawled over two adjoining compounds with interconnected courtyards, water tanks, and iron-roofed sheds. The agent likened it to the historic Mughal forts that guarded the Ganges River. They stopped before a red gate under an entrance arch, beside which a free-standing sign read,

Ghazipur Opium Factory

The elder said, "Very good work in my brother's factory, much money, monkeys know." He pointed to several monkeys lolling on the lawn and visible through the iron gate.

The state of the simians intrigued Bjorn. A hundred little bodies stared blankly between languid sips from the drainage ditch. Their state horrified Richard who saw the similarities with some of his crew on previous occasions.

The guard at the gate, on learning the identity of the visitors, called the plant manager. "Visitors. Your brother and guests are here."

The manager beckoned his brother and companions through the red brick entrance arch. "We make the precious cakes that fill the coffers of India and Britain. Would you like a tour?"

The elder stood tall. "My brother's factory supports India from under this single arch."

They could see the roofs and buildings beyond the gate, the only break in the wall surrounding the compound.

"The harvest for 1854 is underway. Poppies bloom on tubular stems at three months. When the petals drop, they reveal an egg-shaped seed pod. Inside is an opaque, milky sap that oozes out when the harvester nicks the pod. It dries to a dark brownish-black tar which farmers collect with a scraping knife. They pack it into bricks wrapped in leaves. It is your crude opium."

"It's not my opium, but please continue."

Not comprehending the details, the visitors got the idea.

"Busy harvesters seal the bricks in a pot. Of course, the District Inspector demands a form, my God you never saw so many forms, that records each lot. Along with the containers comes a guard to assure their safe delivery and virginity. If a pot breaks it goes very bad on him."

The master of *Agilis* shook his head at the bureaucracy and was glad to command his ship without paperwork.

"Those pots are valuable like silver. Every man present must sign a certificate that the weight is correct, but the factory weighs the pots again to be sure."

The agent smiled at the diligence to protect her Majesty's main source of revenue.

The manager continued, "Every single door in Ghazipur is locked. No one trusts anyone. They are always weighing, testing, and assaying."

Richard and Bjorn nodded at each other, whether from approval or disapproval was unclear.

"The crude opium must be 'alligated' in big vats. We empty the pots into these tubs where coolies work the blend with their feet."

Bjorn said, "Italians make wine from grapes that way, but they had purple feet."

"I do not know about wine or colored feet, but this is opium. We form it into cakes that go to storage in our godown warehouses that contain half a million sterling of product. We treat it like gold."

"With this much work, I'm not surprised. How much is that in dollars?"

"And thus the product is finished that yields income to Britain's government. God save the Queen. I don't know the value in dollars but it is a great deal."

The guide ended the tour with the famous monkeys near a Hindu temple that predated the factory. Overwhelming lethargy possessed the addled marsupials lapping wastewater from the sewers. "Those monkeys demand the run of the factory, eat factory waste, and sleep all day. We drag them out by their tails every night."

The Agilis Three split off after the factory tour and disbursed into the Kumba Mela activities. Many of the tents lining the streets boasted signs written in Hindi, Farsi, Arabic, Chinese, and English, bolstered by images of horses, food, clothes, brass hookahs, Arabian lamps, wooden carvings, knives, games, clothes, religious icons real and fake, all just in the first block.

Offerings to satisfy more discrete urges were out of sight near the edge of town, along with corrals of horses and elephants and a caged tiger. One horse trader said to another, "I am glad to see stock from Bukhara, Kabul, and Turkistan to compare. Mine is better."

A street over, Bjorn looked at the sidewall of a tent with oriental carpets on the floor and a hollow little statue in front emitting streams of incense. "What is that?" as he pointed to an ivory and rosewood chess set.

"What is what?" said Maverick

"A hanging chessboard, but the players stick out flat."

The owner said, "Most valuable, I will show you." He laid the board flat on the table with the chessmen standing erect.

Maverick wandered away to enjoy other wonders.

"Those beautiful carvings look like ivory."

"Indeed they are, sir. This chess set is one hundred and thirty-seven years old. It was carved by a master in Visakhapatnam, the best port city in eastern India. Magnets hold the pieces stable on a swaying ship. You can play during a cyclone."

"I have other duties during a cyclone, but could play with Master Porter during long, lazy days in the tropics."

Bjorn examined the details of several pieces and admired the skill of the workmen who sculpted them over a century ago. "I'll take the set. Somebody will do battle with me, but I don't know how to play."

"These instructions will teach you," as the proprietor took down a dirty, dog-eared little book and pointed to the title, Rules of the King's Game—Chess.

Bjorn added it to his purchase and looked through other titles on the small shelf. A red cover decorated in gold caught his eye. Written on the flyleaf was the inscription, "Royal Library of Prithivi Narayan Shah, 1747." Underneath was a beautifully rendered drawing of a khukuri knife with a note it was the weapon the Shah carried for safety.

Impotent shrimp he thought as he fingered his knife in his belt. Just then, a Gurkha jostled him and he saw a modern khukuri knife in his belt. "Excuse me, would you show me your knife?"

He twisted the knife in its holder to show the general outline. "We swear an oath that if we draw our khukuri it must taste blood before we replace it."

Bjorn said, "I prefer to keep my blood. Where can I get one?"

"A new one is dedicated to its owner, but there is a pawnbroker's collection of weapons with a used one at the end of street nineteen. The owner was killed in battle."

Bjorn found the secret canopy and added the rusty knife to his books and chessboard. Hefting the knife, he was fascinated and said, "I name you Gunnlogi—Battle Flame." The venerable blade was encrusted with a slight layer of rust and stains of blood from the late, unfortunate fighter. "Proven in battle, a heart to be a warrior's comrade, you're mine until I no longer can wield my sword. You will never lie behind my back in a field, but will eternally be ready."

On the way out with Gunnlogi, he saw a scarlet-covered book at the end of the shelf. The title in gold lettering read The Art of War. He slipped Gunnlogi into its sheath on his belt and bought the little red book.

Tired from walking endless streets and deafened by the din, the passenger strutted out of the festival like a proud rooster leading his harem of hens, and made his way to the meeting place. While he waited he looked at the red book. It fell open to a bilingual section with Chinese writing on the right hand page and English translations on the left.

The open chapter was "Waging War". He couldn't make out the Chinese characters but the smudged and well-used translation was clear.

All warfare is based on deception. Hence, when we can attack, we must seem unable; when using our forces, we must appear inactive; when we are near, we must make the enemy believe we are far away; when far away, we must make him believe we are near.

Isn't that interesting? A subtitle on the cover identified the book as The Art of War by Sun-Tsu, written in 500 BC and republished in 1792 in Paris.

Bjorn looked up from the description of warfare when Jones walked up with his arms full of oriental souvenirs.

"Where's the Cook?"

Maverick occasionally puffed a pipe of tobacco and even tried growing some, but usually smoked aromatic herbs from his pantry. Powdered cloves mixed with tobacco was his favorite.

A bevy of smokers looked familiar in the exotic Celestial Heavens Hookah Lounge, but the elaborate water pipes they were pulling smoke from were novel. A scattering of strange towers filled the tent, their use a new ritual. Tribal music and torches enticed passersby inside to experience a foreign land. Lavish entertainment included dueling belly dancers, snake handlers, and a bed-of-nails artist that invoked images of the ancient silk road from China. Ornate hookah pipes sat on low tables as the participants lounged on velvety pillows in the shade.

Entering the canopy of hookah smokers promised a new experience that excited Maverick no end.

Earthenware hookahs with subtle designs and intricate carvings were a specialty. Patrons smoked hookahs and engaged in earnest quiet conversations on local and political affairs, an escape where people could sit, relax, make new friends, and simply enjoy life. The owner stayed busy providing bellows, rugs, draperies, candles, incense, low tables, and many varieties of flavored tobacco.

A sallow Malay assistant greeted Maverick with a pipe and beckoned him to a velvet cushion.

"Thank you. I am new to this custom."

The attendant brought a tray loaded with five blends of flavored tobacco. Maverick picked one at random, and watched the attendant add it to the bowl atop the hookup and fan the charcoal. Watching the man next to him, the cook placed the long, thin hose in his mouth and breathed clouds of fragrant fumes.

The tangle of the flavored tobacco made him feel good until a clumsy patron tripped over his bad leg.

"Ooh, you stupid heathen, ooh, oooh, ..."

He dropped the hose, a serious breach of hookah etiquette, and gripped his leg with the agonized moans.

The manager knocked the patron to the carpeted floor of the tent. "Watch where you walk, stumbling buffalo." He handed the hookah hose to Maverick saying, "So sorry. I have an extra service to ease your pain."

The solicitous Turkistani added to the flavored tobacco in the bowl a pea-sized ball of resin identical to the final product from the Ghazipur Opium Factory.

Maverick breathed deep to savor the healing properties of the tobacco plus the added effect of the little ball."

He liked it—a lot.

Bjorn, arms full of souvenirs, again asked Jones about the cook. They scrutinized the crowds on the ghat by *Agilis* in the river, and festival goers in the streets. "I don't see Maverick anywhere? Why isn't he with you?"

"I don't know. He disappeared in the crowd."

Panicked in the fading daylight, Bjorn and Jones started a frenzied search. A sailor was expendable but a skilled cook was too valuable to lose. Crowds of fairgoers blocked the way rather than parting for important people of ship's masters and above.

Transient foreigners were denied the top levels of cuisine and service, especially in the streets. Bjorn knew Americans ranked lower on the social scale than the British and certainly their wives, but with a status above the caste of shudras, the laboring class. They were never sure where they fit in, and did not care.

Their search scoured the festival tents. Fragrances from leaves and roots grown from the Himalayas to Ceylon wafted in a fragrance of lushness that did not include Maverick.

The sights and sounds were lost on the pair when they reached the spice tent. The vendor disregarded their lack of caste to make a sale.

"Most esteemed Sahibs, what tempts you to enter my humble souk?"

Jones said he didn't cook and Bjorn said his Viking diet was half a world away. "We are searching for our companion. He is drawn to new experiences like a moth to the flame. Food, drink, nuts, or meat all float his boat, and he was desperate to find spices. Where is he?"

The Hindu owner recoiled at the thought of eating meat but resolved to conduct business. "It is my honor to serve you, but I see many customers today and do not remember him."

"Come now, a sailor after eight months at sea walks with a wobbly gait, and no sailor is interested in spices. Jack tars are attracted to spirits and gambling houses, with a trip to the boudoir until they blow their money. I am certain the girls give nothing for free."

"You know the ways of the world, but surely you need tobacco flavored with sweet herbs, for your hookah perhaps?"

"Most honorable, slimy, lower than dog shit, cheating, spice vendor. I am not interested in your dried foliages," said Bjorn with a touch of irritation. "We want Maverick who limps. I know you've seen him."

"These hands are so busy measuring and weighing seeds the mind has no time to watch shoppers."

Mate Jones had an idea. "My good man, might a person of your handsome countenance have a wife and children at home?"

"How did you know? I have seven children, but feeding them is difficult on the meager return from my poppy crops. They eat like a sacred cow and raise noise all day. My wife has trouble handling them and I cannot afford a maid."

Jones pulled three rupees from a pocket. "I am so impressed with your honesty, I want to buy new clothes for your children."

The proprietor bowed as he grabbed the rupees and said they were the most wonderful gentleman he had met. "I almost remember one like you, a man who bought many samples, He left with his purchases.

"Where did he go?"

"He went to the Love of the Celestial Water Pipe Lounge. I can take you, please."

As they left Bjorn said, "Won't somebody rob you?"

"Not permitted. Many in this fair are Muslims. A man who steals with a hand will lose it in a public square."

Bjorn said, "Feet too?"

"Who steals with their feet besides an eagle?"

The shop owner pointed to an open-air display showcasing rows of solid gold bracelets, rings, and charms on horizontal bars. "Those are more valuable than my wares, yet they are safe from theft."

"Let's find Maverick."

The sallow Malay attendant held the hanging beads aside and welcomed Bjorn and Jones into the long carpeted and walled tent. The vendor returned to his souk.

Bjorn and Jones discovered Maverick staring without comprehension at the swirling fumes.

"My God, it's the cook," said Jones. "What is this?"

Maverick mumbled when their questions broke through his stupor, "She is a human angel, a mistress over pain."

The searchers confirmed it was the cook from the knife scars on his hands.

"There you are," said Jones."

"My beat-up body is new."

Bjorn batted the hose out of his mouth. It knocked the water pipe over and splattered little flaming blobs and charcoal to the carpet. Acrid fumes rising from the woven floor covering were not the billows of flavored tobaccos. The manager scooped the blobs into a glowing ball before pouring water on the fire. He yelled words no one understood but emphasized the message in crystal-clear body gestures. As proprietor, he prevented foreigners from interfering in his business. A dagger retrieved from under his robes glinted in the gloom.

Seamen and a seaman-turned-passenger are skilled knife fighters under the most adverse conditions, and the laid-back lounge was not adverse. The odds were two on one, with two really pissed.

Bjorn, the larger, was double the size of the purveyor. He threw Maverick over his shoulder in a fireman's carry, "You're coming with me," while Jones grabbed Maverick's bag of spices and mounted a rearguard action with his slashing knife that parried the dagger. The dagger was sharper, but the manager lacked reflexes from dabbling in opium so long.

Jones charged through the curtain of hanging beads, tearing a few loose, and ran to keep up with the massive Bjorn barging down the crowded streets, straight to *Agilis.* Bjorn hustled the cook on board while the master was still distracted with business in town.

He said to Jones, "This is under control and need go no farther."

They did not notice that Maverick stumbled across the deck without a limp.

That next morning the hierarchy of *Agilis* waited patiently on the strip of land between the factory wall and ghat steps descending to the Ganges next to their ship. Locked gates fit for a fortress interrupted the enclosure in front of an immense building of red brick that was half-hidden in the trees. Richard said, "I'd estimate that structure at three-hundred by eighty feet and fifty tall. It dominates the grounds of the factory like a castle."

"As a matter of fact, much of the design was based on the Allahabad Fort," said the elder.

The EIC agent added, "That fort is the grand depot for the majority of our military stores."

Bjorn examined the construction of the wall.

"Is this a godown, what they call an opium warehouse?"

"That's what our EIC agent calls it if I am not mistaken."

"The godown you see over this wall is the grand depot for her Majesty's revenue."

"Oh."

Creak, squeak, the gates slowly opened and parallel columns of armed guards marched out. They positioned themselves on opposite sides of the short paved path to the river and waited with their weapons at the ready. Two wagons pulled by donkeys creaked from the warehouse stacked with wooden chests two high. An inventory clerk stopped each wagon to count the chests before he allowed it to proceed.

Richard noted the labels glued on each box contained indecipherable Chinese characters and English descriptions, with an exact weight written in Arabic numerals. The caravan proceeded to the stone steps that descended to the water. Armed guards stood on every third step as workers, dripping with sweat, hoisted precious wooden boxes filled with balls of magic onto their shoulders and stepped into two lighterboats.

A strikingly-powerful turbaned man stood in each. Their confident stances radiated authentic strength that hovered over the chests being loaded. *Agilis* hugged the shore as close as the river bottom permitted. Quick oars propelled the boats over to a harness hung from a line slung over a yardarm and rotary capstan.

One of the turbaned men leaped aboard and lifted the hold cover. He was shadowed by an inventory clerk.

Jones scrambled up the ladder and prepared to load a normal cargo in the customary procedure. He ordered two seamen to grab the capstan bars.

Bjorn hollered over the water, "Who are you?"

The turbaned man standing on the deck ignored Bjorn and motioned the stevedores in the first boat to lash a chest in the harness. He rattled a giant khukuri knife that gleamed in the sun for effect. The bright edge spoke to the skill required to hone it wickedly sharp.

"Can't you hear me? I represent the kingdom of Norway."

The turban dropped into the hold.

Richard ran to an idle lighterboat and awoke the sleeping owner. "Take me to that ship."

"Why the hurry?"

"Now!" He held out a stack of money double the usual fare. The weary boatman signaled Richard and Bjorn to climb in. Only a few strokes brought them to the rope boarding ladder. Richard Porter bounded up with Bjorn on his tail.

The custom at sea was to call sailors by their last names, so Richard became Master Porter. Passengers were called by any convenient moniker.

"You are trespassing on my vessel."

In perfect English, the Gurkha in the hold raised his hand and replied, "I am busy. We are guarding this shipment."

"What did you say?"

Jones said to Porter, "Why is this fierce-looking, unfriendly observer in my face? There's another in the lighterboat, and they won't listen to me."

"I had less security at my gold mine."

"Maybe that's why you lost it."

"Nobody around here looks like a thief, Muslim or not."

Porter said watching the next chest, "The market value of each oriental chest beats the year's output of your mine, Bjorn, higher in China."

"Who the hell are these Indian guards?"

"Gurkha soldiers from Nepal. The EIC agent told me about them. They follow the chests from the gates of the factory to the hands of the prefect himself. I didn't invite them, don't like them either, but can't dismiss them."

With arms folded, they watched the wiry arms of the stevedores loop the sling around a box. Two opposite man-jacks rotated the capstan to hoist the hundred-and-fifty-pound carved chest from lighter to hold. The deck men normally used brute muscle power but these were too valuable to risk an accident.

The company agent supervised the operations like a hawk and gestured for another inventory clerk to maintain a master account.

Jones bounded down the hatch to stack the stowed cargo against the aft wall, and up to supervise operations on deck. The stevedores ignored his commands and watched only the Ghurkas.

Bjorn off to the side tallied every chest to show off his writing skills.

Porter examined each chest as it crossed his deck without understanding the Chinese markings, but kept his expert commander's eyes on every movement and the number of chests disappearing below. "What is your total so far?" he asked of Bjorn after every second box.

"Thirty-four boxes loaded from the Ghazipur godown," said Mate Jones and Bjorn together when the lightercrafts were empty. Bjorn and the inventory clerk compared totals under the glaring eyes of the agent. They agreed although the clerk had comments on specific chests. Bjorn could read the English subtitles, Ghazipur Opium, Finest Quality.

After the hold swallowed the last chest, the hidden Gurkha reappeared and locked the hatch cover. His companion in the boat tossed kits of their belongings on deck, clambered aboard, and stashed the kits in a corner.

Jones reported to Porter, "All is snug and tightly secured, with room for common trade goods. I have never met a more unfriendly duo than your wild Indians."

"They're not mine." Porter accosted the Gurkhas a second time, "What are you doing here? I am solely responsible for this command."

A Nepalese Gurkha, showing his station in life and military training said, "Sahib, we assure that every chest arrives intact. We sleep one at a time on deck, and you supply our food and drink."

"I don't have room for two more."

The Gurkha pulled out a contract with the East India Company. It clearly obligated Porter to provide for the guards at his expense. One was named Gaje Ghale, the other Manja Gurung.

"We sleep on deck and do not interfere with operations. We eat morning and night." He spoke in a perfect British tone not to be denied or argued with.

"I deny your boarding request."

The Gurkhas drew their wicked-sharp jeweled khukuri knives and advanced. They had thwarted an Afghan army in the Khyber Pass a month ago and were poised for action.

Gaje Ghale, the leader said, "Permit me to assist your understanding. Our mission is to guard thirty-four chests of opium in your responsible possession. Any intruder will taste our blades. The value at the destination overshadows this entire ship, the cargo, the lives of you unholy white barbarians who sail her, and extremists such as yourself . . ., sir."

Bjorn faced the Gurkhas alongside Porter, but the little knife in his belt felt puny compared to the trained khukuris in the hands of Ghale and Gurung. Gunnlogi was locked safely in his ditty box.

"We have our mission, we complete our mission, we move on. Our loyalty is boundless to the person who pays us. Others are lower than stinking debris floating in the river. We guarantee the chests will arrive unmolested."

Bjorn looked at Jones who looked at Porter who looked ready to explode. "Dammit. I need additional supplies outside the manifest. I am not prepared for two extra mouths."

The Gurkhas smiled and put away their weapons, but only after making a tiny nick in their arms that dripped a few specks of blood. "We have a good relationship."

Jones said, "If you stay against the gunwale under the belaying pins, we can work around your presence."

Neither Porter nor Bjorn had noticed, why should they have, a small junk that shadowed them up the Ganges from Calcutta.

The combined *Agilis* crew and officers congregated back on board every night, and adapted to the Gurkhas in a day or two. There in the morning when they left and still there when they returned, Ghale and Gurung were a solid pair dedicated to their mission. Bjorn studied their interaction and liked what he saw. He thought, the crew should be so diligent.

After breakfast, Bjorn cleared his throat and asked Maverick's permission to enter the galley during cleanup. Being a passenger, not a crew member, and a previous gold-mining partner, Maverick allowed Bjorn into the cramped galley on rare occasions. Anyone else was in grave danger of being hacked with a kitchen cleaver.

"You and your twin brother, Jethro, watched each other's backs when you left Tennessee for the gold rush didn't you?"

"I've felt lost since he got killed in Sacramento by the bloodthirsty goons of Sam Brannan."

"I feel like an orphan too since my parents died."

The pot of salt beef in water was waiting to boil and Maverick had a rare free moment. The two men stared at the chunk of meat dissolving a coating of salt and turning gray red.

Bjorn said, "There's a long tradition among the brotherhood of the brine. Hidden out there are monsters in the deep, marauders on the surface, jack-tars primed to fight, and mutineers plotting to seize the ship. It is a hard passage alone, and worse if you're injured or sick."

"Worse when your pain never ceases."

"I'm sure."

Maverick stirred the meat, threw in a few leaves of dried herbs, and waited. Bjorn sat on the little chopping table.

"You and your brother joined forces with me at the New Viking Gold Mine."

The cook stirred the pot again and turned, "We were down to our last handful of beans. You saved us."

Bjorn tapped a wooden handle on the chopping table.

"Err . . . nothing formal or anything, but we are natural mates."

"How is that?"

Bjorn could see Maverick did not know about the custom of mates. The American south and Tennessee knew and guarded kinship but had nothing like mates. Friends were not the same thing.

"Mates guard each other's backs. One sees one way and one the other like the Gurkhas. He stands by you in danger and covers your weakness. Over in Australia, a mate is a shared experience, mutual respect, and unconditional help during challenges. You are sometimes surrounded by a hostile crowd and need each other for protection."

The two mulled over the idea for a while.

"Unconditional?"

Bjorn nodded, "You never abandon a mate over a mistake, and share what you have, no matter how meager. In combat, your mate might be the only reason to carry on through a hopeless situation."

Maverick added a few more seasonings and tasted the pot. He didn't say anything.

"I look after you and you after me. This is how the world always works and always will."

The salt beef was boiling, so Maverick said they were mates and get out of his galley.

Bjorn's long hair blew into his face and irritated him as he climbed the ratlines to the rigging from the area of the galley. The wind wrapped it around the lines of the sails and threatened to dislodge or entrap him at mealtime. It was the last straw and the long pigtails on most of the sailors gave him an idea. He climbed back down and peeked at Maverick again, "Can you spare another moment now that we are mates?"

"What the hell is it now? Can't you leave a body alone? . . . Come on down."

"Can you braid my hair like the other sailors?"

"It's easier to cut it off."

"Leave your knife alone. Just braid my damn hair."

Well, just how would you prefer it to be done?"

"Look at that lascar fellow. Just like his." He pointed to the head of the lascar visible out the hatch.

"They have cropped locks, the ones I feed. No queues."

"Just do it."

After some unfamiliar tries, the cook got Bjorn's long blonde hair divided into three strands and quickly mastered the technique of braiding them. Tying the ends together with a little cord, the cook stood back to admire his work. "Not too bad for my first attempt. I'll keep mine short." He wrapped his handiwork in sealskin to hold them neat.

Bjorn jumped on deck where several working seadogs commented on his new appearance. "I'd say, mate, you look like one of us. It's about time."

Bjorn was happy to join the camaraderie of the forecastle.

Chapter 3—In Calcutta

"I want to inspire the inhabitants of Uttar Pradesh state during our departure from Ghazipur," said Master Porter from the foredeck of *Agilis*. He directed Jones to freshen the gold paint on the name across the stern and the filigree trim at the bow.

"Pay special attention to the Spirit of Athena, our figurehead and guardian angel. Give her eyes the clearest vision you can. Paint the railings and clean up this clutter on deck. Trim the sails as though we expected the Maharaja to visit.

The renewal made the ship splendid on the eve of embarkation. She was ablaze with lamps to chase away the darkness on the ghat. The guards fought to control the numerous dignitaries and the factory manager offering farewell wishes. Porter gave most of them a brief reception among preparations for departure during their final night in Ghazipur.

Despite the line of guards blocking the rim of the ghat, a crowd gaped at the loaded *Agilis* surrounded by a flotilla of pulwars, single-masted boats propelled by oars and sails. Drummers loudly beat their instruments in the bows of the quick-moving craft to clear traffic from the waterway for the night. Others scouted the navigable channel in the dying daylight and dropped buoys to mark the hazards that might obstruct the egress of *Agilis*. Larger buoys marked turning points with warning lanterns and clanging bells.

Such levels of security made it clear the correct bore a valuable load, even if unofficial.

An unobtrusive skipper of a small Chinese junk brushed notes on a piece of paper and headed downstream as fast as the lateen sail could carry him. Using the lighted buoys and markers in the last light of the day, his speed was remarkable.

Inevitable confusion delayed the departure until the hot hazy sun rose over Ganges the next morning. The red and orange rays of dawn revealed *Agilis* facing the wrong way up the river, and surrounded by the pulwars filled with armed guards and peons. They wielded spears and lathis and bamboo batons to clear away onlookers blinded by the masts silhouetted in the early morning sky.

Porter on deck with Jones tested the light southwest breeze. "Mr. Jones set the fore topsails, the fore topgallants, main and topsails and brace around to catch the wind."

Jones said, "With respect, sir, might this not be more canvas than necessary?"

"It is Mr. Jones, but the winds are light and the helmsman can control the vessel. I want our final image leaving Ghazipur to be the most dramatic vision this region has ever seen. After the first bend, reduce sail to an appropriate level."

Jones agreed to a dramatic display of a square-rigger under full sail would project a rare sight for landlubbers, especially six-hundred and fifty miles from the ocean. "Aye, aye, sir."

Standing shoulder to shoulder, engraving on the ship's bell gave Porter, Jones, and Bjorn a shared moment of inspiration. Bjorn read the words out loud.

Agilis
1841, Johann Lange Shipyard
Bremerhaven

Jones commanded, "All hands to your stations. Prepare to embark."

"Aye, aye, sir," echoed in the chorus from all parts of the beautiful wooden ship.

Sailcloths dropped with loud cracks, halyards creaked when the hands braced the sails horizontally around the masts, the anchor chain tugged tight and groaned.

"Weigh anchor" echoed across the deck. Squeaks from the trusty capstan accompanied the raising of the anchor chain to free *Agilis*.

Porter gestured to Bjorn to ring the bell five times. Clear resonant tones echoed across the Ganges for more than a mile, and the pulwars divided and made a clear path ahead of the bell.

"Anchors aweigh," marked the lashing of the dripping anchor to the railing where the cross of iron rode at sea.

Breezes filled the white canvases without a wrinkle. The hull strained forward into the current to sounds of humming, snapping, and the groans. Bjorn couldn't help himself and climbed to assist the riggers racing to trim the sails.

The *Agilis* turned toward the center of the wide river in a magnificent arc. Clustered proas and pulwars and junks maneuvered out of the way of river traffic and themselves. The crowd lining the ghat cheered a rousing farewell. Many of them had worked hard to manufacture the product in the hold and were proud of their efforts.

Rings of her bell warned the river traffic of her approach through haze or clear.

"Brace the sails." The stately, shiny brig under breathtaking full sail turned for Calcutta, six hundred miles and more downstream.

The pilot cautioned the helmsman to avoid the smoking buoys at shoals, shallows, and hazards.

A proa led another followed as exit security. This was as incognito as *Agilis* could muster, although the entire state of Uttar Pradesh from the Taj Mahal to Lucknow and even Varanasi knew the story of her surreptitious cargo.

The small Chinese junk, racing a day or two ahead, widely spread the intelligence of chests on the water.

After a day on the river, the trip became routine between the attentive river pilot and the expert helmsman. Those onboard relaxed.

"Glad that is over," said Porter.

Bjorn stared at the clouds of sails overhead that blended with the clouds and hazy blue of the sky. "Port, your ship is the most beautiful creation afloat. Far more so than any other vessel. Those bulky three-masted hulls and clumsy transport vessels are not close. No wonder you want to own her, I would too."

Porter looked up through into the billowing sails overhead and was inspired by a poem he learned from the Irish community in Boston.

> "There are good ships,
> And there are wood ships,
> The ships that sail the sea.
>
> But the best ships,
> Are friendships,
> And may they always be."

Jones, the crew, and a momentarily distracted Porter cheered while the lascar crew and the peons were indifferent. Workers slitting poppies in the fields along the shore were awestruck. They had never seen an ocean-going ship billowing a sail from every yardarm on the Ganges and would remember the sight their whole life.

The company just arrived from Ghazipur killed time walking the streets of old Calcutta while the EIC bureaucracy dillydallied through their paperwork. They marveled at the magnificence of the buildings which thundered opulence and power. Mere blocks beyond, the streets degenerated into paths of poverty that changed from dust to mud in monsoon season.

Porter recalled a claim that downtrodden districts fed recruits to marauding pirates. *I wonder if that's true? When I was a young indentured farmhand I was downtrodden but didn't turn to piracy.*

He waved his companions past the Bengal Club. "I'll be in the Captain's room all afternoon and leave you to explore Calcutta on your own. Can you behave yourselves in a strange, unknown city?"

Entering the front portico, the marble entrance hall was appropriately elaborate for an institution that traded half of the world's commerce, supported an army larger than Britain's, generated revenue for India, filled the finances of the home island, and paid for Queen Victoria's accustomed lifestyle.

Porter presented his qualifications to the haughty receptionist clerk. "Your fellow captains are down the hall to the left. Follow the plaque on the door."

The Captain's room confirmed its location by the sounds of good-natured rivalry, jokes, teasing, complaints, a touch of jealousy, and cries to the waiters for refills or cigars that the closed door could not muffle. Clouds of tobacco smoke swirled around the top half of the room.

Porter walked in and found an empty chair. A steady stream of white-uniformed waiters carried trays of cigars, gins and tonic water, IPAs, and requests to occupants of the superbly comfortable chairs scattered throughout the room. In a bastion where no woman entered, not even a female cat, the ring of seated, smoking men welcomed him. The majority of old salts brimmed with narratives drawn from their careers as barons of the sea. Many were barons on land as well.

"-tranquil nights under the southern cross,"

"-a tumultuous run through the Drake passage south of Cape Horn, the outcome of life, limb, or cargo in doubt,"

"-tales of heroism and horror,"

"-no higher concern than the South China Sea."

One stern-looking gentleman took an angry puff on his pipe, ". . . the barbaric Malay pirates. Their bands have harassed every one of my vessels in the Strait of Malacca, if not the China sea itself." He spat on the floor, where an attendant instantly wiped it away, and extended his hand to Porter, "Frederick Hutton from Liverpool on *Sir Edward Hughes*, gun brig. Yourself?"

Hutton had one of those dark, deep voices, the kind that made men listen and women shed their clothing. He acted like the commander of an enforcement squadron which he was. The stout, not tall, man owed his size more to fine cooking than climbing the rigging but was to be reckoned with in any case.

"Richard Porter by way of Boston on *Agilis*, merchantman." His youthful good appearance stood out from the collection of weathered veterans gathered to share news from ports gracing every continent and river delta.

Porter thought That fellow looks like the admirals of history who fought with their minds not bodies but could wield a cutlass with the best if cornered.

"My mission, from the personal lips of Queen Victoria herself, is to eradicate the scourge of thieving ladrones from her Majesty's shipping lanes. I know their devilry. Ignore the flag they fly, if their piss-poor dinghies even have a mast. The depraved peasants use any trick to force a surrender and avoid a confrontation. My advice, if a proa comes at you, make direct contact and sink their damn boat. Don't waste ammunition on warning shots over the bow."

Hutton stood up and reenacted one of his many attacks with wild swings of his cane. "Never flinch at a shout, a wave of their weapons, or a pop from a handgun." He pointed his cane like a pistol. "Pistols back up their cutlasses, so what?" He sliced the air and knocked over a potted orange tree. "Those ruffians aim to disable your crew. Their prey, that is you," he pointed to Porter, "must defend themselves from incoming shots and flying wood splinters."

He waved his free arm and walking stick to demonstrate an explosion.

"Intelligent thieves, an oxymoron, try to disable your sails and prevent escape. Humph." He sat down and took a long gulp of gin.

Porter's acute hearing picked up a pair of white-haired older men whispering to Hutton, "Don't give away everything. We need a decoy to flush out the pirates."

"Uhmm..," and Hutton nodded.

"A horde of bloody pirates bristling with knives, swords, and bamboo sticks boarded *Lalla Rooka* off Hong Kong last month. My *Sir Edmund Hughes* was chasing local thieves and couldn't help. They held a knife to the captain while the bastards ransacked his ship. Those ladrones took two hostages, a Norwegian trade representative, and aide before they cast away the crew. I'm told the Scandinavians planned to initiate business contacts in Hong Kong, with a side goal to analyze security procedures. I and *Hughes* guarantee safe passage and failed. I must rescue those men."

Clouds of tobacco smoke encircled the room in clouds from the ring of pipes.

"How did they attack?"

"Chinese proas are well manned and fast as a rat on cheese. They mount small-caliber swivel guns with a good range. Approaching a target, they storm the stern because the waist is guarded by crossfire, and fighting in the bow exposes the little shits. You don't want to be the helmsman, their first target."

The assembled gentlemen tilted their pipes and cigars in agreement and sipped a gin and tonic or IPA as their taste leaned. Porter pondered his future as the unpopular foreign intruder through the Strait of Malacca, carrying millions in cargo.

"They sweep the timbers of the deck, eliminate resistance, and hold well-dressed persons for ransom. Most leaders accept immediate surrender but will murder you in cold blood if you resist. They kill, kidnap, or push the crew out to sea on a raft. Life is cheap in these parts and we are cheaper as hated foreigners."

Porter calmed his uneasiness with a long draft from his IPA. "A toast to the man who invented this India Pale Ale. He succeeded."

An English captain described the torture he saw while being held for ransom, himself. "Stripped, a common prisoner's hands were tied behind his back and raised backward three feet from the deck. Several men flogged him with twisted rattans, hoisted his remains to the masthead, dropped them with a jerk, and repeated till he yielded or died. Worse was the merchant captain. They shot him on sight since they lacked time for applying gruesome tortures. They burned the ship to hide their crime, as with most unwanted vessels."

"You tire me, Hutton, with your endless tales of pirates. Niek van Diepen of the Dutch brig, Madurense. I imagine the crown on your sovereign's head lies heavy. The weight of those gems is less than the burdens of an empire on which the sun never sets. I'm a simple mariner who loves the sea."

He only owned a thousand acres of prime Dutch farmland and five trading vessels.

Van Diepen took another sip of gin and looked thoughtful. "A commander fears the death of his vessel, but not his own. None of us are prepared to go down, especially at the hands of stinking, bloody, filthy curs of pirates."

He spat on the floor and waved his pipe around the club. "Captains fall into four classes, clever, lazy, stupid, and industrious. Which are you, Peter?"

"Porter. My command is a mountaintop from where the perspectives are different from the valley. A passion to mold the swarming masses is expressed on the summit." He thought That sounds stupid. Shut your face, Porter.

Van Diepen continued, "One jungle tribe chief on Sumatra admitted he had subjects who lived by sea muggings. The villagers got money from raids and the original crew got reimbursed by insurance. Everybody won."

Porter said, "Insurance does not cover all losses, some have none." His ship was naked of coverage.

"No ship is secure without guns if she runs aground or is becalmed."

Porter asked, "What drives these outlaws?"

"They hate each other more than love the thrill of thievery. We Europeans introduced piracy when we usurped their smuggling trade, and ordinary traders shifted to predation. Our concept of piracy is alien to local communities, where maritime raiding is a respectable livelihood. Rich Asia has always attracted pirates, but nothing like today in 1854 with the transport of opium to China.

Looking straight at Hutton of the gun brig, van Diepen said, "Great thieves hang little thieves, as do British navies. I wish you Godspeed to eliminate this scourge."

Porter said, "Can I help? My crew is few in number but stout in character. A passenger is an excellent lookout."

The conversation dwindled as the men pondered the gauntlet to Canton.

Porter broke the silence, "Pirates menace every league from Calcutta to China? Might I request advice for my first passage?"

Hutton said, "This is the cyclone season in the Bay of Bengal, so study clouds on the horizon. Attacks on a slow ship are almost certain. Escape these and fight the infested China Sea to Hong Kong, and don't forget the dangerous coast of Vietnam. Consider everything valuable ripped from your hands, but that is a small thing. You may lose your life or a limb at least."

Porter thought to himself, That is unuseful. He felt the burden on his shoulders to protect his men. Heavier was his responsibility to deliver millions of dollars from Ghazipur farms. Most others likely concealed the same in their holds.

Von Diepen said, "Where is that damned monsoon? I'm waiting on those favorable winds to Canton that break this ghastly heat. He wiped his sweaty brow with a handkerchief.

Porter asked in a quiet voice, since he was the junior member of the group, "How can you protect yourself?"

Hutton said, "Steer a course through the Malacca strait toward the Malay side and hold off from smoky Sumatra. Stop for nothing. The forces of greed, pirates, winds, and contrary tides conspire against you. Good luck."

"Can't the authorities stop them?"

"Hell no. The natives communicate by drums along the shore, shouting between hilltops, and lighting nighttime flares. Keep your guns primed, your powder dry, your men alert, your skepticism high, and allow no intrusion from either shore."

The Bengal Club afternoon wound down. "A final round of drinks, please."

As an afterthought, one sea captain complained with a grimace, "How the bloody hell do these bastards know our cargo," he cleared his throat, "and destination?"

"There are spies everywhere," said his companion. They embed informers in the loading crews on the Hooghly."

"A lascar cautioned that when stevedores mutter among themselves, they are counting Indian silks and chests from the factory. Just because they are low caste doesn't mean they can't pick up information. Even the EIC cannot outpace their communications to Singapore. I find it astonishing when our dispatch arrives in Singapore, it is old news in the streets."

A man in the back retorted, "I know for a fact those booming log drums send messages along the coast at one hundred miles an hour. Our fastest ships only make 10 knots under a ferocious wind. Those filthy tribes flash signals from hilltop to hilltop with lanterns at night and high-pitched cooee yells during the day. Maybe not as fast as a telegraph, and with what information only the Lord knows. I certainly don't."

The first gentleman said again, "If ever her Majesty's molasses-paced social club extends a telegraph line from Calcutta to Burma and Singapore, we can catch up. There's enough traffic to support it. You would think the British Navy could send a letter faster than these primitive savages, but such is not the case."

A prim EIC employee and retired captain said, "There is an investment opportunity here. An enterprising fellow could gain wealth by fighting beetles, evading jungle predators, repelling thieves, negotiating tribal wars among jealous villages, and breaking the union of light flashers. A modest two hundred million pounds plus a few hundred million more to grease the palms of every half-assed bureaucrat along the way would suffice. It's a splendid opportunity waiting to be grasped."

Captains around the room looked away. They did not like ventures on land, only on the water.

"Offsetting this native communication is the slow network operated by the East India Company. We can transmit intelligence to London around the Cape of Good Hope from Calcutta in just forty-seven days, from Calcutta to Singapore in twelve days, and Singapore to Hong Kong in forty days."

Along the way, the most humble native teenager possessed information for sale to either or both sides, but always for pay. No information moved without the lubrication of money.

Outside the Bengal club, an overwhelmed traffic officer stood in the center of a dusty, chaotic intersection where no passerby, donkey, or carriage paid the slightest attention to his waving arms. "Pardon sir, can you direct us to the marketplace?" said Jones walking with take-it-all-in Bjorn and gaga-eyed Maverick.

The beleaguered cop wearing a red hat looked at the trio through a smile of gleaming white teeth behind a trimmed black mustache and said, "The major marketplace in Calcutta is five blocks down this avenue and four to the left. Look for an arch proclaiming the Chowringhee Market. You're on your own when you get inside. Beware of pickpockets, tricksters, and enjoy yourself." He spoke perfect English as he had worked for the East India Company for many years before retiring to a less stressful traffic job.

Calcutta, the largest city in India, welcomed visitors from all over the world. Everyone spoke a unique language and yelled above the din. The rule was if a listener did not understand the words as spoken, a higher volume would aid communication. It didn't.

Elegant English horses and carriages shared the streets with donkeys and ox carts, merchant wagons, people on foot, dogs, sacred cows, dust, and clouds of buzzing, biting flies. The range of smells was the widest on earth, from heavenly perfumes to animal droppings and everything between. Street vendors offered exotic shish kebabs seasoned with herbs from the Himalayas to Indonesia. Garlic, pungency, curry, and ginger pervaded the air.

The Chowringhee bazaar in downtown Calcutta was a revelation to the Agilis Three. A popular gathering center for an international city, the collection of shops and cubicles that swarmed with diverse cultures was more than they had seen in the combined ports of the world. Impressive entrance arches welcomed shoppers from all directions. Compared to the Kumba Mela festival in Ghazipur, it was a different world of vastly larger organized chaos.

"I hope those bureaucrats take their time with Porter," said Jones as they plunged inside and joined the maelstrom of activity. The intoxicating atmosphere of dust and noise permeated the shops and crowds of people. "We'll meet back here at the end of the day." Bjorn wandered off down the aisle where weapons of many sorts were displayed.

Maverick interrupted, "My sauce begs for flavorings. Where're the spices?" A sensitive nose led through tunnels of exotic shops. Elbowing through the crowd, the cook arrived at a stall where his sensitive nostrils wallowed in aromas of exotic herbs, seeds, leaves, roots, and bowls of fragrant but unknown substances.

The proprietor screamed at the customer ahead of them over the price of nodules of frankincense. Back and forth the heated negotiations flew until the proprietor threw up his hands and gently placed several nodules of aromatic resin on his scale. "You ruin me."

Transforming his face into a smile he looked at Maverick, "Behold the glory of our Bengal dishes. Do you like our food?"

Maverick said, "Tell me about your flavorings. I want to improve the mess I serve my sailors."

The shop owner rubbed his hands, "Most certainly, honorable sir. What do you desire to know?"

Maverick pointed to the first jar, "What are those?"

"Excellent choice, Sahib."

Maverick tasted samples from each container, asked what it was good for, and how to use it. His mouth salivated at the exotic flavors his future shipboard fare would have.

"My God, those are hot. What are they?" fanning his mouth.

"Naga Morich ghost peppers to treat fever and insomnia and digestion. They are the hottest peppers on earth."

"I'll take some." The proprietor filled a pouch and tied the top with a bright red cord as a warning of the potent contents. Maverick appreciated the caution.

"What do you have for body pain and sore muscles?"

"Nothing better than the leaves of the eucalyptus tree. Smell these." He held crushed green leaves under Maverick's nose.

"Give me a bag." The proprietor filled a little pouch.

Proud of his Bengal cuisine, the owner explained which dishes contained what spices and how they were served. Have you tried our food, sir?"

They shook their heads no.

"Come with me." Speaking in Hindi to the man tending pots of steaming stews in a nearby booth, he said, "My friends are strangers to the delights of Bengal. Please to serve your best."

The cook handed plates to the mariners of rice pilaf smothered by heaps of pork vindaloo, butter chicken, tandoori fish, vegetables, and naan flatbread. Tempting aromas made their mouths water. No chopsticks or eating utensils were in sight but they were used to primitive dining aboard *Agilis*. Other diners washed their right hand in a bowl of water and ate using scoops of naan flatbread to pick up morsels of food. They did too.

Maverick dug in with gusto. That is until he took a big serving of the vindaloo pork. "Aaah! . . . ooah! . . . oah! . . . oaaaa!, water!"

"What's wrong?" said Jones.

"My mouth is afire. Water!"

The proprietor handed him a small bowl of yogurt. "Smoother than water to cool the bite, sahib."

Maverick smeared the yogurt around his tongue and lips in blobs and felt the pain gradually subside. "That goes in my secret barbecue sauce, but not so much."

"You like my ghost peppers, I see." He laughed at his little surprise for the foreign tourists.

The rest of the meal was an eye-opener. After cooling off with yogurt and washing their hands, they agreed it was the best meal ever. Back in the spice shop, the proprietor said, "See how good are our delicious spices." He pointed to thirty-one bins of offerings.

"There are cloves for toothache. Bye, bye, gone. Stiff hands? Cloves cure arthritis too." Jones tasted a little and noted the bite, although it was nothing like the vindaloo. He rubbed the powder on his hands and enjoyed the tingling.

"I need a good handful of your cloves." He handed the bag to Maverick for safekeeping.

With a lowered voice, the vendor said, "For men only," as he slammed his left fist into his right elbow and raised his right arm upright. Maverick and Jones got his aphrodisiacal meaning.

"Green cardamom." He poured a handful in their outstretched palms. It clears your head and your love life is much strong."

Jones said, "No thank you. I don't have a love life. This one?"

More good is bhang lassi, the sacred hemp from the body of Shiva, to heal the spirit and the body."

Maverick said, "This matches the natural cannabis that grows wild across Tennessee and California. It treats dysentery, rheumatism, and malaria. I made a salve for snakebites with it." He took some.

"The best is last."

"More?"

With a flourish, the vendor presented a small bag of seeds, "khus khus." He gave a few poppy seeds to each customer.

"Tastes like nuts," said Maverick with closed eyes.

"Calms anger and lice."

"I like the taste," said Jones. "Give me some." He added the pouch to the mess cook's bulging collection.

With a worried look and pointing to Maverick's leg, the proprietor said, "Your foot, it walks with a limp. It gives pain? Here, must try khus khus. Maverick added another bag to his bundle.

Just as the Agilis Three returned to the central area, a loud cry echoed through the market and grabbed peoples' attention.

A loud cry echoed through the market and interrupted their wonder. Allahu Akbar! Scattered members of the crowd pushed their way into the central open area and were joined by many merchants who closed their stalls. The westerners could barely see over the heads of the crowd, even though they were a foot taller than the average Indian person. Men all around them unrolled worn prayer rugs and knelt facing west. A Buddhist observed that Muslims pray to their Allah facing Mecca five times a day."

Fascinated and tired after the prayers, Jones carried his bundle of souvenirs to the entrance to wait.

Alone among the noisy cubicles, Maverick spotted a tiny carpeted vestibule that piqued his attention. Interest in barbecue vanished when a grinning genie rose from a stool and beckoned him to a beaded door. Chinese markings on the entrance were identical to those on the box of the little balls in the hookah lounge that eased his sore leg. He pushed through the door beads out of curiosity.

Back at the meeting spot, Bjorn walked up to Jones. "Where the hell is Maverick? You've got to watch that cook like a hawk."

"He disappeared during the prayers, but promised to meet us at the entrance."

"You left him? Companions always stick together in a port like Calcutta. We've got to find him before dusk."

"You were with us."

"I'm not an official officer, just an informal passenger."

"You're his friend."

"Damn him. Where did he go?"

Bjorn dropped a few rupees into the hands of the traffic officer to guard their purchases and grabbed Jones to search for Maverick.

Not like the EIC in the Bengal Club, a nearby institution lived by a different habitude. The small but elegant Indian School for Commerce promoted the smuggling of contraband as their prerogative, using techniques honed to perfection over generations of marauding ancestors.

Certain families of enforcers dominated the larger piratical rings, but their control was far from absolute. Operating just outside their clutches were myriads of part-time freebooters dealing in assorted forbidden goods. Items moved through their hands to new owners without the burden of a sales transaction or taxes or paperwork. It was very efficient.

Amateurs challenged the enforcers for the thrill of competition more than loot. Smaller families considered the illicit movement of contraband as their entitlement. Since abject poverty was their alternative, they were determined to escape. The skills of smuggling passed from generation to generation in the small elegant building.

A teacher of aspiring marauders faced a room of eager squatting apprentices who hung on every word.

"Mimic the surrounding crowd to avoid detection. Near a mosque, you are a Muslim. Alongside a manastambha column of honor, a fellow Jain. In the house of sahibs, a cleaning servant."

"How do we do that, honorable leader?"

"You are a chameleon who changes color to blend in the background. Say nothing when accosted, mumble, never make eye contact."

"That is not action."

"Listen to conversations whether in Urdu, English. Hindi, or Sanskrit. Be aware that words are not enough. Observe a gesture, a grunt, a physical touch? Do they speak quietly but build to a shout?"

One squatting student slapped the head of another. "I'm observing your attention."

"Quiet! Walk like them. Manners betray a person, but the observer cannot say why."

"The big project?" a student asked with wide eyes.

"Smuggle when the inspectors know nothing. To move treasures outside the system is to move invisibly. A disguise diverts attention from the surprise inside. Hide in plain sight.

"How can I do that riding a cart?"

"Any common conveyance is enough whether a pack, a goat cart, a railcar, a floating vessel. The Chinese paint eyes on their boats for good luck. We also appease the gods of luck, but help them as well."

Scores of little eyes glistened in the training for sea mobbing.

"Search hidden routes and unexpected times of movement and always keep your guard against sleeping inspectors. A final warning. Any habit which alters your mind, never use. Always be alert."

The students nodded. Addicts were below untouchables.

"Make every man comfortable but forget when you're one step away." The Guru motioned for the students to rise and bow.

"Welcome to the brotherhood and sharpen your knives daily."

"Your vessel is a small bucket to have braved the Cape of Good Hope. I am surprised you made it from London to Calcutta, Mr. . . what was your name?"

"Master Richard Porter of the brig, *Agilis*. I go by the title of Captain."

Sitting behind a carved mahogany desk with an inlaid leather top in the elaborate office of the East India Company, the agent handed Porter a sheaf of papers. "This is the manifest of your shipment to Canton. You agree to absolve the East India Company of any liability. You are mandated to guard this merchandise with every resource at your command. Sign each page to accept, please."

The agent placed another legal document adorned with flourishes and a portrait of Queen Victoria on the stack.

This loan for sixteen thousand pounds covers the value of your shipment. You agree to repay £1.2 million less your fee of one hundred eighty-five thousand to the office of the Oriental Bank of Commerce in Hong Kong or forfeit your floating wooden timbers."

Such draconian terms and the interest rate over seven thousand percent set Porter aback, and he hesitated to sign. He stared at Queen Victoria on the wall, who stared back.

"Her Majesty's coronation portrait painted in 1837."

"That red ruby in the crown?"

"The Black Prince's Ruby. A gift from Abu Said, the Sultan of Granada in 1362. It is priceless."

Porter leafed through the sheets with a blank line for a signature at bottom of each page. "By your leave, I want to understand this."

He read the manifest of ordinary goods through to the last item.

"What! Thirty-four little wooden chests that are valued higher than the silk, salt, wheat, cotton, saltpeter, tea, and the vessel altogether. What is in them?" he said as if he did not know.

The agent cleared his throat. "A natural plant product. Her Majesty's government has declared it legal in the international market and is pleased to contribute to a modest quantity to willing buyers in China. It is opium."

The East India Company prided itself on a clean image that the directorate of public relations was ferocious to protect. Outright smuggling was considered a crime and castigated offenders with public floggings or held in solitary confinement on bread and water.

"You require me to smuggle opium? The club talked about your obscene profits and laughed at the feeble Chinese warships trying to halt supplies to greedy middlemen." Porter looked at the documents, "Am I as corrupt as a slaver in the Caribbean?"

Arrogantly, the agent said, "They designed your *Agilis* in Bremerhaven to transport black slaves from West Africa to the New World. I reject your high and mighty attitude."

The agent had a well-oiled procedure to overcome objections. Lowering his voice to a silken flow, "In no way does her Majesty impugn the integrity of yourself, Mr. Peter."

Porter said nothing.

"The Celestial Kingdom leader bans certain materials, but a foreign ship imports nothing to Canton. Particular crates may line the deck, but no Master should force them into a country where they were banned. Why, who would unload them? The sails, the anchor, the storage, and the winds require the full attention of the crew."

"Correct. Mooring a ship occupies all hands."

The agent continued, "It cannot be the fault of the owner if a swarm of coolies absconds with the chests during a moment of inattention. It is no fault of ours if thieving hands pass them to Chinese junks, or whatever the hell they're called. We reimburse the theft with a deposit in favor of the vessel to the Hong Kong office of the Oriental Bank of Commerce, James Matheson, owner."

Troubling thoughts swirled inside Porter's head. He knew the confusion of an addicted crew on his ship but used the same product to comfort patients when removing a limb.

"How much profit is there?"

"Mark up the value seventy-five times over."

Master Porter did some quick mental figuring. On this note for sixteen thousand, my return is one hundred and eighty thousand, and ownership of *Agilis* free and clear. Chests are legal commerce for the entire seven thousand miles. Did somebody on the tiger hunt say karma? Each person deals with his own. Those vague whispers that captured smugglers are vigorously disciplined are surely exaggerated.

"May I borrow your pen?"

He dipped the trimmed quill feather into the inkwell of black India ink and signed a bold Master Richard Porter on each page. A second unsigned copy he kept for his records aboard *Agilis*. Without a moment's hesitation, he signed the loan.

The agent shook hands. "It is a pleasure doing business with you, Master Pinker. Godspeed on the wings of the monsoon. I trust you will have a fruitful voyage to a mysterious oriental land. I have not been there myself."

"Splendid."

Porter boasted about the profit on his return to Bjorn's question of the meeting.

"Good for you, but I see problems."

"Nonsense. These chests are commerce, and the other end is not my problem. I don't consume it, and neither do you. Monkeys love the factory waste, and who am I to question a monkey?"

Porter planned his activities for the rest of the day after leaving the impressive headquarters of the EIC. Shaking his curly head at the grubby advice from the captain's meeting, he said to himself, I must arm my command because my pistol won't stop a boarding party. The brigands will laugh when their sharp knives slit my throat.

He surveyed the deck filled with two masts, capstan, cabin, fife-rail, binnacle, Ghurka's belongings, livestock cages for swine and chickens, hatch covers, coiled lines, planks for an occasional hornpipe, and the tiller. "The deck furniture only leaves room for a six-pound cannon, not a carronade. The lascar carpenter can knock together storage chests for the weapons, projectiles, and gunpowder. Too bad I can't use Bjorn's stateroom for storage, but he's my only friend on board."

Porter ran down a mental list of the limited armaments that could only fit like a jigsaw puzzle since *Agilis* was a merchantman designed to carry paying cargo, not military weaponry.

He strolled the waterfront to observe how other vessels protected themselves and stopped at a sign that read,

Armaments and Weapons
of All Kinds

The store displayed enough weaponry to fight both sides of a war. Porter carried a letter of credit on the Bank of Calcutta that was enough to cover one side of a conflict. Grizzled captains in the Bengal club had inundated him with conflicting advice on defense measures, so he used his own list.

Laying the handwritten sheet on the counter, he explained his brig had restricted deck space. "I limit the weight of iron topsides that would make her unstable in a cyclone. What do you suggest?"

"To keep those slimy bastards as far away as possible, rely on the medium-range ordinance. Pistols and daggers are effective in hand-to-hand skirmishes but you have lost the battle by then. Shoot them in the ass before they kill you is my motto."

"Sounds like a plan."

"Here is my selection of swivel guns. They are modest caliber but rotate through a circle. How large is your deck?"

"I can install your mid-sized weapon, but no more. My sailors need space to fight."

"Keep your access open at the gunwales to repel grappling hooks and to toss the intruders overboard. Slash them first so the sharks sense blood. I suggest fore and aft guns for the bow and cabin roof."

"I'll take two swivel guns. With myself, mate, passenger, and Gurkhas, we are well-armed, but I should like five of your largest pistols. Add two hundred pounds of black powder and five hundred pounds of lead balls."

"I suggest doubling those quantities. Pirate action is fierce, and death and theft is your lot if these ruffians should gain the upper hand."

"Do you know armorers to install them?"

"I have a crew who arms her Majesty's hulls and related vessels, God Save the Queen. You are in her Majesty's service and qualify for their expertise."

Two days later, *Agilis* looked like a miniature version of a man-of-war in the service of the East India Company or at least one of her Majesty's lesser-equipped support vessels.

Bjorn looked at the weaponry on his return, "My God, she's a little fortress. I don't know about pirates but I hesitate to confront myself. She can hold her own."

"Bring up those old rotted hogsheads and anchor them in the river for gunnery practice," Porter said to Mate Jones.

The mate promptly ordered the man standing at the medium-range artillery piece to shoot the heads out. "Fire at will."

A firearm commotion shook the timbers of the brig like never before. Native fishermen stood aghast in their floating fishing boats, blackbirds fled screaming away from the shores, monkeys hid in the recesses of the forest, and bottle fish alarmed at the commotion dove violently into the muddy bed of the Hooghly River.

Warning the spies watching and pirates lurking in the maze of river traffic, Porter's navy continued blasting random debris in the river during the afternoon. Rotating through the armaments trained new gunners in the skills of accuracy, aim, and recoil of the pistols. They sunk debris near the ship and blew up wooden boards or occasional fish farther out. The crew cheered at each successful hit and groaned at each miss. It was great fun converting flotsam to sinking rubbish.

"Shiver me timbers, incoming on the water." The cannonball fired in response bounced five times across the Hooghly River and disappeared into the distant trees, where a chatter of simian insults arose.

Clouds of smoke hung in the still air and hid the body of the vessel. Monkeys squawked from the treetops when balls ricocheted through the park. Flocks of birds flew off to escape the monkeys. Ragtag children cheered both. An enraged policeman berated the ship from the top of the ghat in every language he knew but English. He didn't want the guns turned on him.

It was a good but awful time for the crew, particularly those who supplied shot, cartridges, wads, pitch, tar, grease, sweat, dirt, powder, grape, and all the complex agents of death related to the swivel guns.

"Here comes a pirate," yelled a deckhand. The hogshead exploded in a cloud of splinters.

"I've got you, Blackbeard." Five pistol shots dispatched the invisible attacker.

"Breached on the starboard quarter," shouted the Captain through a speaking trumpet. To the attack ran every tar armed with a cutlass or pistol. Valiant sailors tumbled down from the topgallant yardarms overhead or stormed out of the forecastle, laughing as they engaged the unseen and unyielding attackers. After hand-to-hand fighting to exhaustion, the brave *Agilis* navy drove the enemy back to their invisible proas.

A final roar louder than the artillery of heaven burst from stem to stern, and enveloped her masts and rigging in a cloud of smoke. The victory was assured by the broadside into the last floating splinters that cause their complete demise. The battle over, Porter called the fighters aft and addressed them with a glowing speech.

The oration had a wonderful effect on the sailors who shouted, "Hurrah for our side."

It was a foretaste of fighting marauders.

They concluded the best part was the order for a gallon of whiskey distributed among the crew under the technical policy of splicing the main brace.

Maverick capped the operation with the announcement that dinner was ready. "I went easy on the spices."

"We're glad."

A patron of peace desiring to restore calm after the show of force, the Brahmin sauntered along the crowded street behind a sacred cow that grazed on bits of grass with his staff in hand. His faithful Chela attendant toting a small bag trailed by a respectful distance. The stream of humanity opened to let them pass. Some approached the holy man with a small coin request a blessing because they worried about their reincarnation as a rat or roach. The Brahmin, always grateful to accept the offering, gave each supplicant words of hope.

> May every creature look at me with a friendly eye,
> May I do likewise, and
> At each other with the eyes of a friend."
> To hurt another is to hurt oneself.
> (Hindu saying from Ahimsa, the spirit in all living
> beings.)

Watching from the other side of the street, Richard shook his head, "I don't understand it. India is overrun by sacred cows they never use for work or food, yet are protected to the last animal."

Bjorn said, "I favor a dinner of red meat, more than the lingonberries I munched growing up in Norway. Holy cows are not bad and I urge tolerance starting with the elephants and their mahouts." He pointed to an elephant working nearby under the guidance of his trainer.

Richard shuddered in sympathy with the draft animal. "Can elephants sweat like I did pulling a plow through sticky, stinking Massachusetts mud? That indentured elephant is no better off than indentured me. I want the blessings he receives."

Most protective were the mahouts who cared for their elephants. They were dedicated to each other from the time both were toddlers. Their loyalty was to the karma of the shikari leading them in hunts or pulling stumps.

"Mixed points of view drive the world," said Richard. "Land disputes interrupt my command, but a tiger attack on a person is positively disastrous. After it tastes human flesh it never returns to hard hunting they say. God forbid it ever tastes a displaced Norwegian."

Karma I've never had, good or bad," said Bjorn.

Moving with the crowd, Bjorn said to Porter, "They have holy men, Buddhists, Fakirs, Muslims, and sacred cows everywhere, Yet a sahib in the marketplace is cheated or considered an outright fool. This is a strange culture that leads the world in religion."

"Jesus' notion of good and evil is directed in this multitude. What's this?"

A colorful structure displayed rows of arches on the side and front. Thirteen steps climbed from the street to the entrance. Spires decorated the corners and rose at least a hundred and fifty feet toward the hot blue sky. More spires completed the forest in the center of the top.

They entered the temple of unknown persuasion. Lavish carvings covered the interior with gilded abstract designs, people, flowers, and decorations over which floated the fragrance of incense. A holy man approached from the depths and bowed deeply. "Welcome to the House of Kali Kula Learning."

The mariners stared at the statue of the goddess, Kali. She was deep blue with a face grimaced in rage. Solid gold carvings outlined the idol's three enormous red eyes and made a long tongue and four hands. Fangs protruded out of her mouth and her golden tongue lolled over them. Disheveled hair with a garland of human heads was as startling as her skirt made of human arms. Four arms carried a

Khadga (crescent-shaped sword), a trishul (trident), a severed head, and a bowl or skull-cup that collected the blood dripping from the severed head.

"I don't think she likes us," said Bjorn.

Kali's extended yellow tongue seemed to express embarrassment with her foot planted on her husband's chest.

"I think she is rude."

The priest explained in halting English that despite Kali's origins in battle, she was a symbol of Mother Nature in her creative, nurturing, and devouring aspects. Many Hindus referred to her as the great and loving Kali Ma, Ali Mother. He chanted a mantra that ended with, "You gain merit in this holy place, but you have a long journey to wisdom as a sahib."

Captain and friend watched troubled souls enter the temple. They seem to receive comfort without saying much. Maybe their voices were too low for the visitors to hear, but they left refreshed.

A table beside the altar held a pitcher of white liquid surrounded by small cups. The priest filled a cup and motioned for Bjorn and Porter to share its contents. Porter said he was not thirsty, but Bjorn tossed it down. "This is the strangest bitter tea. It puckers my mouth and tingles everything."

The communal cup was used before germs were invented.

"Teach us the mysteries of good and evil."

The priest pointed to murals on the wall that illustrated deep significance. "This is the hell to punish bad men". He pointed to one notable scene dominated by a grand vizier. A scribe read charges to his right and an enforcer with a horse head mask stood to his left. Underneath him were gruesome punishments. A man was suspended and jerked by his feet, a curved hook ripped flesh from a man's face, a long thick bamboo staff beat a prone man's naked body, two prisoners carried boards of wood around their neck, the top of a man's head was squeezed off by a tourniquet, a man inserted headfirst but slowly into a bowl of boiling oil.

Porter said, "With these paintings, you never need a sermon, do you?"

"Vishnu affects all people for good or bad. A beating by intent is evil, but teaching punishment is good. Is evil to tempt a man into bad actions and abandon his duties. Vishnu says, 'Wrong to erode a man's soul with sweet-smelling temptations.'"

"I flogged a sailor on rare occasions, but it strengthened the crew against tough times."

"Love of a woman is good unless she robs my money as a bad gesture."

The holy man said, "Bad for a man lost in the strong drink or heavenly opium with ganja. Both must enter the temple of Kali to recover."

"Maybe the bureaucracy has stirred," said Bjorn. They turned to go.

The priest stopped them, "Sahibs are always impatient," but they still left.

Porter abandoned the concept of good and evil on the way out of the temple. He said to Bjorn, "Concealed from spying eyes in my hold are thirty-four wooden chests I'm to transport a few leagues away. The destination benefits from the silk that becomes beautiful kimonos for the ladies of the land. The profit covers the debt of Agilis, and I shall be an owner and Captain."

"Captain, is it? You are getting a little too big for your trousers, Richard Jeremy Porter. If those chests with hieroglyphics pay so well, why don't more people deal with them? Maybe sample the purity along the way?"

"Not on my ship. I prohibit the use of opium on board."

"Porter, my friend, you are becoming the tyrant of the ocean. Discipline is necessary, but a touch of understanding makes a happier crew."

Maverick parted the strings of beads hanging in the doorway and stepped over the threshold, worn hollow from endless feet. A flickering smoky oil lamp on the wall dimly lit a long, low room, thick with brown smoke. Maverick's eyes, accustomed to the brilliant sunlight of the sea, did not register in the dusky atmosphere for several moments. Eventually, scattered benches covered with thin blankets like the hold of an emigrant ship beckoned his presence. He limped in and grasped a little statue for balance.

Lumps of flesh lay motionless on the benches. Their faces wore a vacant look of ecstasy with barely enough interest to keep a small metal pipe burning. The manager circulated through the muck to check each pipe, dropping a pea-sized bit of resin into any that burned out. He wanted no interruption in the experience of the user. Maverick turned to thank the shop owner, but he was long gone.

Some clients appeared to be euphoric or drowsy like the reputed monkeys of Ghazipur, but all lay alone. Dark, lack-luster eyes turned upon the newcomer, unsurprised, unknowing to see a foreigner.

Most lay silent, but a few muttered to themselves or attempted conversation in low, monotonous voices that came in gushes before falling silent. At the far end sat a small brazier of burning charcoal, beside which a tall, thin old man was seated on a three-legged wooden stool. The jaw rested on two fists, elbows on knees, eyes stared into the orange lumps.

Greeting him with feigned enthusiasm, the manager bowed. "Welcome to the seven heavens of serenity." He motioned to an open bench.

Maverick placed the bag of precious spices at the foot and pressed a bundle of money into the outstretched hand. A tray appeared with an assortment of long-stemmed, beautiful dream sticks fashioned from ivory, bamboo, tortoiseshell, and even porcelain. "Most excellent from Burma, just for you." The jade pipe with a bamboo stem caught his attention and he picked it up. It was as strange as the hookah had been but the style of use was the same and easy to understand. He sucked a breath of air through the bamboo stem to judge the draw.

On the same tray, balls of opium beckoned in a multitude of varieties. Maverick pointed to one at random since they looked alike and led to the same destination. The manager stabbed the selection with a pin and held it over the brazier until it gave off vaporized fumes. Placing it in the carved jade bowl decorated with the iconography of dragons representing longevity, wealth, health, and happiness, he handed the stem of the loaded, smoking pipe to the man on the bench.

Maverick sucked deep breaths and held them in as long as he could before coughing. His stomach revolted, but the magic streaming through his system triggered waves of glory. The leg pain dissolved into the bliss of the garden of a thousand eternal delights.

The progress of time stopped and his world shrank to a glowing orb in his pipe bowl, around which dragons chased phoenix birds.

In a moment came the words aloud, "Blessed relief at last! I don't hurt and mysteries of the universe overwhelm me."

His body returned to reality and started sweating. Every muscle relaxed one by one and euphoria triggered a pleasant laugh. Smoking the pipe packed with tobacco, he held the vapor in for several heartbeats. The taste was bland and the fragrance was similar to incense. Tingles raced up and down his body and the exterior felt light and smooth, but his chest was heavy. Vague figures melted into the shadows and sparkled in silhouettes outlined with a greenish glow.

Maverick yielded to ecstasy.

Limp limbs wrapped around his chest and stomach. The hugs came in waves, one moment intense with arms squeezed tight, only to float away. An enormous smile embellished Maverick's pain-free face.

Life was good.

Smuggling was an ancient tradition by the time rifles and gunpowder, labeled as snuff and umbrellas, were smuggled to the Taiping rebels in China by English traders. Supplies came from surplus equipment sold by western companies or thefts from military stores. They ranged from small arms up to artillery. One shipment from an American dealer, well known for his dealings with the rebels, included 2,783 percussion caps for muskets, 66 carbines, 4 rifles, and 895 field artillery guns. The loyal prefect signed their passports, while the mercenaries described their traffic as merely plundering an evil country.

Porter confronted this tradition. "What a crazy world is commanding a wooden community. I negotiated a load of cargo, arranged payment across the ocean, and pledged to deliver it, but this is beyond my ken. I'm sitting on thirty-four chests of a secretion I've never used. I armed my vessel against naked pirates and trained jack-tars to massacre them. Every nook is crammed with practice gunpowder that wiped out a troop of monkeys and terrified oxcarts, river junks, and natives in the street."

Maverick delivering morning coffee to the cabin the overheard Porter talking to himself and joined in, "Sir, I know guns. I've shot four-legged critters from squirrels to bears."

"And cooked them," said Bjorn peeking through the door. "You should have opened a smokehouse in Sacramento instead of panning yellow corruption from the river."

Porter complained, "Who knew I'd be feeding two Gurkhas capable of slaughtering an elephant by themselves and eating it."

Bjorn and Maverick said together, "Gurkhas again?"

"They're idlers."

"We've got eighteen able-bodied hands on board. Why do we need Gurkhas?" said Jones.

"EIC requires a guard for our cargo."

"What part is that," said Bjorn?"

"Those red ornate chests under the bales of cotton. We're crossing dangerous waters."

"Your policy of no shore leave to prevent hands getting shanghaied is unpopular. How long can the damn paperwork take?"

"Promised this afternoon late, and I don't give a damn about popularity. Besides, my friend, everybody hates the captain when times are tough."

Bjorn heard the crew grumbling loud enough to be heard when he and the captain went ashore.. and left them stranded in the middle of the river. Most ordinary seaman couldn't swim and wouldn't jump in the filthy river if they could. The lascars were loyal and content with their position in the crew.

Porter and Bjorn walked boldly through the imposing Grecian marble columns to enter the doorway of the East India Company headquarters. The attendant directed them to their agent sitting behind an immense desk covered with papers. His manner exuded efficiency and no-nonsense.

Porter said, "Good day, sir. I trust business is brisk."

"And you are interrupting. What is your concern with the EIC?"

"I am waiting on my manifest from Ghazipur to Canton for Agilis."

The agent mumbled as he shuffled his papers and retrieved a page. "Seventeen bales of cotton, a hundred and ten bags of rice, twelve skeins of silk, seventy-five bottles of perfume, products of handloom weaving, and thirty-four chests from Ghazipur. Ah yes, the opium. The fee is five hundred pounds, plus two hundred and fifty pounds for each chest."

"What! Where is this from?"

The agent looked at Porter in disgust, "Surely you understand that her Majesty's government incurs costs maintaining this enterprise so far from London. The Honorable East India Company must remit funds to pay for our humble operations. The total charge to exit Calcutta is ten thousand, five hundred pounds."

Bjorn sucked in his breath and Porter pounded the table. "The whole damn ship only cost six thousand dollars in San Francisco."

"The fee is ten five or the port authority sinks her in the Hooghly River."

"That's a traffic hazard," said Bjorn.

Porter fumed but finally said, "Can I put the charge on account? That sum exceeds my resources at the moment? How much is that in American dollars?"

The agent consulted a table and said the conversion to dollars was fifty-one thousand, two hundred. Porter was stunned.

"Because this is your first visit to Calcutta, I am authorized to open an account with your ship as collateral. Sign here."

After intense negotiation and plowing through innumerable pages of legal language over his head, Porter signed until he wore out a quill pen and requested another. His hand felt ready to fall off. The agent handed a final sheet to Porter saying it was his approved manifest and to guard it carefully.

A clerk whispered in the agent's ear.

"What on earth for? We have negotiated the fees." He said to Porter, "The director wants to see you. I cannot imagine why."

Porter clutched his copy of the manifest and followed the clerk to the director's office. Bjorn stomped after him.

As they walked down the hall to the head office, Bjorn said, "I never realized a Captain faced such difficulties."

"Petty tyrants of the port that you see everywhere, but worse in Calcutta. I'm not worried about the mortgage on the ship because Captain Macintyre's company owns her, not me, not yet."

Porter knocked on the door with the sign on the frosted glass,

Director

"You wanted to see me, sir? I have paid your permits and fees."

"That is her Majesty's business. Might I offer you a cup of tea? We grow the best in the world in Darjeeling, you know."

The three sipped cups of tea from hand-painted cups and matching saucers in bone china from the Spode company. Over small talk as they sat around a circular table, the director leaned forward and motioned their heads together to hear a whisper, "I have a mission of sweeping importance." "We know your ship for its speed and maneuverability, and you, Captain Porter, are famous for your navigation skills. Mr. Amundson, as the Norwegian trade representative we welcome you to the international community and look forward to many years of cooperation." Bjorn nodded. Porter looked skeptical. What was he up to?

Bjorn and Porter stared at him from six inches away. His breath smelled strongly of exotic spices and garlic, but they were indifferent, shipboard was worse.

"The prefect of Guangdong province, Xu Guangjin, has a debilitating fondness for fine gems"

Bjorn's eyes sparkled as he also liked gems, especially those extracted personally from the earth.

"Burma has opened a new deposit. Among the enslaved miners was a new recruit waiting for his iron mask to prevent swallowing raw rubies. The overseer did not notice when he tried to eat several stones. Men don't need gravel in their craw to grind their food like chickens. Of course he choked and died, and his companions tugged the body to the graveyard. Deaths occurred every day and this caused no undue attention, even when the workers ripped open the stomach open and recovered the stones."

Porter said, "How does that impact me?"

Still whispering, "The prefect has spies scattered everywhere. He knows of these stones and craves to own them. Their color is deepest pigeon's blood red."

"What can I do."

"You with your swift boat can deliver these gems to his eminence. It will be worth your effort."

Bjorn said his Norse ancestors smuggled gems to France, but not he. It was inappropriate for a trade representative to engage in smuggling, although high-level people always grasped business opportunities.

"It delays your departure by one day. Under the cover of darkness, a chest of opium carried in a dinghy will come to *Agilis*. Listen for a signal of two short and two long whistles. Two men will boost a chest over the railing that is identical to your cargo. A character in the lower-left corner of the label has an extra dot." He drew the character and added the mark.

"The stones are in the top ball behind the label. Guard that chest with your life. It is worth more than your ship, this building, and the island of Sumatra."

"Who knows about this?"

"The original thief is dead, his companions cannot read or write and have no tongues. Only the Chinese spies and the pirates infesting the South China Sea are aware."

Bjorn said, "I overcame exiled south sea pirates in Honolulu. Bring them on."

"Humph. The same scum, no doubt. I strongly recommend you arm your merchantman well. The Oriental Ironworks here in Calcutta manufactures many weapons that merchants find useful for protection."

"Accomplished. Delivery?"

"Contact my man in Hong Kong. He has forged papers to allow bypassing the port of Canton directly to Zhaoqing."

Returning to Agilis, Porter wiped his brow. "Whew, this is our wildest endeavor ever, my friend. Opium is bad enough, but contraband is another story."

"I wish we had a native for guidance in China."

"We will manage."

Across the Bay of Bengal on the southern Malay peninsula, Si Rahman, a minor warlord, and local village headman addressed the skippers of proa boats. They were idle farmers with wet fields.

"The monsoon is here, your sugarcane is planted and ready to drink the rains, and pepper trees can't be harvested for two months. Are you ready to raid the river of vessels passing your fields?"

Rahman controlled the area around the Muar River halfway down the Malay coast. The location was prime to move stolen goods over the well-used trade route to the sultanate. What did it mean that he was a warlord, even a minor example?

He was the enforcer over a local territory in favor of the sultan, to whom he owed frequent tribute of money and men. Responsibilities offset his local power, and an exiled brother warlord down the coast hounded him at every opportunity.

"Ready and armed," came the chorus from the boat owners. "I still need more weapons."

"Strip arms from your target before you burn it."

The proa owner replied, "Good idea as usual. When can I start?"

Warlords were men of diverse talents, powerful instincts, political skills, and absolute ruthlessness. Rahman was an expert at charm and gracious companionship, with a demeanor that imbued his presence with a feeling of amity as though visitors were his best friends. He lubricated the wheels of human interaction and controlled people into following his will as smoothly as the finest oil.

The opposite mood was a towering rage that generated a fear more potent than charm. The customs of Si Rahman filled the consciousness of everyone around him. Some he knew personally, but perceived enemies he executed on the spot. There were other punishments available to induce followers to obey his dictates. But where did such dictates come from?

Si was enraged. "More! always more. The Sultan demands additional tribute. It's all he ever says. 'I must have army recruits,' For his satanic rituals no doubt."

The ruler called often on the local warlords to defend the honor of his realm or expand his territory. Continual fighting was normal.

"How about my territory? Dragon shit, I have enemies too."

Death was the inevitable outcome of these conflicts. Elite warriors set the culture and made death honorable. Trivial if an enemy, killing was as commonplace as a yawn. But how much greater was killing in moments of passion and armed fury? Their opponents bowed or fell to the ground.

The surroundings of the warlord were natural thatched roofs instead of blocks of quarried stone and witnessed swirling stories of passion and intrigue. The architecture of tree branches and bamboo resembled erections by nomadic tribes, only more permanent.

Rahman seated himself on his customary chair of authority, his personage surrounded by people always present. Many had a specific desire to plead a favor or correct a crime. Others were advisors and entertainers.

Rahman settled in for a long afternoon of resolving disputes. His eyes bored into the first man with a grievance. "Talk."

"Your honor, Hazer put a curse on my fighting rooster and killed it." He pointed to a person in the audience.

"How do you know?"

"My gamecock rooster died. He put poison on his bird's spurs."

The warlord motioned for the accused to come out.

"What did you do?"

"It was not my fault. My gamecock, Yellow Terror, was stronger and faster than his sorry competitor, Red Cackle, who ran loose in the yard. They naturally fight."

"My son opened the cage by mistake."

"Can't you control your kids? You have enough of them."

Before the warlord could settle the dispute, a loud shout interrupted from the entrance. "A messenger from the Sultanate demands an immediate audience."

The warlord raised his hand to stop the argument and invited the messenger to sit on his right in the best seat available. In response to Rahman's hand clap, a captured enemy slave brought cups of tuak, made from fermented rice, and pistachios to mark the time, while the host cracked jokes. The warlord had a unique way of looking into someone's eyes. Tiny half-closed eyes seemed to see right through the visitor's soul, and the threatening black irises exuded intelligence and power.

The official visitor announced. "The esteemed great Sultan of Negeri Sembilan demands more loot this year because he must impress foreigners with our growing power. An expanded meeting place is under construction, so the Muar River district will make the required contributions."

After pleasantries and discussions, the messenger left to visit the competing warlord down the coast. The exiled brother held sway over the region of Batu Pahat, named for the salt-makers on the Batu Pahat river. The fiefdom was the poorest in Malaya and housed vicious bands of the sultan's private militia. He mistrusted them.

Up the coast, Si Rahman addressed the gathering to announce the additional tribute. Since it involved raiding foreign vessels, they were enthusiastic to start. But before he could begin, another local messenger arrived from a local hilltop with fresher news. "Drumbeat messages say a small brig comes with chests of opium. Compact, not too heavy, prized by customers, the chests are a fine loot.

Rahman gave a wild cry. "It pays our contribution to Sultan Negeri." He rubbed his hands together and spread his arms wide. "You heard the news. Gather raiders of the sea to man the boats. Use their brains because the farmers, fishermen, and sailors are dull. Include ex-militiamen for their muscle from fighting other warlords."

He directed several men to organize their attack. "Good luck to crews and their debauchery after they restock our supplies."

The village cheered at the chance for their members to strip foreign vessels in the Malacca Strait, notably *Agilis*. "

"Can we start now?

"The ships out of Calcutta arrive on the monsoons like hoards of wild wasps. They fill our seas with valuable cargo, but we'll take them like ducks in a pond."

The farmers didn't look like hungry pirates but hooted to celebrate a new 1854 hunting season.

"Sergeants, divide these men into training cadres. We must reclaim the bounty stolen from our lands for China. We all know what a worthless, stinking race of degenerates they are."

"Death to the interlopers."

Morgan Fore 'n Aft named himself King of Cats and protector of the sea. He surveyed the ghat from a perch on the head of a Hindu God and stayed dry.

Born in Bremerhaven, Germany, won by an itinerant sailor in a poker game, adopted by Richard Porter as his owner and guardian, and eloped to Jamaica with an Italian carpenter, Morgan Fore 'n Aft had a history.

Morgan loved to go ashore with the sailors of the Madurense. Changes in food and new sites did him good. He found the atmosphere of Calcutta exciting but a little dangerous, so he stayed clamped on the shoulder of the man he selected to carry him. Clamped-like claws dug in a little bit, but not too bad.

Returning to the ghat to rejoin the ship, he saw the flowing tresses of a figurehead he remembered well from San Francisco. Many other ships welcomed him but he never forgot the Spirit of Athena on his first ship. Or his rescue by the indentured farmhand named Richard Porter.

Could it be the same vessel? It could and a lighterboat was pulling away from the ghat. Quick as a cat, which he was, Morgan leaped into the boat. He seduced one of the stevedores and enjoyed the short ride to his first ship. His wicked-sharp claws carried him up the side, over the railing, and into the arms of his long-lost owner wearing a hat decorated with gold. The scrambled eggs on the brim meant it had to be Richard Porter.

"Purr, purr."

"Morgan Fore 'n Aft, you're back. I'd know that white nose and white-tipped tail anywhere. You've aged because I see a gray hair or two and carry new scars, but you're as ferocious as ever." He placed the cat on the capstan and bowed. "I present to you a smorgasbord of rats and cockroaches that we saved since you left. Don't get fat like me."

A combined white spot on the black cat's nose and the white tip of his tail gave Morgan the nickname of Fore 'n Aft. Four white feet marked him as a feline of distinction. Lover of rats, hater of parrots, boss of the boat behind the scenes, he left his calling card in the uneaten tails of the rats.

Greetings aside, the most lonesome soul on board was Richard Porter. Morgan's spirit-healing nature bubbled up. Acting as a totem animal for Porter was a big job he tackled with the energy he used to chase rats. Porter was a night person, typical of those born with the cat as their totem animal. Nocturnal walkabouts with no particular destination filled the night hours and worked personal magic on the crew.

Totem traits made Porter an ardent adventurer, including visits to his inner space. Porter had been naturally agile and able to land on his feet in impossible situations until he gained weight on Maverick's cooking.

Unique perspectives showed the cat checking out the angles of the timbers and brushing them with sensitive whiskers. The cat portended an unpredictable life filled with antics, risks, and a bit of craziness. But he had nine lives. "Be careful how you use them," was Morgan's unstated admonition to Porter on his nine lives. Porter wasn't sure how many he had.

The spirit animal purred the lonely captain to sleep every night, to relive the memory six years before when Porter mended his broken leg from the kick of a horse. Fore 'n Aft's super-sensitive instincts warned the captain of upcoming dangers by disappearing from sight. Morgan's retreat to some unknown cubbyhole saved him more than once, and maybe *Agilis* too.

The close companionship and rich smells of the forecastle suited him after tucking in Porter and making a quick side trip to the galley for a late-night snack. He spread his spiritual blessings from hammock to hammock for stroking and loving. The lascars favored him as a gentle respite to the harsh masters and overbearing mates. Morgan was unaware that cats were a food item on the menu in their destination of Hong Kong, where they raised cats for food.

Curious to a fault, Morgan loved playing with the priceless carved chess pieces. The magnets that held them to the chessboard gave just enough resistance for him to get a solid hit from a paw. For a more peaceful recreation, he moved chessmen to new squares when the human players were distracted by mundane duties. He never put them back, but he always took time to comfort any person in pain on board. He could smell hurt on anyone.

In the doctor's bag of tricks he carried,

1. Purr
2. Soft fur
3. Sharp claws for bloodletting, never used that way
4. Spiritual communion.

They were ready at a moment's notice, but the rats disapproved as it interrupted their occupations of hiding and reproducing.

The King of Cats believed every human being should love him, yet there were a few like Bjorn who rejected or actively hated cats. Bjorn was only indifferent.

An overwhelming drive to convert non-lovers compelled Morgan to rub up and down a leg as the opening phase of rehabilitation. Bjorn was his first target.

"I need six able-bodied hands for a run to Canton," said Porter to the serang leader, Akbar Mohamet, of a group of itinerant hearties known as lascars by the British, and sepoys or soldiers by themselves. Heeding the advice of Captain van Diepen of the Madurense who described their traits and uses, "Pay them half what a white man demands and feed them cheap rice, not dear salt beef. I daresay at least half of every crew is indigenous Indian sailors called lascars. They make your profit."

Only half of Porter's crew was signed and he was unsuccessful at rounding out his complement. Fellow sea captains had discussed the pros and cons of the indigenous sea hands and agreed they were essential to a successful trip.

Bjorn knew several lascars from his time in the forecastle and enjoyed listening to the serang's pidgin words to Porter. He nodded at the leader and interrupted, "If I may, Captain Porter, this crew worked with me in the past, and I can give good recommendations. They tell stories and boast, these small-limbed, tawny men. They mangle words from English, Malay, Hindustani, Chinese, Filipino, and Arabic but they understand each other. I can interpret what you don't know."

"I told you," said the serang in excellent English, better than most seamen.

Porter was reluctant to send crimps into the brothels and bars of the Calcutta waterfront. They dropped drugs into the drinks of the patrons or worked in cahoots with the madams and saloon keepers to steal crew members who would wake up with a splitting headache, a third of their wages gone, and on their way to China. Such men were not the best crew.

With his thumb on his chest, one said "I be your serang, Akbar Mohamet, leader of men." He pointed to the group behind him. "We load ship, and sail away."

"But can you manage on the open sea?"

Mohammet's happy, open manner turned as dark as his skin. "My men are the best sailorsmans you got." He repeated the insult in their pidgin language and caused an instant reaction. Leisure waiting, smoking, gossiping, and telling tales turned to shouting and beating their chests. They considered themselves excellent sailors and said so.

Bjorn said, "You're the greatest sailormens there are," and presented them to Porter with a flourish.

Porter knew lascars associated themselves in a unit and refused to split up. Cheap, they had stubborn ideas of work they would do and the number of hands required on a job. They walked on naked feet with few clothes beyond a piece of white cambric fabric around the middle, held by a red sash. Complexion showed a rich dark brown, short straight black hair, more nimble afloat than anybody else, their mild, good faces promised a good passage.

Captain Porter and Mahomet signed the crew log and protection papers for all six, designating Akbar as their serang. His betel-red teeth belied the stream of red juice he sputtered into the ocean from time to time. Sharks snapped at the red spittle like it was real blood

"What kind of habit stains the sea to red and fools the shark?" Porter added another vice to his list of disapproved behaviors.

Bjorn greeted the line of lascars as they boarded and spoke to each other. A quick once over let him judge the character of each man. One of them seemed a part of the group, but yet different. The fellow greeted Bjorn in a foreign accent.

"Where are you from?"

"Far away from the island of Samoa. I kanaka, not lascar. Work hard, read sea, navigate."

The serang, Mahomet, interrupted, "Get along. No time to waste."

Bjorn felt the group who he assumed were Muslims, Hindus, and Christians were likely the best of companions but wondered how they would react to the officers, other seamen, and himself as a passenger.

They in turn wondered who was this strange blonde sahib who looked like a mariner, acted like a jack-tar, and did no work.

Thirty miles down the Malay coast from the Maru River a separate fiefdom held sway at the Batu Pahat River. Its region was the poorest in Malaya. The leader, Riayat Shah, was exiled after he tried to assassinate his brother, Si Rahman, the warlord on the Maru River. Such a custom skirted the open retaliatory conflict mandated by their traditions but allowed continuous low-level guerrilla attacks. His clan did not rise to the official status of a warlord but he pretended in every way, if not in actual power.

His forces included vicious bands who also served the Sultanate as a private militia. They gave and received every day of battle, tribute, women, slaves. Secondary status made them try to outdo Si Rahman in viciousness. Their limited resources never allowed them to keep a hostage, never.

The motley gathering of pirate farmers was young, idle, poor, and hopeless. They struggled to make ends meet in the pelabuhan tikus (rat harbor). Their idols were seasoned older fishermen who raided ships of opportunity with a small crew and built mosques for believers.

A ragtag sergeant instructed the gang in the well-honed techniques of boarding their prey. "Throw the grappling hook, overpower the crew, and ransack every part, open and concealed. They fight, they die. Torture will loosen their tongues for hidden bounty."

The clan headman pounded the table, "Prepare for the coming treasure. Those bandits of Maru can't intercept our rightful ships this time." He demanded of his grizzled sergeant, "How many men do you need?"

A runner burst into the meeting with a message from the drums that noted a rich prize was coming their way.

The sergeant continued, "Keep a lookout in good weather and foul. Our good luck will triumph over the sorry efforts from the Maru River. I should have killed him when I had the chance."

Shielding his face with his hand, he pointed to the horizon, "Where is your lookout? You fail already." He cuffed the sergeant.

A distant mast top peeked above the horizon and grew into a cloud of sails picking their way among the shoals. Even from a distance, the bristling array of guns on deck and the glints of sunlight off sharpened daggers discouraged an attack.

Speaking in Indonesian and Malay, the sergeant said, "I need thirty extra farmers, swords, and daggers. I have to post lookouts along the coast from Pelabuhan to here. Unfortunately, messages sent from our drums echo at Maru, but that is nature. We will raid the ships when they get here. Let this armed intruder pass as they are too strong."

He did not stop to think that the Maru River group would see ships from Calcutta before Batu Pahat.

The parting admonition from the headman was to practice their fighting skills in hand-to-hand combat and refine their torture techniques on captured prisoners who refused to pay a ransom. Shah never took prisoners, although the other warlord, Rahman, did occasionally for sadistic fun and training in persuasion.

"Hold races between proas to the waiting grounds to train for the surprise attack. The Sultanate demands more bounty to build his forts or he will burn our village."

Chapter 4—Tides of Bay of Bengal

Far north in Upper Burma, within the Mogok Stone Tract, a dispirited Chinese man scraped a hillside alongside other exhausted captives. They struggled to breathe the humid jungle air through iron masks, made worse by the afternoon rainstorm. A sudden flash of crimson lit up his tired eyes. All of creation was concentrated in that tiny red fragment. Hiding it from the guard, he said in a low voice, "Behold, I see the face of God," and dropped the fragment into a tiny sack at his waist. He resumed his search for small red stones, clawing loose rock with blunt iron tools and his bare hands. In water every day his hands were gray, calloused, bloody, and peeling.

The miners started their day with little breakfasts of rice before they trudged to the Magok ruby mines. Pigeons joined their breakfasts and pecked one another in competition for any loose grains of rice that fell to the ground. The drops of blood matched the little red stones the diggers gathered from the slopes. Red pebbles in the stream between hills were long gone, and the tired miners were forced to dig the hillside searching for their daily quota of gems. "The overseer demanded a double quota from the hated Chinese captive in return for fewer beatings.

The guard started every day with the same story for the benefit of any new captive. "A tradition speaks from centuries ago that a man discovered a stone the size of a small egg in this hill. It blazed the color of blood when it rolled downhill to the water. The governor confiscated it, applied the name Ngamauk Ruby, and sold it to the Sultan of Granada who presented it to England in 1362. England renamed it the Black Prince's Ruby and mounted it in the center of the crown jewels. It shines from there to this very day."

None of the workers had ever seen the British crown. "How much did the worker get?"

"Get to work."

The Chinese citizen said to a fellow worker in halting Burmese words, "I am a slave, not a prisoner. My skin goes Grey and peels off in the water. They won't even give me a name, only 'Chink.'"

"Who are you then?"

"My parents named me Liu Fong. We are descended from the Emperor, many generations back."

A companion gem miner listened in and claimed descent from ancient warriors. "My father told how Burmese soldiers offered rubies to Krishna to gain invincibility. Their bodies absorbed the power of the gem by inserting them into their flesh."

The Sino-worker sweated in the hot sun reflecting off the clay and rock and stone underfoot. Any multi-colored rock that appealed to his spiritual nature went into his little pouch. He gathered everything because he had a larger quota than anyone else. Fatigued and in a hurry to fill his quota bag, he stumbled and kicked a ledge of gravel into a puddle. Seeing a flash of aquatic red fill the puddle, he made a quick step to restore his balance and plopped a bare, yellow, chapped foot over the flash. With a swipe of copious sweat from his brow, he snuck the stone up to the sun. Large as an egg, it was as clear as the pigeons' blood drops at breakfast. A star shimmered from deep inside when he bent over and rubbed it on his waistband.

Liu was clever and a survivor. He charged a nearby worker with a sharp broken rock and made a cut on his back. The worker screamed in anger and responded with a slash to his leg with a tree branch. Liu Fong limped to the overseer, "That man cut my leg and it wasn't my fault."

"He cut my back with his rock first."

The overseer rushed to the culprit. "Stop fight now!" and laid his whip across Liu's shoulders. "Worthless chinko scum," and to the injured worker, "You too, no rice tonight for fighting."

Liu Fong bowed and said, "Most sorry, sir." Doubled over to avoid the whip and feigning stomach cramps, he asked the overseer's permission to visit the waste area. "I have to shit most bad." He clenched the stone in his fist away from the overseer.

"Make shit before work. No play in the toilet."

"Sorry master, it will not happen again."

"Hurry up and dig dirt."

Near the waste area when no one was looking, he enlarged the slash wound in his thigh with the same broken rock even though it stung like the fires of ten thousand suns. He inserted the stone with gritted teeth. Tearing his thin shirt into strips, he wrapped his leg tightly. The blood soaking through was the color of the stone in his hand and obscured the bump in his thigh, but the flow stopped.

Liu Fong limped with real and exaggerated pain from the waste area past the suspicious eye of the overseer but slipped into the trees when another fight diverted the overseer's attention. Among his many talents was that of locksmith. Quick manipulations released the rudimentary lock on the iron mask. He flung it so far into the jungle it would rust before discovery. No distant target was safe from his thrown spear, a skill that earned him the respect of the monks in the Shaolin Temple of Kung Fu during his training.

Now free to breathe, he hastened down the road to his humble hut and retrieved his most prized possession, a little lump of resin, from a hiding place and chewed it. The pain in his leg eased off.

He wrapped a small pack of naan bread into the last remnant of his shirt. Alert for bounty hunters who collected runaway slaves for bounty, he kept to the trees along the road to Kyatpyin. It promised to be a long seven miles until he came upon a mahout trying to secure a teak log to an impatient stomping elephant. Liu offered a hand and they together tethered the log behind the elephant amidst loud grunting in multiple languages.

The Chinaman cursed in Mandarin Chinese and the mahout responded, "China? I work with Chinese companies. We can talk to each other."

Chest heaving, "I am injured. Can I please ride your elephant?"

"You help, I help, be mahout." After a quick readjustment of the loincloth and the addition of road dust to Liu's skin where the shirt had been, the Chinaman emerged as a mahout. They proudly dragged the valuable teak log past the village of Kyatpyin to Thabeikkyin on the Irrawaddy River.

Fong cleverly talked his way onto a riverboat downriver to Rangoon, the major port of Burma. From there he stowed away on a Chinese junk headed for Calcutta.

He made his way through the crowded Indian city to the shop of a famous gem cutter, the most important in the Orient. The proprietor growled, "Another filthy urchin. What the hell do you want?"

"I have a stone."

The cabin where Porter lived was constructed midway above and below decks with a sunken doorway. Windows looked out both sides and aft, while the entrance faced four steps up. The interior was elegantly spartan with dark polished wood paneling on the walls. A dining table greeted visitors entering the door, while items of wooden furniture and a locked liquor cellarette lined the walls. A desk large enough to unroll charts lay along the starboard bulkhead. Adequate lanterns illuminated the room and bed where the Captain slept and sometimes read. The feeling was warm, comfortable . . . and lonesome. It was home.

One lazy afternoon waiting on the Calcutta tax collector, bored and lonesome himself, Bjorn knocked on the cabin door.

"Let's learn the game of kings."

"Mr. Jones, please remove the folding table and two chairs from my cabin to the deck. Get the passenger's new chess set." Porter did not socialize with the crew but enjoyed having them around to soften his solitude.

Bjorn proudly placed his new magnetic chessboard on the table with a black ivory square to his right. He brought a well-worn book from his ditty box titled Royal King Games Rules—Chess and opened it to drawings of the carved ivory figures in black and white.

"Hmmm . . . ." He lifted each miniature sculpture from its felt-lined recess and placed it on the board at random. Their magnetic bases popped them upright. "The first pages of the rules describe the philosophy but don't explain the rules." He stared in confusion at the chaos, while Porter on the opposite side did the same.

Gaje, the Gurkha on guard duty, stepped to the table wearing an amused smile. "Do you play?"

"We want to learn. Can you help us?"

"My great, great, great grandfather carried the first chess game from India's Chandraraja to the Caliph of Persia as a gift. Each king wore an emerald in his crown. The two red-hot queens had rubies in their royal tiaras. That intrepid man traveled throughout the land to train suitable opponents for his royal majesty."

"My set lacks jewels."

"The ruler of Persia learned fighting strategy from conflicts on the chessboard. He applied the insight to attack us in Nepal and captured our treasury of valuables. Incidentally, he gained insight into the character of his opponents. There are rumors he decimated his court afterword."

Bjorn envisioned similar applications in his nautical world and Porter wondered if he might repel a pirate attack.

"Permit me." The Gurkha turned the board to a white square at the right of each player and lined up the smallest eight men in the second row, placing white in front of Porter and black on the opposite side.

A lascar who knew chess and crew members who were bored crowded around the little table to watch.

"Once upon a time, two great armies met on the field of battle," said Gaje.

The lascar spoke up. "The chessboard holds many deep secrets. Mr. Bjorn has sixteen black men and Sir Porter has sixteen white, half of them wondering loose in the middle of the board.." He wore such a serious face that it was clear something momentous was at stake.

The two battle coaches lined up their respective white or black pawn figures across the second row of squares on the board.

"Who is scattered across the back?"

"Like I was saying," the Gurkha frowned, "Your pawns need a place to hide, so their castle occupies each corner." He placed a castle on each corner square and demonstrated how they moved, "Straight up and down on open squares."

"The horses?"

"From out of the castles charge warriors on horses that are knights in armor." He placed a knight beside each castle. "They jump one square forward and one diagonal in any direction, even over other pieces." The black knight jumped over the pawn in front and landed one square diagonally. He jumped back over the pawn to his starting square. "A horseman is a man of action, but reckless. He needs the bishop next to him to give tactics. They stay on their color and slide diagonally, which makes them dangerous."

He placed the bishops next to the knights, which left two empty squares in the center of each back row.

"The last two?"

"The regal queen always sits in her own color. Powerful, she can move in a straight line anywhere. The lady defends the king at her side at all costs."

Porter said, "Behold my red hot queen on her own color, yours on black."

"This last piece goes in the last square, right?"

"His majesty, the king, plans the strategy but does not actually fight. If he gets trapped and cannot escape, the opponent wins."

"This is how the story of chess unfolds," intoned the Gurkha standing behind Porter.

". . . Once upon a time, two great armies met on the field of battle."

Porter held up his hand. "Wait! I want to name my players."

"Listen to me first," said the Gurkha with agreement from the lascar.

". . . Once upon a time, two great armies met on the field of battle. Chess is a ritual that ends in victory or honorable defeat, like all grand stories."

The lascar punched his fists like a boxer and said, "We fight the battles in the field of the board."

Bjorn and Porter looked skeptical. They wanted to play chess.

"I start the first phase of about twenty moves."

"First phase?"

"We engage in massive battles during the middle game. Victory is our goal in the endgame. A white pawn starts." The impromptu white instructor moved a pawn in the second row forward two spaces.

The black lascar instructor moved a black pawn forward two spaces opposite its white counterpart.

"The armies surge onto the field of adventure and make a mad charge to control the four center squares of the board because the strategy revolves around this area. All battles eventually end. So too in chess. one side must fall. The epic tale ends with a checkmate where one great ruler concedes to another.

Chess is the game of kings.

Gaje the Gurkha jumped a white knight over the row of pawns to menace the center.

A Calcutta gem dealer working a modest stone cutting shop was famous for fencing irregular goods from Mogok.

"A beggar like you has nothing of value you did not steal. Show me your stone."

As Liu Fong unwrapped the bandages and pulled slabs of dried blood from his thigh, the disgusted jeweler said, "Inflammation in your leg looks like a piss-poor ruby with pus oozing out. You trick me." He raised his fist to strike Liu.

Chewing on a ball of resin to dull the pain, the ex-miner now smuggler dug the ruby from within his thigh. The shop owner was shocked at the audacity of the procedure, even more so at the pebble. Despite himself, he gasped when he wiped the corruption off to reveal the blood-red star.

"Two rupees and no more for this pebble," with feigned disinterest, but the pumping blood vessels in his neck and arms betrayed irresistible excitement. Liu for his part knew the value from years of trading Asian gems.

The Chinaman grabbed the stone from the jeweler's hands and shouted, "You insult me. I have dealt rubies my entire life and this is superior to all of them. The color is deepest pigeon's blood red with a purple undertone that complements a pure gold mounting. I will pay you a hundred rupees to polish it."

"You are above your caste level."

He shoved the jeweler away with his powerful arm, strong from work in the mines, and stalked out leaving a stream of blood across the floor. The shop owner was beside himself and chased the red star, "A hundred rupees and my healer treats your leg to save your life."

Fong thought to himself, This man seems no more corrupt than others and has an empathetic heart. The pair walked back to the shop where the stonecutter summoned a healer to complete the transaction. Loud chants announced the healer carrying an enormous bag of healing potions slung over his shoulder.

The jeweler mustered every technique he knew to polish the rock into the most beautiful jewel the world had ever seen. It took him three months to prepare the ornament for a final lucky owner. The Fong watched by day and slept in the shop by night. He never once took his eyes off the work in progress.

The stone carver and observer experienced a moment of pure terror when a cadre of British soldiers searched the premises and almost discovered the stone. They were famous for appropriating special jewels for the English crown, but the jeweler was the essence of slyness and secreted it where only he and Fong knew.

The same jeweler grew wealthy supplying gemstones to a powerful ruby-addicted prefect in Zhaoqing, China by the name of Xu Guangjin. That august official maintained a clandestine network of intelligence which listened to rumors from the stevedores of the docks, jewelers everywhere, and spies throughout Asia. He knew *Agilis* would bypass Canton and deliver a gift directly to his palace in Zhaoqing, but those rumors knew nothing about a world-class star ruby.

Impatient, Fong grabbed the gem after its final polish. Quick, sticky fingers grabbed a red reject from the waste pile on the way out.

Liu changed from a lame mahout to a hard-working stevedore. The polished stone was smaller and fit well in his thigh, now healed. He wrapped a decorative bandanna over the slit and danced a few steps to show off his new style. It was easy to join a motley lascar group of stevedores whose serang was negotiating with Captain Porter.

By the end of the day, every lascar on the waterfront sported his own colorful leg bandana and started a new sartorial trend that made the serang famous throughout Asia.

Awe swept through the throngs lining the ghat steps on the Hooghly River as an elegant horse reined to a halt in front of *Agilis*. A few short strokes of a paddle brought the messenger to the starboard railing where he requested and received permission to board. He handed an engraved envelope to the Captain.

Porter opened the invitation addressed to Messers Captain R. Porter and B. Amundson, Norway Patriciate—California, and read the elaborate enclosure.

Lord Prabhubhai Kapoor and Mrs. Dishna Kapoor

request the pleasure of your company
at the marriage of their son
Dipak Kapoor
to
Reena Prabhati
daughter of Dr. Gamesh Prabhat and Mrs. Sheena Prabhat
Saturday, the seventeenth of June
One thousand eight hundred and Fifty-four
at half-past four in the afternoon
Auckland Hotel, Calcutta

He was quite unprepared for the second page that detailed events far beyond his limited experience of Indian affairs, especially weddings. Arrangements for departure on the morning after the wedding demanded his full attention, but the bride was the daughter of the most important merchant in Calcutta and he felt obligated to attend. With a sigh, he reflected that the wedding would be an interesting finale to their time in India.

"Mr. Amundson, we have received an invitation to a wedding. The celebration will be our parting image of Calcutta. Can you go?"

"In a heartbeat," came from the deck outside the cabin.

Eavesdropping from his station on deck, Ghurka Manju Gurung smiled and said, "Your invitation is a great honor, sirs. Have you been to a Hindu wedding?"

"No."

"No."

"I can help you." Pointing to the invitation, the Gurkha said, "We call this invitation the Pooja. Prepare for a good time in the most prestigious hall in Calcutta."

Porter had misgivings. Bjorn was enthusiastic.

"Expect a king's ransom in gold jewelry, red clothing, and dark maroon henna. The bride decorates her arms and legs the night before and tells a love story in the patterns. During the ceremony, you will smell incense sticks. A Hindu marriage is a covenant between two souls in the presence of the Hindu gods."

He explained the program for three days of festivities. The first day was Ganesh Pooja and private to the family." The public celebration started on the second day and was called the Sangeet Party.

"You sing and dance with a thousand other guests. Songs relate jokes about the groom and in-laws to have a successful marriage, followed by songs about the bride leaving her parent's home. Sample the food first for seasonings. Flavors can surprise foreigners."

Bjorn said, "My friends say I dance like a tree, but I can sing."

"Not to worry, Sahib Amundson. All eyes are on the professional dancers. No one will notice you."

Bjorn looked down at his clumsy feet and was relieved.

"The following activity is the Mehendi to prepare the bride, but visitors are not participants."

Porter shook his head at the stream of unfamiliar words. He said to Bjorn, "I can't remember all this. We'll have to follow the crowd as best we can."

"That's my course of action too."

"On the Third Day, the groom arrives at the Baraat ceremony to receive blessings in the Haldi. The couple meets under a canopy. The sacred fire is lit and the ceremony is concluded. After the Saptapadi sendoff comes a gigantic wedding feast. The guests and families let loose, drink spirits, and dance the night with the newlyweds."

Porter said, "Our schedule presses us but we will stay at the Baraat as long as we are able."

Bjorn said, "What do we wear?"

"I have a uniform, and you have a dress suit. These are the best we have."

On the day of the Baraat, Bjorn went to his tiny cabin and dusted off his good clothes. Porter retrieved his uniform and polished the brass buttons with a bit of seawater and salt. After a quick touchup by Mate Jones, they made their way to the Auckland Hotel.

It was shortly before the ceremony of the second day. The bride stood out in a red sari and red veil. A tangled carved headgear like a milky white sponge covered her head. Likewise, the groom's headgear was conical and intricate. They noticed the groom was attired in the customary rich Bengali fashion. The traditional couple looked beautiful and amazing.

Neither Bjorn nor Porter had seen a civilized female person for many months and gawked at the gorgeous bride. Bjorn said, "I could fall in love in a heartbeat."

"No, you could not. She almost has a husband, but her beauty is breathtaking, especially to me."

The actual ceremony was in Urdu and they did not understand the dialogue. They did understand the next ritual.

"What on earth are they doing now?" said Bjorn. "I want to help."

"They do not want your assistance, I am sure."

"I can offer, can't I?"

The bride was seated on a wooden plank and covered her face with large green betel leaves. A group of relatives raised the plank and carried the bride seven times around the groom before bringing them face to face. As the bride slowly uncovered her features, the bride and groom could finally see each other for the first time that day. They exchanged glances and floral garlands, except the brothers lifted the wooden plank higher than the groom so that he could not place the garland.

"It's about time. Maybe they need a hand."

"They don't."

The day was saved when the groom's friends lifted him up to exchange his garland and win his bride. Bjorn relaxed.

The crowd moved to the fun and frolic hall where a huge gathering of family and friends prepared for several days of revelry with unlimited food and drink. Laughter, noise, and fun surrounded the newlyweds.

The breath of heavenly perfume mixed with fragrances of incense. Music, laughter, and sarongs in brilliant colors on the ladies blanketed the classy ballroom in the Auckland Hotel.

Porter and Bjorn sampled the proceedings in variety and depth. They felt underdressed among the brightly-hued clothes and heavy jewelry and were amazed at the choreographed dances and colorful and loud proceedings. Neither wore a single gold bindis nor a pair of jhumkas for the ears, even though they once owned a gold mine. Bjorn did not have a gold chain with a pendant. Porter's buttons on his uniform were not jeweled and made of brass, not gold.

A burst of laughter caught their attention. Dancing from the group in high spirits, a young woman pranced to the blonde-haired passenger and took his calloused hand. "We celebrate together, no?"

An embarrassed Bjorn stood hardly moving among the swirling people while his new partner swayed and circled around him.

"We don't fit in so well, do we?"

"I feel as welcomed as I ever have. Perhaps I should learn to dance."

The night was late when Porter ended the evening, "My friend, we have an engagement tomorrow with the Hooghly river and best see to it."

They missed important happenings onboard while attending the wedding.

Elsewhere, Maverick floated in a field of dreams where days had no beginning or end.

Maverick could not know his companions waiting at the meeting place were worried about him the day of the wedding. After a decent wait, they carried bags of gifts for their wives, lovers, family, and friends back to *Agilis* and assumed Maverick had returned on his own. He was a grown man, wasn't he?

The next morning Bjorn held his head in a hangover headache after the wedding festivities the night before, "I need a cup of coffee." He called down the galley, "Mate, a cup of coffee if you would."

Nothing stirred.

He looked down the galley hatch and saw a cold stove. "Where's Maverick?" He called out in his famous voice, "MAVERICK!"

Nobody replied again.

The obscene pilot, prepared to guide their way downriver to the ocean, cussed through two ship's bells. "Let that worthless deserter ass go. You see them abandon their posts all the time. We have to catch the tide."

"We can't lose our cook," Jones said to Bjorn. "Where is he?"

"Not again. Let's go."

They hurried back to the chaotic marketplace and tried to retrace the steps their cook might have taken. It was no use and they asked a vendor about an opium den. The shop owner pointed to a beaded door in a remote corner of the market. They pushed their way in.

A sallow Malay attendant hurried up with a tray of pipes pointing to samples of ecstasy and beckoned Bjorn and Jones to recline in empty berths. "I am not staying," said Bjorn. "I'm looking for a friend."

The proprietor persisted, "Most welcome esteemed gentlemens, I saved a special bed just for you and have your choice of the finest imported pipes from Burma to bring you pleasure."

"See here, you slimy slug of a snake, where is our friend?" They waved through the fog, both smoke, and mental. In a voice that could carry away the topsail in a gale, "MAVERICK! WHERE THE HELL ARE YOU?"

In a little higher alcove at the back, barely visible through the gloom, they heard a small groan from a pale, haggard body.

"My God! It's you," said Bjorn.

He looked down at the incoherent vague form staring into nothingness. "I told you 'No more of this shit' in Ghazipur and here you are."

He was in a pitiful state of inaction with every nerve atwitter.

"Wh . . . what day is it?"

Jones looked at him. "You're a worthless waste and lost to this world for a day or more. Get up."

"I just got here. I've had only three pipes . . ., four . . ., I forget exactly."

"We're leaving this den now!"

Mumble, mumble, "I . . . am in . . . heaven. You come too?"

"You're coming with us," said Jones.

Bjorn batted the opium pipe out of his mouth and heard the precious jade bowl and bamboo stem shatter on the floor. "That's one down."

Roughly grabbing Maverick by both arms, they pulled him to his unsteady feet. The angry manager approached with his dagger drawn to eliminate a brazen attack on his dope business.

Bjorn and Jones hustled their companion toward the exit, leaving the old manager standing in his stupor by the opium lamp. He hesitated at the source of his profit and comfort, but only for a moment before he came for Bjorn.

With Jones supporting the weight of the cook, Bjorn, who outweighed the manager by double, fought a rearguard action through the sweet haze. They were getting good at these rescues.

The manager's rage grew as their efforts stumbled over comatose patrons and knocked a string of pipes to the floor spilling little burning balls. Several of the precious imported pipes broke which further stoked the anger of the Celestial proprietor. Bjorn was groggy from the never-before-experienced sweet floral fumes but defeated the manager who was weak and fossilized from years of low-level addiction in the den. The headache from the hangover was erased.

Bjorn cut a gash across the proprietor's forehead with a swing of his knife and crossed it with a reverse swing. "You've got the scar same as me. Never show your marked face to my mate again, not here, not in China, not in India, not in San Francisco, never."

They charged into the crowded marketplace, followed by the bleeding manager determined to prevent any further inconvenience to his patrons.

Bjorn yelled at Jones, "Never leave your mate like you did last night. We guard each other in these strange ports."

"Aye, aye, sir, never again."

Dragging Maverick on the ground, they hustled through the streets and bumped down the ghat steps to an empty dinghy in the river. The rower conveyed them to the rope ladder hanging over the side of *Agilis*. Staring down the rungs were the bloodshot eyes of a monumentally angry Captain Richard Jeremy Porter.

"Where the bloody hell have you three been? The tide is running and we must catch it or lose a day. I'm ready to embark." He pointed to the full, straining sails overhead and the stretched anchor line. We cannot wait.

They pushed an incoherent Maverick over the railing and joined him.

The manager of the den vowed to never again serve sailors unless they came in singly, without friends. and brought plenty of money.

More serious activities were underway on *Agilis* during the night Bjorn and Porter partied on choices of Bengali wedding cuisine.

The motley crew and chanted sea shanties to harmonize their exertions of hauling stay lines to the masts. The choir of the deck erupted with a new version of an old song.

> Oh was you ever on the Hooghly River
> Black fever makes the white man shiver
> A Yankee ship came down the river
> Her masts and yards they shone like silver
>
> (chorus)
> And blow me boys, and blow forever
> Blow, boys, blow!
> Aye, blow me down the Hooghly River
> Blow, me bully boys, blow!

They were harmonious enough the Gurkhas distracted themselves into listening and overlooked the quiet dripping of water from the little Chinese fellow climbing the stern. They did not notice when he slipped under the hatch cover the cook forgot to lock. Feeling through the cargo for anything like a chest, his hand grasped a warm foot. The owner of the foot made a quiet exclamation in Yue Chinese and repeated it in Malayan. "I am not here."

"How many chests of opium do you guard?"

"The mate said thirty-four plus a late addition."

"I did not see you."

He slithered up the ladder as smoothly as Morgan stalked a rat. The Gurkha's backs were toward him, and he oozed through the shadows like a spirit. He took away nothing but the count of thirty-five chests of prime opium and the knowledge that two ferocious guards enjoyed sea shanties. He headed uphill to the School of Commerce building that overlooked the Bengal Club.

"Tell me what you saw." The spy explained everything to the distant chant of the sailors in the forecastle.

What do think she had for cargo
Why, black sheep that had run the embargo
And what do you think they had for dinner?
Why a monkey's heart and a donkey's liver.
[Chorus]

Captain Porter studied the horizon and felt the local wind winds were unfavorable for maneuvering through the press of traffic in the moonlight, on returning to the ship in the wee hours of the morning. Jones suggested they delay their embarkation until the morning. The two drunk gentlemen were satisfied with the delay and went to their respective quarters. Morning broke far too soon.

With the river pilot manning the bow and Bjorn alongside, Jones called the hands to their stations. The helmsman gripped the tiller. "Mr. Jones, prepare to set sail now that we have the queen of the caboose back amongst our company."

"Lay aloft and loosen the topsails. Let fall the fore-topsail. Let fall main topsail. Set all topsails."

Willing hands, common and lascar, hauled the lines to brace the canvas and watched them bulge with the wind.

"Weigh anchor." Four hearty sober seamen turned the capstan and raised the anchor to the railing singing Hanging Johnnie.

They call me hanging Johnnie,
Hooray, Hooray!
They call me hanging Johnnie,
Hang, boys, hang.

They say I hang for money,
Hooray, Hooray!
But saying so is funny;
Hang, boys, hang.

Porter said, "Our pace down the Hooghly will be slowed by the traffic and the daily tidal wave rushing upriver."

"There were more boats than water coming up," said Bjorn.

The anchor chain disappeared into the hawsehole and a rusty anchor dripping mud and muck from the river bottom rose from the river. The little brig did not qualify for a spot near the wharf that would have allowed actual mooring lines to secure her position.

> Come hang, come haul together,
> Hooray, Hooray!
> Come hang for finer weather,
> Hang, boys, hang.
>
> I'd hang to make things jolly,
> Hooray, Hooray!
> I'd hang all wrong and folly;
> Hang, boys, hang.

"I have reengaged our obnoxious cussing river pilot for three days to guide us downriver to the River Pilot Boat. He was the only man free for days to come. I'll be glad to drown that son-of-a-bitch in the Bay of Bengal, or at least be quit of him."

A roar came from the open deck, "You think I curse? My descriptions of the floating debris, derelict men, and junk shit on the flowing mud of the Hooghly are the only language they understand. I'll knock your head off if you criticize me again."

The pilot was his usual pissed-off self and chewed out Jones, Porter, Bjorn, helmsman, and the ship's cat.

Bjorn said in a low voice, "He knows red-blooded words the hearty jack-tars don't know. I want him gone, myself."

Jones assumed command to hear the announcement, "Anchors aweigh."

Despite delays, the masts and yardarms reluctantly creaked into action in the red dawn, the hull popped and ached, the rigging whistled and moaned in the wind. *Agilis* pushed through the fleet of palwars with their single masts and made a grand arc across the Ganges and headed downstream toward the Bay of Bengal. Leaving behind the tall ships preparing to carry the world's commerce, they waved at *Sir Edmund Hughes*, gunboat, ready and armed to eradicate rascally pirates.

"Go get the bad guys," someone yelled.

The last view of the ghat was a cloud of smoke from a cremation whose stench followed them downstream for miles.

The helmsman obeyed as best he could the profane orders of the pilot to minimize serious collisions on the clogged river. Minor bumps were inevitable, but *Agilis* was en route to the Celestial Kingdom of China and could not afford a delay.

The pilot knew intimately and hated ferociously the changing river, yet between every fourth curse word gave accurate guidance to the helmsman along with every one of the ninety-six miles to the Bay and forty more to the Pilot Ridge lightship.

The sailors jabbered about combats with pirates, shoals, Sino warships, the adventure of it all. Bjorn climbed the foremast to enjoy the fertile plain silently slipping by.

Porter prepared for the unknown with Morgan Fore 'n Aft giving advice in the middle of his desk. His tail smeared wet ink on the page from time to time to which he responded, "Purr, Purr." After crumpling the ruined sheet and starting a new one, the scribe said, "Why do I put up with you? Get off." Morgan moved all of six inches to the side of the desk. "Purrrr, purrrr, purrr."

When Jones addressed the crew on deck, Bjorn noted the difference from Porter. Instead of shouting and cursing at the men in an overbearing display, the mate stated their success depended on them, the members of the crew, and emphasized that commands "Will be promptly obeyed."

Porter stepped forward to end the session with, "Any sailor who willfully disregards an order will answer to me." He thumped his chest and dismissed the men, "Set the watch, Mr. Jones."

In the meantime, they contended with boat races among the junks, fishermen with scattered nets, and river chaos. The writhing river bottom was an extra hazard among many others.

After two hectic days and one hundred and thirty-eight miles weaving their way down the muddy, shifting Hooghly River and the tidal bores flowing up, they greeted the River Pilot brig moored in the open blue waters of the Bay of Bengal.

Jones called down the hatch to the forecastle, "I need a rower to the River Pilot brig."

Men in the forecastle pointed to a man asleep with his back against the bulkhead. "Him," and shook him awake, saying he was required on deck.

The crew guffawed at the blue creative profanity the pilot shouted across the entire stretch as the rower pulled harder than chasing a whale. The profane pilot climbed on board the brig with the red stripe, ready for his next victim, before the inhabitants of *Agilis* gave a hearty gone-at-last cheer. The returning rower pumped his oar overhead three times and joined them with a wide smile.

Porter faced the Bay of Bengal alone, with only the cat for company.

"I wish you spoke English, Morgan, because we are in this together. Are you a leader or just naturally the king of the hill? Am I king of the hill? My character and honor are steadfast. My word is my bond. On rare occasions, I might need to communicate my orders a bit better, but that is all. Uncompromising integrity is my standard."

"Come in, I have not talked to a living soul this entire blessed day, not even the cook at breakfast or the damn cat. I'm trying to leave India in one piece," said Porter.

Bjorn, passenger and friend, had privileges to enter the cabin informally but still remembered that Porter was the master with responsibility for the wooden community of souls. "I'm not sorry to leave. The weather is hot, the food is strange, and I don't care for their culture. What's coming up?"

"Call Mr. Jones, if you would."

"Jones on the double," bellowed Bjorn out the door.

First Mate Jones entered as Captain Porter unrolled on the highly polished walnut tabletop a sheet titled,

A Chart of the Bay of Bengal, from False Point to Cheduba Island, with a Plan of the Port of Aktab and the Aracan River &c. Revised from the late Surveys by J.S. Hobbs, F.R.G.S. Hydrographer. Publication 1850."

It only covers the northern part of the bay," Porter sighed, "and ignores the rest."

They unrolled the second sheet that Bjorn and Jones held down.

"James Rennell published this helpful chart thirty-five years ago with routes to the Strait of Malacca. My third chart by Lieutenant J. A. Heathcote, H.M.I. Navy is marked with hand-drawn wind arrows that are helpful, but why can't the damn mapmakers put all the information on one chart?" He asked Jones and Bjorn to hold open another well-worn rolled sheet.

Chart of the Northern Part of The Bay of Bengal, Laid down chiefly from the Surveys made by Bartholew Plaisted and John Ritchie, London / 1772.

"It was a splendid effort when my great uncle crossed this very body of water, but seventy-four years ago . . .?"

Jones said, "Can't trust an old chart."

Bjorn added that observations of the waves, the color of the water, birds, and fish, clouds, and their combined briny instincts constituted their best guide.

Porter traced their route with his finger. "We raise the Andaman Islands in six days and fight the contrary currents through the Alexandra channel between Great and Little Coco Islands. They grow food for the penal colony down at Port Blair."

He stabbed the location of the port. "Repel the local pirates and we'll enter the Strait of Malacca five days out of Port Blair. The advice at the Bengal club was unhelpful. 'Stay alert day and night, keep underway at all costs, and prepare to fight.'"

"Good advice, I volunteer for a watch."

Porter shook his head. "Commanding a vessel is complicated. The Malacca passage is coming up in seven or eight days with well-known contrary currents, unemployed farmers infesting both shores, and changeable winds. The next three weeks will challenge our bodies and vessel."

Jones said, "*Agilis* construction is strong, our artillery can fight a war, and our mariners are young and strong if untested."

"They are that, and the best I could find. Those six vagabond lascars make skilled sailors but seem to be difficult to command."

"The best in Asia when you talk to them and occupy their hands," said the mate.

"You have my service. Life as a passenger ill suits me. No one to talk to."

The sailors were busy, and resented Bjorn as an idler, although his fine singing voice with proud and profane verses helped, and the chorus on deck welcomed his harmony to their working sea shanties.

As an ex-able-bodied sailor, Bjorn preferred the camaraderie of the forecastle to the formality in the cabin. He missed the ancient seafaring tradition of swapping stories and tall tales, especially with the lascars. They bitched about the captain and the officers for recreation, danced and sang, gambled, and wrestled. Bjorn didn't dance.

Even friends for half a decade, Bjorn was surprised at the chang from a reasonable companion onshore to a bully tyrant at sea. Porte possessed no qualms about using force to maintain obedience. H genteel language spilled into words that shocked the hands whe necessary.

"Damn, the old man has been around," was an opinion voic below decks on occasion.

Bjorn watched a handful of lascars play their familiar games of d a pair settling a playful dispute on the foredeck straining in impromptu wrestling match. The new queue in his hair indulged presence in the forecastle to join their games and learn their lore

His nautical instincts picked up a lascar swaying in time the waves splashing the hull and he asked the serang to explain rhythm. The serang said the man navigated by the forces of natu

"How?"

Akbar motioned Bjorn and the lascar from Samoa to the where they sat on the railing and admired the stars overhead reflected in jumping diamonds on the water. "I will tell you Samoan carried a latticework of sticks and shells.

The serang waved his arms and said, "Forces of nature tall you hear them?"

"Sometimes. How do they talk to you?"

Akbar touched Bjorn's eyes, his ears, his fingers, his nose, t on his forehead, his heart, his hair, his body, his mouth. "Her

Pointing to his ear, Akbar motioned silence to listen to the waves on the hull. He pointed in the direction they arrived from and traced a trio of swells with his finger. They made two gentle rumbles and broke in a swish before the sound faded to await the next set. Major waves arrived from one direction, but cross waves superimposed themselves from another. The serang and Samoan hummed a tune in rhythm with the slapping rollers.

In a moment of inspiration, Bjorn said, "Song and ocean are the same. Different songs for different waves."

"Sahib be smart. Touch water to feel of land, clouds, wind, tides, animals, swimmers." The serang instructed Bjorn on feeling the forces and their messages. He said complete instruction would span many years but started now.

"What is that frame for?" Bjorn pointed to the latticework, "It is a strange sculpture of art."

"The navigator memorizes star figures in night to steer by. He holds sticks and shells in day to show directions, and marks patterns for ocean swells when islands are there."

Bjorn turned the latticework over in his hands and tried to line up on a distant reef.

Akbar translated the cowrie shells that marked the islands and the connecting sticks which marked tides and currents. He laid it flat, pointed forward. "Natuna island is two days to come," when the map tells the winds of air and curved strips the currents.

From studying the charts, Bjorn knew this was correct and complemented the navigation skills of the Polynesian navigator.

Bjorn soaked up every shred of knowledge about navigation by the forces of nature. He suspected the information might be valuable in the future.

The knowledge came in bite-size bits, almost slogans.

"Follow birds to discover unknown lands."

"Clouds surround distant islands, and seabirds, turtles, coconuts, and twigs confirm the land."

"To see the weather, look over the side."

"Feel the perfect clarity of the tropical oceans from the side of a boat, close and personal water by you."

"Sea birds fly home to land at dusk and from land at dawn in the morning."

"Temperature changes and the colors of silty river outflows tell the story of life on the island."

Bjorn became instructed to a minimal level of knowledge and was dangerous.

"We have navigators' songs, information remembered in chants, the points where stars rise and set, and the sway of the boat with the song. If water and wood are out of rhythm, in wrong part of the ocean."

Rumble, rumble, swish continued one after another in a regular pattern that put Fore 'n Aft to sleep in the sun.

"We study before the voyage. Sahibs follow the map during navigation. We go good. But, I no like a big ship. No can feel the soul of the water."

Lascar life in the forecastle came in many guises depending on their tribe. The Hindus coexisted with the Muslims who tolerated the Christians who avoided the renegades. Their common goal was to fill their days and nights at sea with various endeavors, such as they might be. No stent at sea lasted forever and neither did a wife.

Harsh Masters, easy Masters, all had a place in the karma of things. Australians were proud of their one-on-one mateship, the lascars were crewmates within their nautical kinship, regardless of their tribe but independent of outsiders. Able to wring the last knot of speed out of a clipper or other assembly of boards and canvas on the water, working companions all, they had collective wisdom in their ranks that survived through the centuries, wars, assassinations, intrigues, betrayals, and friendship.

They even played chess on occasion, at least the thinking ones did. The clicking of dice were more active games than chess, and friendly arguments ended in wrestling matches. Occasional bumps in the cramped forecastle interrupted their style.

Porter signed them as a group under a three-year lascar agreement from another vessel, aware of their nature.

Headed by a serang, lascars were born gamblers and entertained themselves with pastimes that Bjorn learned in the forecastle. Their skills in fighting pirates held his attention more than anything else. Many of them improved their strategy and tactics by studying games of chess, but it was essential to tease each other with truthful but harmless jabs over the outcomes.

Lascars were skilled at everything except cold weather. Porter's group included a cook, carpenter, and sail mender with traditions of poetry, storytelling, and autonomy. They would work for you, support you, fight for you, teach you navigation, but refused domination and were experts at small-scale resistance.

Each group had a head serang who knew enough English to communicate with shipboard officers. His intermediary spoke the languages of many tribes and communicated orders from the officers, reasonable orders, but if an order was outside their tolerance, the lascars resisted.

Did they ever.

Bjorn witnessed the lascars dragging their feet, showing false compliance, feigning ignorance of orders, refusal to turn out on deck, hiding from officers in the forecastle or cargo. Each individual was an expert in these techniques, but only against unreasonable orders.

Mutiny might manifest itself in collective measures. A favorite fun was engaging in time-consuming celebrations related to religious festivals that dragged on for days. Claims of their deep-seated seafaring beliefs required them to avoid work but filled the day with long songs accompanied by lively dances and processions around the deck for Saturnalia and other holidays.

They would sometimes resort to a blanket refusal to eat or go on a strike. In extreme cases, they demonstrated on deck with threatened verbal and physical threats, not actual violence. Necessary violence, they might direct at officers, the ship, or send physical fists against weapons from the armory. Long-developed martial arts often prevailed. A really hated officer they threw overboard.

Even with the ship potentially sinking and them with it, they could be difficult, but in extreme situations, nobody thought of consequences.

That is when the serang, with a wink and knowing look, said the sahib must take lessons in navigation. "We do not use fancy metal gadgets."

They ate a diet of rice, flour, dull, key, curry kinds of stuff, dried fish, vegetables, and sometimes a little meat in line with their diverse religious and cultural preferences and practices. These comestibles were cheaper for the ship-owner than the standard fare of salt beef, dried peas, soft butter, or hardtack without weevils.

As a group, they were decent swimmers in contrast to the average sailor who sank like a rock. Honor kept them from deserting ships in a port like their white companions.

Chapter 5—Malacca

Facing calm bay seas as *Agilis* sailed for the Andaman Islands, the officers and passenger sat outside the cabin and turned philosophical. Raising a glass of wine, Jones started a poem he learned on an earlier trip.

> Here's a little red song to the god of guts,
> Who dwells in palaces, brothels, huts;
> The little Red God with the craw of grit;
>
> The god who never learned how to quit;
> He is neither a fool with a frozen smile,
> Or sad old toad in a cask of bile;
>
> He can dance with a shoe-nail in his heel,
> And never a sign Of his pain reveal;

Porter had learned the same poem from a literate sailor on an earlier voyage and continued in a bold voice,

> He can hold a mob with an empty gun
> And turn a tragedy into fun;
> Kill a man in a flash, a breath,
>
> Or snatch a friend from the claws of death;
> Swallow the pill of assured defeat
> And plan attack in his slow retreat;
>
> Spin the wheel till the numbers dance
> And bit his thumb at the god of Chance;

Maverick drew on his proud background as a moonshiner in Tennessee. He really understood the next verse,

> Drink straight water with whisky-soaks,
> Or call for liquor with temperance folks;
> Tearless stand at the graven stone,
> Yet weep in the silence of night, alone;

Bjorn, also known as B'horny from the mispronunciation of his name by a Mexican friend, picked up the thread in a sonorous voice,

> Worship a sweet, white virgin's glove,
> Or teach a courtesan how to love;
> Dare the dullness of fireside bliss,

> Or stake his soul for a wanton's kiss;
> Blind his soul to a woman's eyes
> When she says she loves and he knows she lies;

> Shovel dung in the city mart
> To earn a crust For his chosen art;

Commander Porter understood the brush of responsibility and spoke the next passage with great feeling from his heart,

> Build where the builders all have failed,
> And sail the seas that no man has sailed;
> Run a tunnel or dam a stream,

> Or damn the men who finance the dream;
> Tell a pal what his work is worth,
> Though he lose his last, best friend on earth;

> Lend the critical monkey-elf

A razor-hoping he'll kill himself;
Wear the garments he likes to wear,

Never dreaming that people stare;
Go to church if his conscience wills,
Or find his own-in the far, blue hills.

Maverick whispered as he missed his brother, his wife's grandmother in the hills of Tennessee,

He is kind and gentle, or harsh and gruff;
He is tender as love-or he's rawhide tough;
A rough-necked rider in spurs and chaps,

Or well-groomed son of the town-perhaps;

They jointly recited the final verse united in spirit with the words of the unknown poet,

And this is the little Red God I sing,

Who cares not a wallop for anything
That walks or gallops, that crawls or struts,
No matter how clothed, if it hasn't got guts.

Porter said, "Well enough, but guts hit-or-miss are mostly a miss. The lads in the forecastle are fearless, but they require my command for direction. Join me in the cabin."

The four returned to the table with the charts of Malacca stretched out. *Agilis* was centered between Point Batee, the northernmost point of Sumatra, and Phuket Island off Thailand.

"Geography makes this passage vulnerable to pirates. Mr. Jones, you will maintain diligent watches for the next three weeks. We should be beyond Singapore by then. You are a lookout Mr.

Amundson, even as a passenger. Mr. Hatfield, I expect extra coffee and food to be available at all times for the crew. You have weapons in the kitchen, be ready to use them. I will muster all hands on deck under attack including the Gurkhas. They are the best fighters on board."

They studied the inlets and shoals, observed notes from five previous years along the five-hundred-mile-gauntlet to Singapore. They are mentally prepared to vanquish any challenges.

"The strait's wide mouth narrows to about a mile at Singapore, within spitting distance from the raiders to the south.

"Keep calm and carry on."

The Gurkha Manju pointed to the empty chessboard and reviewed the rules. "White player, you have sixteen pieces, so does black. You vanquish your opponent when you move into their square and remove the piece from the board." Two eager faces absorbed his words with confidence. He drew himself up to his full erect height and started the story of chess as though he were addressing hundreds of men.

"Once upon a time, two great armies met on the field of battle, ready for the inevitable clash. I was there myself a month ago alongside Gaje, here." His demeanor and charisma affirmed his statement and the jeweled khukuri knife in his waistband backed it up.

"The field is a board of battle eight squares by eight, black and white. The army demands soldiers we call pawns." He filled the second row in front of Porter with eight white pawns and eight black in front of Bjorn. "We recruited them from the farms of the countryside."

Porter said, "My peon pawns can whip your lazy lascar pawns."

"We'll see about that."

"Wait for the other pieces."

The passenger and the captain looked bewildered but interested. They practiced moving the chess pieces around and learning the moves under the guidance of Manju. Fore 'n Aft was too busy chasing rats to attend the chess lesson. He followed his own rules anyway.

A white pawn starts. The impromptu white instructor moved a pawn in the second row forward two spaces.

The black lascar instructor moved a black pawn forward two spaces opposite its white counterpart. Manju jumped a white knight over the row of pawns to menace the center.

Bjorn jumped his black queen over her pawn and took three white pawns in a row.

"No, Sahib. The queen does not jump pieces, and you get only one move at a time. You trade maneuvers with your opponent."

"Why can't a pawn move more steps?"

"Because they're pawns."

"But you say they can take other men crossways?"

The Gurkha got exasperated and said the rules came down from antiquity and he didn't know why they were that way.

Porter asked Jones to retrieve paper, an old handkerchief, paint, and glue. "I want to name my players."

"Sir King, I christen you the master of the ship." He painted a tiny captain's hat with gold braid around a green emerald in the brim and glued it on the king.

"M'lady the queen, you are my chief mate masquerading as a midshipman with a plain hat and gold band. I can't imagine two bishops becoming bosuns but here they are, on white and black squares." He glued a gold scepter on each bishop and a cape in the right color for their square.

Amused, Bjorn said, "You want horses befouling the deck?"

Porter glared at him. "They're fine. The castles are cooks, and the pawns are farmers." A torn piece of handkerchief became an apron on the cook castle and a red sash converted each pawn into a peon farmer. "My little peon lads, ye be."

Manju folded his arms at the debasement of his chess players.

Bjorn said, "I don't play with dolls and my pieces will memorize their own names." He held up the king, "A sultan." The queen became Madam Ching, the famous pirate woman. Bishops stayed priests, knights became pirates and castles turned into proa rowers. "My pawns are the lascars."

With Porter naturally strategic and Bjorn naturally intelligent, their understanding of chess maneuvers advanced rapidly. The Gurkha was a disinterested bystander, offering less advice as time went on. The serang took pride in his lascar pawns.

The competitors were anything but disinterested. Bjorn lost the early matches because his natural aggressiveness was over-matched by his partner's strategy.

Bjorn said one exasperated day, "You cunning son-of-a-bitch, I see how your pieces defend each other. The knight joined your bishop to block me. I will keep to that strategy for the future."

Porter remained silent but the Gurkha nodded agreement and the lascar looked amused. His lascar life flowed smoothly among sailor, farmer, marauder, spy, depending on the season. An actual battle identical to the ongoing drama on the chessboard left him scarred for life.

Bjorn made four reckless moves and lost both knights. Always on the defensive, he lost again. "My cavalry can't run ahead of my soldiers. I have to balance the attack."

The winds picked up, and Porter ended their lesson. He had Jones carry the chessboard back to the cabin with the players magnetically anchored in position. "We'll finish our competition next time."

Bjorn took every lesson to heart and replayed the moves in his mind, whether standing in the rigging or sleeping in his bunk. A dream of armed chessmen disturbed sleep by advancing without following the squares.

That is unorthodox, he mumbled in his sleep.

"Oh bloody hell, get away from me. The captain is an idiot."

A shipboard cook crossing the Bay of Bengal was convulsing, befuddled, feeling sorry for himself, and hated every prior Hatfield living or dead. The cook chewed the last of his magic medicine from Ghazipur and had long since finished his willow bark tea. His appearance was between a slug and a twisting maggot.

Confusion turned to obsession with the chests of opium lurking in the hold behind the food stores. He tapped his fingers on the cutting board and took a drink of grog to soothe his nausea. Depression followed him to the head to relieve his diarrhea.

"Damn, I hurt."

The day was warm, the next meal for the sailors was due, the sea was calm, and the following wind was benign. The seamen were working up an appetite with their duties.

Maverick stumbled to the locked hatch over the hold. His way was blocked by two each, well-armed, heavily mustached, fierce-looking, taciturn Gurkhas. He could see the sparkle of the jeweled handles of their weapons and noticed their dark eyes sweeping the deck for any threat to the integrity of the chests.

"Some afternoon is it not." One grunted and the other looked violent.

"How am I supposed to cook tonight? I need to enter the hold."

The Gaje and Manju looked Maverick up and down, visually searched for weapons, communicated in body language with each other, and relaxed their vigil a tiny amount. One unlocked the hatch for Maverick.

Wearing his stained apron, he opened a barrel of brine with as much noise as he could muster and withdrew a slab of salty beef. Fire shot through his veins and he thought while peering through a gap in the cargo at the red carved chests with Chinese hieroglyphics, these boxes are full of escape and I need a sample.

Next to the wall behind the bales of cotton, he found a little tunnel. Feeling more than seeing in the dim light, the herb master wiggled through to the first chest. With care and by feel, he pried the bottom corner of the label loose that recorded the weight of the contents. Pulling a long thin paring knife from his apron, Maverick dug a hole through the wall of the chest. The first contact brought out leaves, but the knife penetrated a firm resin halfway in. He twisted and withdrew a bite-sized black substance on the tip. Slipping the knife and the sticky prize into the pocket of his apron, he licked his finger to moisturize the label and paste it back down.

Interesting, thought the Chinese stowaway, cowering in a corner that was the only unoccupied space in the cramped *Agilis*. Maverick did not see him in the gloom, but Fore 'n Aft did. The cat purred so loud that Liu Fong was sure he would be discovered. For the addict, the anticipation of the fix obliterated everything else.

The chef shuffled the bag of feed for the pigs and chickens, dropped the slab of dripping salt beef to make noise, cursed, and exited the hatch mumbling about the sloppy loading of the stevedores. He threw a handful of grain to the chickens and greens to the pigs but looked down from the gaze of the Gurkhas.

Gaje said to Manju, "A very slow cook. How does he ever cook a meal?"

Back in the galley, Maverick wrestled with his personal devils and slew some, but not all. Starting a big fire in the stove with clouds of pungent-smelling smoke, he banged the stove a few times. It was only then that he swallowed another tablespoon of raw, yellowish, sticky, poppy sap in an easy bite. It wasn't tasty and he gasped for air.

The salt beef was boiled and clean by the time the effects kicked in. His body heaved and he sweated diffusely before turning ill. Even with the knowledge of where the situation was heading, it was too late to fix his mistake. He was hooked for now and forever.

Sounds from the deck overhead sounded like Satan wanted in. Maverick puked corruption and yesterday's meals into a spare pot along with more from the last week. After a few spastic heaves, he fell to the bench in front of the galley stove and entered a gorgeous dream experience, relieved that his intestines were intact.

He felt good, chill, happy, and simply mellow. Humanity was beautiful with love and peace. No longer trembling, he mashed the slab of beef to wash out the salt and prepared the beautiful evening mess for his mates. All was well.

The pain in his hip and leg was gone.

Hungry men coming off the watch grumbled about their missing dinner and didn't notice a few missing ingredients.

The leadership and passenger crowded the binnacle compass near the tiller and jammed the helmsman to one side, leaving him barely able to control the seller. Jones pointed to a point on the binnacle and directed the helmsman to maintain that course, come hell or not.

"Aye, aye, sirs."

Porter called them to his cabin. "Let us review our course for the coming days." They studied the stack of contradictory charts over the six hundred and twenty miles to the Alexandra channel. "I expect to reach there in six days, but this bay is famous for currents, squalls, variable winds, and severe cyclones."

Fortunately, the voyage was uneventful outside of the usual afternoon downpours, strange waveforms, and a shakedown of the crew as they threw off the effects of their overindulgence in Calcutta. Fascinating features captured their attention through the windows of the cabin. Houndfish jumped at Agilis, barracuda charged, the aggressive saltwater crocodile swam across the ocean.

Gentle waves marked the tranquil surface after the storm yesterday, and the idle hands were passing time as they pleased.

"Sail ahoy," broke the monotony. The quiet swish through the water and the mariners' well-trimmed sails contrasted with the slow, lumbering vessel they overtook. The sharp-looking *Agilis* put the dilapidated vessel to shame if they had any shame.

On a closer approach to the clumsy ship, Jones made the first assessment, "A lousy run-down tub who can't rig sails." He saw desolate souls shuffling in a tiny pattern under the bosun with foul language in his mouth and a whip in his hand.

The rowdies ran to the railing and shouted across the waves despite the protests of their overseer. "Help us mates. We're bound for Port Blair and the prison colony on Andaman, but this ship can't make it. Take us aboard and we'll raid the bay for you."

"I'm innocent of killing that man. Besides, he deserved it."

"You're our last hope. Help us, please."

Not a seaman among them but shuddered to think of punishments they received in the past. A couple rubbed the scars from the cat 'o nine tails on their back while others looked in the opposite direction. No one felt good about the convicts they were seeing, none of whom could swim to *Agilis*.

Said Captain Porter, as he now demanded to be called, "They want to convert us to a pirate ship. We decline."

Roars of agreement rose from throats of the men. Maverick's cooking was too good and they were healthy to a man compared with the emaciated prisoners on the other ship.

The captain teased Maverick with stories that he hated jail after previous incarcerations in Tennessee lockups because of his moonshining career. "It seems your time of confinement did not have the desired effect."

The cook was unreformed. Jail cells were comfortable enough for a mountain man and better than the bunk in the galley, but were confining to Maverick, a free spirit. He could not tolerate loss of freedom for years surrounded by a steaming tropical jungle guarded by shark-filled waters. The prospect appalled him no end.

Jones' own rescue from a thrown-overboard situation made him acutely sensitive to floating in the water. "No!"

The prison bosun with a mighty swing of the whip knocked a man over the rails into the ocean.

"He can't swim!"

The man dog-paddled furiously to stay afloat against the iron manacle on his foot that dragged him under. Crews from both ships watched as three fins sticking out of the water converged not twenty feet off the hull. He gave a single yell as the teeth in front of the fins slashed chunks of flesh from his body. Other gray swimming machines joined and he was gone before you could say Davy Jones locker.

"God rest his soul," said Porter.

Bjorn summed up, "No one deserves that kind of treatment, and there's not a soul over there who deserves the hell they face. But there is no earthbound way I would turn us into raging pirates."

"Piracy is fueled by desperate people. You can understand why, but they are still dangerous." Insightful words from Porter.

The prison ship slipped astern and the watery blood spot became hidden beneath swells of blue water. The hull sank below the horizon followed by the tips of the masts leaving only the memory of the underbelly of civilization.

Porter returned to his cabin to ponder his situation. *I am not prepared for the burden and discipline of twenty souls on a wooden vessel carrying millions in contraband. I must guide us through the most treacherous waters of the planet. My crew is strong, but the scavengers of the sea are descended from generations of brigands skilled at overwhelming us.*

He pulled out the agreements he had signed with the EIC.

"I have a loan against my hull of sixteen thousand dollars and a promissory note to deposit six million dollars in Hong Kong in two months. I won't sleep until this caper is completed."

Head bowed he said, "Dear God, protect *Agilis* and her inhabitants. We need your help as never before. Amen."

Boundless water everywhere, beset by storms when two friends embarked together from Boston, Bjorn and Porter stood up from the chess table and surveyed the immensity of the horizon without a speck of land, a rock, or a landmark to guide their floating community.

Bjorn said, "The nature of the sea this evening is mysterious as it was for my Viking forefathers, only warmer."

"Hear, hear," responded his companion of many years.

They marveled at the courage of the early seafarers, who sailed vessels smaller than *Agilis* to explore unknown shores. To their contemplative minds with diverse outlooks, the immensity was a creation of their God, whoever that might be.

The wonders, they understood as sailors on the level deck, but the supreme beauty they appreciated from the masthead, although Porter with his plump body rarely ventured into the rigging. Vessels on the undulating surface gave confidence, security, and reliance on her gentle character.

"So ends a good day on a good ship with a good friend. I am fortunate,' said Bjorn.

The sun sank below the horizon, the ship pressed on through the ripple of the waves. The deliberate tread of the watch, the flap of a sail, the ring of the bell every half-hour marked the passing of time.

Porter said, "This calm may end with an exceptional rush or the elements can heap wrath on our staunch wooden ship. I've seen faithful logs of the sea that recorded hurricanes, shipwrecks, and sufferings. Chronicles relate stories where crews were massacred, of dark cruelty and oppression, of pestilence without medical aid, no balm to soothe the pain or whisper peace to the dying.

"Don't talk like that. It is bad luck."

"Will not we mariners develop traditions peculiar to ourselves in the face of danger and death, never to be heard again? Our failings are familiar, but those men pursuing our seafaring life perceive redeeming traits among our blemishes. Others harden their hearts against our suffering without respect for our worth."

Puffing on his pipe, Bjorn mused about sailors like he that might be rough, but were conversant with far-flung regions of the world, their moods, their culture, their mercies, their avarices. "He serves where firm hands and bold hearts are required. That man is worth more than a land-bound leading a life of dissipation and degrading habits. We unpolished men of action will lend a hand to the weak, spend our last dollar encouraging the unfortunate, and risk our lives defending the honor of our country."

Pointing to the sea with his own pipe, Porter said, "We cherish those who go down to the sea in ships and do business on the great waters."

A shout from aft interrupted their reveries. "We caught a fish."

Common knowledge among sailors held that several species of fish were palatable and welcome to eat. They knew the art of fishing required a line attached to a hook baited with a meat carved to resemble a fish. Seldom a day passed that such a bait on the line didn't trail astern when the crew had time.

It was afternoon when an excited shout from aft interrupted all activities. "We caught a fish."

Rushing to gaze on an intruder wobbling from side to side, everybody threw discipline overboard. A shark relaxed on the line. The catch was passive until the united efforts of the crew hauled it toward the brig with inevitable shouting. Annoyed by the restraint or disliking the motley collection of shaggy heads bending over the railing, the fish took a swift run to starboard. The hated monster snapped the hook and swam off, wagging her tail out of the water. "I am free, nah, nah . . .."

"Never mind," said Jones in consolation for his disappointment, "We'll hook that rascal yet. He follows us like a pet dog."

The shark had no intention of abandoning his food supply. The fish hovered near the vessel and moved with a fin and tail above the water, mouth open to gulp garbage. He was hungry and proud, not finicky as to the quality of food, edible, indigestible, or over-spiced, and greedy.

Minus a shark hook, Bjorn still determined to capture their sworn enemy. He fastened a piece of salt beef to the end of a rope and threw the bait straight into the wide-open, tooth-lined mouth. it lodged in a swish and triggered a suspicion food was too easy if not pursued.

The shark swam in company. Several small fish, mottled and less than the length of a lascar's foot, attended it. They swam around the shark's teeth, sometimes above or beneath and sometimes in front. These were pilot fish and a shark seldom went anywhere without one or several. Two of the pilot fish rubbed their noses on the sleek hull and returned to whisper, "All's well, only a monstrous whale." They betrayed the triangular-tooth-carrier to its doom.

The shark swam forward to bite the sculptured beef, but Bjorn hauled it hand over hand until the meat bait dangled at the stern. Jones tied a running bowline loop in a small, strong rope. This loop, he lowered over the stern. Bjorn jerked the bait and coaxed a leap from the water.

Jones loosed the running part of the bowline.

"Trade these." Bjorn switched the bowline from Jones and slapped the bait line into his empty hand and Bjorn roped his tail like a cowboy roping a steer, a skill he remembered from his California cowboy days. The deception made the gray fish furious, and he thrashed to escape, but the rope was strong and only tightened the noose that was gripped by several stout sailors.

Eager hands hauled the shark on board, but danced a lively jig to avoid the slashing teeth. Sailors set on the plopping bundle of muscle with an eagerness to subdue the beast that astounded the officers. Especially after the prison ship, they regarded this flapping fish as their mortal enemy at sea and welcomed a chance to reduce their numbers.

Even though the gray beast was strong and covered in leathery defensive sharkskin like sandpaper, it finally succumbed but not before the parallel rows of triangular teeth severed a line as completely as Maverick's knife, and released a gallant-sail to flap in the wind.

Maverick swung a meat cleaver like an executioner to separate the dangerous head from the powerful body and the shark eventually quit twisting. Some of the crew gagged when a knife wielder slashed open the stomach. Not a seafaring man among them, but forfeited his hunger for shark meat that day.

Pieces of a human leg bone enclosed by an iron manacle spilled across the deck.

Captain Porter pondered the freedom of owning his own vessel from the comfort of the cozy cabin. That privilege was encumbered with demands and responsibilities, and he wondered whether the illusion of freedom was really the gilded bars of a prison. Looming in the front of his thoughts was the obligation to bring *Agilis* safely through the strait, balanced with loyalty to the men under his command who worked the ship to make it happen.

The more he thought about it, the more the armaments shrank and the more vulnerable he felt. Compared to memories of the early years with a mate to guard his back and listen to his concerns, the comfort of the cabin made a poor substitute.

Porter was lonesome.

"Richard Jeremy Porter, you've got to fortify yourself with experience and knowledge from the mariners you have known. Your beatings as an indentured farmhand were nothing against the rigor of the schoolmaster. You lit the fire in the Franklin stove every morning and greeted Becky Revere on the rare occasions when she attended school. Common sense warns it's unwise to have a confidant under your command." He sighed and leaned on the table with his chin in his hands.

Unrolling the chart for the tenth time he studied the channel between the Little and Great Coco islands in the Andaman Archipelago. The chart showed no particular hazards and the depth soundings were ample. He muttered to himself, should be a swift passage down Malaya, and with the grace of God through the Malacca strait to Singapore. I see two ports on the way, each flanked by innumerable inlets and infested with idle farmers marauding in their off time.

"Today we start our grand adventure."

Agilis passed smoothly through the Alexandra strait and enjoyed two days of clear sailing past the prison colony in Port Blair. They approached Port Pelabuhan in Malaya where the strait of Malacca narrowed to thirty-five miles. but the smoke from the burning fields of Sumatra reduced the visibility to a few hundred feet. Only the binnacle compass guided them from hazard to hazard.

Jones ordered the sail area reduced because of congestion near the port. Moving carefully through a deep channel with frequent soundings of the depth, a flotilla of proas paddled swiftly toward her. Unfortunately, the smoke-filled wind stopped dead and the ship found herself becalmed in a listless sea.

Porter was concerned in light of the warning from the Bengal club and assigned guards in all directions. Cautious as the ranking and only captain, and encouraged by Bjorn, he refreshed the weapons training. "Mr. Jones, please assign the crew in squads of four or five. We will train to fend off boarding attacks."

Jones lined the crew up. "Starting on this end, count off one at a time." Pointing at the end man, "You're number one," and to the next, "Number two, and so on." The count reached eighteen, without the Gurkhas or the concealed stowaway. "The first five are the Sea Scorpions. The next five, you're Seagulls. Eleven through fifteen are the Mad Dogs, and everybody else is the Gray Dolphins including myself."

"Scorpions, Gulls, and Dogs will stack supplies of gunpowder to shoot blanks. I want to conserve our ammunition for actual combat.

"Quite so, sir."

Off the land flowed slight wafts of humid, dripping atmosphere laden with the fragrance of tropical fruits and flowers so heavy with perfume as to intoxicate the senses. This mingled with the earthy smell to which they had been a stranger since Calcutta and now inhaled with pleasure.

Any visiting vessel near Port Pelabuhan attracted boats from far and near, and *Agilis* was no exception. Men scrambled over the rails like a clutter of cats from little trading boats filled with tropical fruits and livestock that jostled for position. Ducks, geese, chickens, foals, goats, and pigs made a tempting chatter that portended flavorful meals from Maverick.

The Malayans in the fleet especially interested Bjorn. They were an undersized class of tawny men with coal-black hair and small piercing eyes, well-formed and featured, nimble as cats. They swarmed on board asking for the master. The bold spokesman made his way aft to Porter, and with a winning smile over red teeth, held out recommendations from captains he had supplied previously. He could not read the notes but emphasized their endorsement as one who could fill their needs. Porter said, "This is first-come, first-served."

The natives packing the deck appeared to be friendly, were certainly good-looking, and pointed to their boats stacked with fresh fruit of every description. Jones lost his battle against the flood of intruders even as he protested, "We are fully provisioned and permit no foreigners."

Porter observed the boats had no decks to hide malfeasance. He ignored the rhythms of a tribal drum in one boat, which if he had understood, would have described the ship and surmised a valuable cargo because of the two Gurkha guards.

It was amusing to see the serang smiling while the captain read the recommendations. Written comments denounced the vendors as swindling cheats and the greatest scoundrels ever encountered. Nevertheless, Jones accepted fruit and vegetables and crowded the Gurkha's space for livestock. Porter said, "It is cheaper to feed the men fresh produce than salt beef that costs so dear. I wouldn't want anybody tempted to dine on Morgan Fore 'n Aft."

Bjorn tried a banana which was a strange fruit to him. He traded an old pair of trousers for a whole bunch and ate nothing else for several days.

Porter decided to end the marketplace chaos, "Fire the bow gun for effect. I want no injuries." The gunners fired a warning shot over the canoes. The farmers in the proas scattered with frantic paddling. It appeared they didn't expect to be fired upon and were only trying to sell produce from their little farms. It was when the aft swivel gun fired out to sea that the paddlers scattered like a flock of birds and returned to shore.

"Bad-tempered foreign devils," several men commented in Malay during the paddling.

The scare over, Porter was dissatisfied at the performance of his crew. For the rest of the afternoon, under the direction of Porter, Jones had each man practice shadow fighting with opponents, shooting the pistols at imagined targets, and repulsing attackers from all directions.

The momentary deafness of arms' fire drowned out the rhythms of drums along the shore, but news of the rich plum traveled down the coast to every waiting warlord. Two were situated on the Muar and Batu Pahat rivers, which lay a day or two ahead. They hated each other but salivated at the coming plunder.

Under a fresh breeze the following morning, *Agilis* sailed into their competing territories.

Bjorn was edgy from looking at the horizon and not thinking about games. Captain Porter stared at the magnetic chessboard in his comfortable, lonely cabin, too occupied for a match until today.

It was enough to drive idle ivory chessmen to drink. They craved action.

The row of eight black lascar-pawns sent a mental message to the passenger in the rigging that they wanted to exit their trenches and engage the enemy.

"Hey Port . . . ly, my men are bracing to take on yours. What do you say?"

"I'm free."

"Coming down." He plopped onto the planks. "Let's go."

The chessboard reappeared on deck. Both contestants were eager to start.

Porter's ivory attack troops faced Bjorn's ebonized black forces.

Ghale, behind the Captain, faced the shrewd lascar supporting Bjorn. Fore 'n Aft saw thirty-two standing rodents and jumped into the middle of the board before the players even sat. One quick paw batted a black pawn into a white knight that stood his ground. The reeling little soldier stumbled into a white counterpart, and the magnets locked them into a wrestling clinch.

Bjorn swatted the cat aside. "Go find a rat." Fore 'n Aft hissed as he slinked off to chase conventional rodents while Porter rearranged the pieces.

Bjorn opened the rulebook to starting moves, but the lascar offered a quicker lesson.

"Pawns block the important characters." The Gurkha touched the white peon pawn in front of the king and folded his arms, "One or two squares." The student moved it two toward Bjorn. "This loyal soldier defeats an enemy in a diagonal move.

The lascar pointed to an ebonized pawn with pride. "We leap into action." Bjorn moved out his pawn two spaces.

The Gurkha explained a player that enters an occupied square captures the occupant.

Bjorn said, "I like no bloodshed."

"Why so many pawns, Ghale? They obstruct everybody."

"These fellows are tough, violent, and confrontational, but need the strategy of the bishops. Porter advanced the pawn in front of his queen two squares.

"Release the bishop," said the lascar, and Bjorn moved a sideways black pawn forward two spaces.

Centered on the board was a cluster of two white and two black pieces together.

Porter followed the finger of Ghale and moved his queen to the edge of the board.

"Checkmate."

"What is that?"

"Your king is under attack by my queen. You must respond or lose the game.

The lascar teacher said, "I'm afraid they have tricked us, sahib. We cannot protect your king. You lose the match."

"What! We just got started."

"Always defend your king. Your ancestors knew diplomacy and fighting, but not war. The Art of War cautions a general must control the center of the battleground or chessboard, or he will have a hard time and likely lose."

"I'm studying it."

Ghale restored the chess figures to their original positions. "Watch."

The Gurkha also knew the Art of War and said, "Fight a war with orthodoxy, win the war with unorthodoxy. Sun-Tsu defeated the Mongols with this philosophy."

The group talked about warfare with occasional references to the game. In the meantime, Fore 'n Aft rejoined the board and played an unorthodox match with himself using random player attacks. After he won over himself, Morgan disappeared with the white queen in his mouth.

Porter toyed with his pawns with the thought of getting these farmer pawns out of the way, "so I can unleash my power."

Bjorn moved his opposing pawns with the thought, fight bravely, my loyal lascars, and good luck.

The game continued with frequent references to the manual and advice from the loyal lascar and Ghale. Interested bystanders who did not understand the game spouted jovial, ribald jokes to intensify their gambling excitement. Each lascar picked a favorite pawn and put a mark on it, followed by a bet.

The strategies of the Gurkha and lascar ended in a stalemate. All the bets were moot, leaving the bettors disappointed and poor.

Dusk fell rapidly on the chessboard battleground, as it does in the tropics. The fascinated soulmates Bjorn and Maverick studied the bioluminescence on the ocean that warm tropical night. In the fresh breeze, every part that foamed during the day glowed with a pale light at night. *Agilis* drove two pillows of liquid light before her bow and left a milky train in her wake. As far as the eyes could see, the crest of every wave was bright, and the sky reflected the light back.

Maverick brought up cups of hot coffee and said, "This reminds me of the fireflies in the Smoky Mountains of Tennessee. The woods fill with clouds of glow worms flashing together for two weeks."

"Dried fish skins give off light in the mines too, but not bright like this astonishing ocean," said Bjorn.

"The entire forest seesaws between light and darkness."

"Not in Norwegian forests."

The mates' minds encompassed the nautical display in silence. Parallel bands of light rushed toward the ship at forty miles an hour. They skimmed a yard above the sea surface. The bands changed into rotating wheels, and a third wheel formed. They turned on hubs three hundred yards from the ship, spokes reached the horizon. The sea was calm, visibility was excellent, atmospheric electrical activity was everywhere.

Jones at the helm exclaimed in alarm, "There is a shoal ahead."

A tract of water was light green, leaning to yellow in that direction. Its edges were well defined but irregular and contrasted with the general pace of the ocean. The mate had not seen the phenomenon before and supposed that the strait was shallow. A heavy swell and no breakers showed the depth of water was enough for the little brig.

Jones asked Bjorn to drop the deep-sea lead overboard. It paid out a hundred fathoms of line to the seafloor. The peculiarity in color was from luminous electric particles floating on the water.

Their conversation turned philosophical, with the seafarers posing as amateur philosophers.

They could not match the imagination of the sea.

Bjorn considered cats as indifferent compared to his beloved dog, Boudica. Morgan Fore 'n Aft determined to convert him.

Saying to Fore 'n Aft when he climbed the rigging with him, played with his queue on a yardarm, purred while reading books, and harassing Bjorn with love, "There's not enough of you to go around."

The passenger pulled his beard out of the cat's furry clutches. Fore 'n Aft clawed up Bjorn's queue, "Meow, meow."

"What are you bleating about back there? I have work to do."

The cat climbed onto a broad shoulder and dug in his claws. Bjorn would love him face to face. He had to.

"Meow, meow . . .."

"Meow to you. Leave me alone or sail to the deck and forfeit one of your nine lives. I have one, and I want to keep it."

The last cherished animal contact of Bjorn's was two years ago when his dog was shot during a raid. It was futile to wrap his enormous arms around her sixty-five pounds and raise her to a sitting position. "Stand or sit or anything."

Her life drained away with each drop of blood over those work-scarred hands. He hugged the limp bundle of tan and black fur and rocked on the ground. His lingering vision was of Boudica's three puppies nuzzling her body, but their mother slept the endless sleep.

Arrested during the raid and alone in jail, Bjorn hung his head in a corner. He sobbed masculine grief for a long time.

"I will avenge you, no matter how long it takes. Goodbye, my faithful Boudica." His clenched crooked fists showed his depth of resolve, but no one in the cellblock bothered to look.

Today, half a world away in the Bay of Bengal, the man abandoned the black cat with white fur and made his way down the ratlines with clenched fists.

The King of Cats surveyed his wooden and watery domain and chirped at a bird he could not reach.

Bjorn closed the door in his tiny room to keep the cat out and sobbed at the memory of Boudica.

Morgan Fore 'n Aft scratched at the door to give comfort, but Bjorn was inconsolable. He remained indifferent to any animal he could wrap only a single palm around.

Chapter 6—Winds in Strait of Malacca

Sumatra. The very name evoked images of distant, mysterious Asia. Porter's knowledge of Sumatra was the source of culinary black pepper and predatory ruthless pirates. Perhaps the pirates farmed the pepper when they were not marauding or were the farmers playing pirate when their fields were growing a new crop?

Bjorn didn't know but was familiar with the black peppercorns so prized in the kitchens of Europe and America to enhance their food. He said aloud, "I want to see where pepper comes from. Are we nearby?'

"No closer than necessary. Lining the Strait of Malacca are farms in Malaya on the north and Sumatran pepper plantations to the south. I shall split the difference down the middle, except for dangerous shoals. The monsoon winds are unpredictable and can stop us altogether or blow backward. We are square-rigged and sail poorly into headwinds."

Navigation was difficult between torrential rains that whipped them daily, plus the limited visibility obscured by smoke from the burning Sumatran fields. Frequent waterspouts provoked ominous images of dancing sea monsters for which the strait was famous.

Porter commanded Jones to focus on the horizon for the next three days, and the same for every hand working the sails and helm. They were fighting hard waters against a powerful reverse current from the southeast.

Bjorn passed part of his watch chatting to the cook. Maverick was preparing the evening supper, in separate batches, of course. Wilted fruits and salt beef at the end of their life were adequate for the crewmen, but bubbling on the other side of the stovetop was a pot of tasty cuts from two chickens, just beheaded out of their dwindling flock. As an honored passenger, Bjorn dined with Porter on the better half of the mess.

"Hot enough for you?"

The vessel lunged like she was in the teeth of an obstinate sea monster with a mind of its own, and the able-bodied helmsman at the tiller struggled to keep the *Spirit* of Athena pointed at Singapore. The pots on the caboose slid from side to side, front to back.

"Go to hell, you worthless bag of seaweed. All you do is harass us working hands instead of helping." He moved each pot back over the fire.

"Worthless? Not on your ass. It's a hell of a climb to the top of the mast, where I watch for scoundrels trying to sink us. Your galley is below deck and hits the seafloor before me. The water will drown that stinking fire of cow shit and you with it."

"Leave me alone. I'm cooking chow to keep you clowns from gnawing on the railings. The paint is bad for your digestion."

"No worse than those god-awful spices from India."

"I'm warning you B'Horny, get outta here or your dinner will give you the runs from here to Singapore."

"There's already a line waiting to use the head. If the seas weren't so rough and they weren't so damn busy, the men could sit on the railing."

Bjorn quit teasing the cook and climbed the foremast as they glided deeper into the Strait of Malacca. The winds were angry, blowing from one direction, then another, swirling from the stern for good measure.

It was a bad omen.

Chapter 7—First Pirates

Plotting their position on the Heathcote chart covered by hand-drawn arrows that indicated the ocean currents, Porter commented to Jones, "The approach to the strait is tens of miles wide at this point." He marked their position with an X.

Jones traced their expected route with his finger and said, "Greater danger is a day and a half down here when the passage narrows to fifteen miles. That's within robbing range of both shores." His thumb on Sumatra and index finger on Malaya made a little arch over the Strait of Malacca under which they would pass.

"Quite so. The captain of *Sir Edward Hughes* explained their tactics. The rowdies lurk near the shipping lanes in proas with no obvious mast you can spot from a distance. Their well-honed instinct latches onto any approaching sail like a bird following a fish. They slither over the water, climb aboard, and eliminate the crew. You don't want to hear what they do next."

Jones shuddered because he knew what they did next. "I must check the watch, sir," and left to confirm the lookouts were scanning the horizon in all directions.

The contrary ocean current reduced their forward speed by half and formed rough swells against the monsoon winds. Momentary dips in the wind contributed to their slow headway. The air was quiet apart from the low slap of waves against the hull and a low hum in the rigging except for faint throbs of log drums echoing across the water from the Malay shore.

Porter remembered hearing about similar sounds along the Congo River during an argument over the language of jungle drums. A river captain said, "Their messages are simple, but those deep resonant booms carry immense distances. Drummers keep a sharp-eared spotter nearby to listen for incoming messages. He relays the information to the next drummer miles away with taps from drumsticks on a hollow log like a telegraph station. Is it accurate? I don't know?"

A musical rhythmist added higher and lower tones with patterns of short and long beats, pauses, and shifting tempos and rhythms speed messages at a hundred miles an hour to the next drummer seven miles away."

Porter heard the resonant beats scudding ahead through the Malay jungle in some dialect that neither the Gurkhas nor the crew understood. It was a new lascar that translated the words as, "Small, rich vessel to Singapore. Two masts and fast. Hurry." The fading rhythms alerted every warlord, pirate, farmer, and opportunist on the Malay coast to *"Agilis* is coming, *Agilis* is coming ."

Idle village farmers toiling in their plots understood over the rustling of the jungle and welcomed the news. She was overdue and their warlords demanded tribute now.

The lead farmer relayed the news from the jungle listening post to the overseer who reported to the warlord, Si Rahman. "By a day and a half comes a rich prize. Strong guards watch but we can take them." He flexed his biceps and punched the air.

The warlord mobilized the locals and explained his plan. Early the next morning, they paddled six miles offshore with provisions for a day. Three proas filled with men, ammunition, and weapons dispatched to the interception point, where an occasional slap of an oar maintained their position against the contrary current.

Even though the booming message reached Singapore and alerted bandits all the way, the transmission was garbled. *Agilis* grew an extra mast and swelled to a monstrous size with bars of gold stacked on the deck and chests of opium filling the hold. The crew devolved to a gaggle of schoolgirls in petticoats.

The wiser second warlord, Raiyat Shaw, had his own strategies for plunder that discounted the drum message. Supported by his own observations, his instructions were the same and three competing proas waited a short distance from the opposing group.

Rahman and Raiyat called an uneasy truce waiting for the cloud of rich sails to rise over the northwestern horizon.

In the constricted channel, currents roiled and canceled each other as opposing winds fought to a stalemate, and stranded *Agilis* in a slow, pitching wobble.

Captain Porter paced the deck and wore a path around the cabin. He trained his spyglass forward toward the Malayan shoreline, but his vision was blocked by haze. At least the drums were silent. The view in the direction of Sumatra was obscured by choking smoke from burning sugarcane fields. Behind them was an empty sea with no hope of help from fellow merchantmen or gunboats. Nervous, he had Jones revise their position based on logs and sextant readings and stomped around the cabin once more. He worried their progress was slower than the proas. "Damn those pepper peasants, their fires make so much smoke I can't see a bloody thing." Ahead through the haze, something lay low in the water. It could have been a log but that was unlikely with no storms.

Rahman's rowers of sea rats reacted to the approaching sails first. The trio of boats threw up spray from multiple paddles and closed on the brig in a heartbeat. Two instead of three masts and relatively clean decks didn't matter, she still made a good target.

Each proa contained a larger gang of hopefuls than a fishing boat, all poised for action. A similar storm erupted from Raiyat's proas and they stormed from the opposite quarter.

"Boats ahoy, two points off starboard bow. More boats ahoy to port."

The merchantman company, able-bodied and common, lined the railing with knives or the first weapons they could muster. Bjorn from high in the rigging hollered to the helmsman, "Keep moving at all costs. Bloody pirates, every last one. Prepare for attack."

Porter looked overhead with a flash of anger and was about to speak but Bjorn was too fast with his cupped hands in a manual megaphone, "Sorry, sir, I didn't mean to intrude on your authority but I've been in this situation before and know the danger. We're midway between the Maru and Batu Pahat rivers and both harbor marauders."

"See that you don't. I'm the only captain aboard." He directed the gunner, fresh off his hour of training, to load and fire at will."

Porter looked at the serang, Akbaar Mohamet. "What are they saying?"

"They are competing majahs that claim this stretch of strait for themselves. They hate us foreign raiders and even more."

Addressing Ghale and Gurung, "What say you?"

"I do not understand the Malay language, but they are in serious conflict, even while ransacking us. We repel both or we are lost. Each will outdo the other in viciousness."

Porter hollered to Jones, "Assault imminent." He glared at Bjorn who said nothing.

The force from Batu Pahat arrived first, the hull hiding the attacks from the Muar force. Jones ordered the hands, "Engage portside, engage starboard." The crew split and faced off against each attacking force. Porter said to Jones,"Give them lead, give them hell."

"Fire at will."

The first proa abandoned any pretense of a peaceful approach. Skilled hands clamped grappling hooks onto the bow railings and mounted the lines to the deck. Porter ordered the Scorpions and Dogs forward to neutralize them and the Gulls and Dolphins to the aft railings where the stern stormers traded threats with the crew.

The lead Muar from the opposite side responded with a swivel gun over the port railing to demand immediate surrender. This was not going to happen from either the victim or the Batu Pahats. The projectile splashed between two boats not far from Porter's swivel guns. An evil eye painted on ball looked where it was aimed.

The deck defenders fired pistols and the stern swivel gun, along with a musket or two, to show they were armed, ready, willing, wanted to fight, and surrender was not a possibility. The rising cloud of gunsmoke aroused anger in the proas. Batu fired a shot across the bow that narrowly missed a proa from Maru. Their hatred of each other was as great as their thirst for a prize, and the warlords exchanged volleys over Agilis, who returned fire in both directions.

The attack broadened into a three-way shooting match. Lead flew through the air like clouds of mosquitoes, although the gunsmoke, pepper field smoke, and natural mist obscured the scene. Land-based hostilities broke the truce, and both sets of thugs divided their forces, sending two proas to sack the prey and one to fight the other warlord.

Ugly, sweaty, swarthy pirates clambered over the railings from two directions and overwhelmed the defenders. Hand-to-fighting was the Gurkhas' natural element and they enthusiastically joined the melee. Intent on forcing an immediate surrender, the boarding parties attacked but divided their forces to face the crew, the Gurkhas who fought like three men each, and competing thieves from the coast.

Bjorn slid down the stay line from the masttop and seized a cutlass from the stash on deck. He plunged into action with all his considerable strength and attitude.

One pirate slashed a new gash across his back but he twisted and stabbed back with conviction. Two sailors pushed a maimed brown body overboard to make more room for fighting. Porter at starboard raised his cutlass and plunged into the action, but shouted when he slipped on a pool of blood. Bjorn plunged through densely-packed looters to confront a vicious pair poised to dispatch Porter with raised knives. The hat with gold braids marked him as captain.

Bjorn stabbed both, but before they hit the deck the Gurkhas slashed their guts out with instinctive swishes of their khukuris. Astonished companions next to them called a retreat because of the loss of men and fled overboard in all directions, even as Bjorn and Gurkhas tossed torsos into the ocean with yells of victory. A traveling saltwater crocodile sensed food and scavenged the ocean of the floating bodies.

The short, swift attack did not damage the rigging, and *Agilis* pulled away from the action in the freshening winds. Smaller predatory fish followed the scuppers that drained blood from the deck on both sides. In their frustration at losing their prey, the competing warlords mounted a mutual naval battle among all six proas. They exchanged shots, taunts, and actions before returning to their villages on the coast.

Unnoticed in the combat, two large ships almost invisible in the haze and gunsmoke managed to slip by without notice. As *Agilis* entered an area of clear sailing, Bjorn pointed out the distant sails to which observation Porter said, "The skippers in the captains' meeting wanted a decoy in the Strait of Malacca and we have been honored by that designation. Ungrateful sons-of-bitches. If we don't hang together in these dangerous waters, we can most assuredly sink separately. Full alert men."

An able-bodied lascar, carpenter by trade and impromptu sailmaker by custom, arranged a triage center on deck. He sewed up the worst, life-threatening wounds, amputated mangled limbs, and turned to the merely injured. Ghale and Gurung cleaned their weapons and resumed their defense of the cargo. "Action is action," one said to the other, "regardless of the attacker."

Porter stood by Bjorn at the railing who was repaired with five new stitches in his back.

"You saved my life. Thank you."

"What else could I do? You're my friend."

Chapter 8—Accident

The seas were not rough that evening though squeezed between shorelines only five miles apart. Little white clouds dotted the sky and signaled good sailing conditions for a change.

Jones said, "I say hug the shore at Singapore as far away from Pirate Island as possible. Barring delays, we'll enter the Pearl River off Hong Kong in eighteen days."

Porter sat at the head of the table with the idlers of the crew, Jones the mate, Bjorn the passenger, and by special invitation Ghale and Garung the Nepalese. Hatfield served a meal not different from what the crew was getting, only fresher with garnishes.

The cook was a strapping fellow from the labors in the galley. This was all the more remarkable for a man disabled in his leg. Maverick was a quiet individual who didn't normally speak when serving food and drink, but hummed folk hillbilly tunes throughout the day, and whistled in tune with a familiar shanty. It was just as well since the table conversation was mostly about navigation and business matters. Server and served might make eye contact from time to time and show off his sparkling sense of humor and devilish backwoods wit, but tonight was different.

With a few mumbled words, he placed a highly-seasoned barbecue chicken dish, a bowl of fruit, and side dishes on the table. There were vegetables and oranges, a little cheese, potatoes, butter, and plum pudding.

Porter said, "Let's pop the cork on a bottle of St. Regis." Maverick stumbled to the normally-locked liquor cabinet called a cellarette and fumbled for a bottle of wine. He moved to fill the captain's glass.

"I said St. Regis and you brought us a St. Julien, dammit." He pounded his fist on the table and made the classes jump. "We will go with it since it drinks well with dinner, but pay attention next time, hear?"

Hatfield managed to spill a spot of crimson at each glass around the table. At the last seat, he dropped the bottle and watched it shatter on the wooden floor.

"Please clean that up before somebody slips on it."

Mate Jones scraped the broken shards into the trash basket and mopped up the traces of Saint Julien. "What a waste, St. Julian is one of my favorite wines."

Porter said, "Since you are up, let's try again. Please pull a bottle of St. Regis, my good man." Jones handed the bottle to Hatfield to open.

The second pour of wine made the glasses . . . mostly. Porter emptied his first glass by the end of the round and raised it for a refill.

"What is wrong, Hatfield? You've missed every glass and broken a bottle. Do you know how much they cost?"

"No, sir."

Are you drunk?"

Hatfield mumbled, no sir, and emptied the bottle down Porter's shirtfront.

"It was an accident, sir. I am so sorry. Please deduct the cost of a shirt from my account. This won't happen again."

"See that it doesn't, and consider your account more than fully debited to cover my humiliation. I doubt this was an accident, you're acting strange."

Gaje whispered to Manju, "That cook is diligent unless he samples the fruit of the poppy. Better check the chests. A massive flogging or death awaits us on the other end for missing any product." The companion cast a knowing glance. They both peeked at Bjorn who had similar internal suspicions but not enough evidence for a solid opinion.

The dinner concluded in silence. The Gurkhas left before the others, followed immediately by Bjorn. Together they carried a swinging lantern and clambered down the ladder to inspect the goods stacked to conceal the precious chests. Bjorn's instinct warned him something was amiss. The Gurkha's intuition kicked in too. Maverick dallied below decks longer than necessary and always picked a time when one Gurkha was asleep and his cohort distracted. "He must have his own supply. The cargo is undisturbed, but he lives in an opium dreamland."

"From the odor of the air and arrangement of the cargo, a stowaway is hiding in here," said Gaje. They shifted the bales of cotton and silk, rolled out the barrels of wine, and worked a channel to the wooden back wall, actually the front sides of the opium chests. As Bjorn lifted the final bale, the Gurkha who could see like a cat in the dark said, "There's a foot."

Bjorn pulled on the other foot. They yanked both and pulled a muttering man into the circle of light from the lantern. Examining him closely, Bjorn said, "A stowaway."

Ghale unsheathed his khukuri knife and prepared to use it.

"No, I want to talk to him."

The Gurkha reluctantly sheathed his knife. The creed of the khukuri was that once drawn it could not be replaced until it had tasted blood. But in the secrecy of the hold with Bjorn and the stowaway as the only witnesses, he decided to violate his oath this one time.

Bjorn held the terrified man against the ladder, "What are you doing here? We thought our water barrels were evaporating too fast and shrinkage of our foodstuffs was faster than rats could eat."

The stowaway spoke passable English with a sing-song oriental accent. He gave his history in a few words and pleaded for his life.

"We have to reduce rations to feed you."

"Oh no, sir. I catch rats and cockroaches unless the cat gets them first. He is the fat one, not me."

"Ugh."

"I sip only a little water.

Morgan Fore 'n Aft was definitely getting heavy on his diet of bugs and treats from the jack tars.

"You do look like you haven't been eating much." The Gurkha nodded.

"We should throw you overboard."

"Please, sir. I am a merchant from Zhaoqing. My business is to smuggle snuff and umbrellas to the Taiping rebels. My family sells arms to the revolutionaries of the Guangdong province for many years. The regime in Beijing hates us."

"Snuff? I don't believe that?"

"You westerners call them guns and ammunition. No good, my English, but I read labels. I hear through the cabin floor you go to Zhaoqing. Much difficult to avoid Canton."

"What is your name?"

"Liu Fong."

The Gurkha said, "You have big ears. I cut them off."

Bjorn stopped him. "Let him speak."

The Chinaman trembled for a few minutes before recovering his composure at the pardon of his death sentence. "To enter China beyond Canton is tricky. The government watch the Xi River, but Fong know way to Zhaoqing from Hong Kong. I make careful smuggler."

Bjorn and the Gurkhas looked at each other to debate nonverbally the fate of the stowaway. The Ghurka shrugged since it was not his vessel.

Finally, Bjorn said, "You can stay if you eat little and bother no one."

"And never molest the sacred chests for any reason," said Gaje.

"Never, honorable sir. Thank you, thank you, thank you."

The Gurkha rubbed the jeweled handle of his clean khukuri to reinforce his point. He insisted they tell Jones. Jones told Porter and everybody knew immediately.

Later, Bjorn made a surreptitious search of the galley while Hatfield was gathering provisions in the hold, but found nothing suspicious.

Porter strategized with Jones quietly in the cabin about the discovery of a second passenger. Bjorn eavesdropped through the window.

"Another mouth to feed. How in bloody hell can I make a profit with so many drains on our expenses? Can he cook anything besides garlic-dripping Chinese food?"

Jones said from personal experience it would be inhumane to throw the interloper overboard. "I can find work for him."

"If you say so, but I expect to see every crewman occupied, never idle, even for a breather."

It's a long haul from Calcutta, over nineteen hundred miles, but we slipped through Malacca without serious damage. That's the advantage of an innocent-looking modest merchant brig. It took only twenty-three long hard days and sleepless nights against contrary currents, headwinds, drifting backward, and minor skirmishes.

Bjorn called through the window, "Can we visit Singapore?"

"No. The East India Company demands all possible haste for the delivery. They're afraid our cargo is perishable."

Porter cleared his throat and said, "Mr. Jones, we are entering the home waters of professional sea looters. These put to shame the amateur fighting fishermen off Malaya. Stash lead balls and gunpowder near the swivel guns. Instruct each man-jack of a sailor to watch for suspicious activity from every quarter, especially Chinese fishermen, and be prepared for hand-to-hand combat. They want to stay among the living, don't they?. Times are hard and these are vicious professional pillagers. Their proas are faster than hell and they maneuver them with consummate skill."

"Gurkhas?"

"They guard our special cargo, but their lives are in danger so instruct them too. Jeweled or not, those swinging knives made quick work of intruders.

"Aye, aye, sir. That they did."

Bjorn leaned his elbows on the open window sill, "Stack bricks along the gunwales. That unconventional trick will surprise the bastards. You know a gun's target and where a cutlass slashes, but a flying brick can go anywhere. They hurt like hell and the edges rip the flesh off your arm."

"You are on duty, Mr. Amundson. The dangers require your skills as lookout, passenger or not."

"I am an honorary seaman but glad to help."

"Call the hands, Mr. Jones."

Porter addressed the company in a loud voice, clad in his Captain's hat with the fancy gold braid for authority. "Listen up. We are sailing the South China Sea, home to the most vicious pirates in the world. The first danger is Bintan island thirty-five miles from Singapore. Mr. Jones is doubling the watch until further notice. The notorious Anambas and Besar island archipelagoes are coming up, whose shores are jammed with watercraft ready to rob us. Man your stations."

Not to be outshone, Bjorn held up a brick from the floor of the galley. I have watched every man-jack standing on this deck pitch their over-seasoned food to the fishes . . .,"

Several of the crew laughed.

". . . and know you have a strong arm. This brick is a weapon for that arm. Watch me." Bjorn held the brick in his fist just so and threw it the length of the deck with a spin. It knocked a splinter from the deck plank where it hit.

"How did you do that?"

"Wrap the thumb around the side opposite the fingers." He planted his feet apart." "Hold it behind your shoulder. Swing and just before you release it roll your fingers underneath, and follow through." His fist made an arc from behind his ear to the knee in one swift movement.

Repeating the movement in slow motion with a second brick that split the first one. "Like that. Line up and take a few practice throws."

Bustling men took turns ripping up the brick floor of the galley and hurled full-fledged brick attacks. The targeted section of the fore-deck lost the battle in a pile of splinters.

The lascars who kept the fore-structures repaired protested, "Aim your blocks to one spot because we have to fix your damage."

Their combined aims and spins improved from wild misses to dangerous.

Porter said, "Fun is over. Replace these bricks in the galley before we burn us to the waterline."

The brave brig sailed through the Strait of Singapore, outran menacing pirates, and only thirty-five nautical miles out of Singapore repulsed a visit from Bintan Island thugs with no losses. from notorious Bintan island nick-named Pirate Island.

Guided by the binnacle, the helmsman turned north without incident. There was not a person but knew firsthand stories of the ferocious bandits, had drunk spirits in waterfront taverns with some, and eaten fish from their nets. You could not tell who they were.

Jones was optimistic, "Two thousand miles and three weeks to go. We can make it."

Porter leaned pessimistically, "The monsoon winds are unreliable and every little spot of land scattered along the route vomits armed pirates with pointed arrows. They plunder ships without bothering to enslave people.

Bjorn said, "Who are these thugs?"

"Two types. Local taxi-boat drivers or fishermen of the area. They are barbarous, rapacious, faithless, and ruthless. Mangrove swamps hide them, but they have chopped outlet channels to the shipping lanes, the better to prey on honest commerce like ourselves. Cowards covered by a mask and armed with household machetes strike at night. Local witch doctors spout superstitious black magic spells to bolster their confidence. They believe the shaman's magic water makes them invisible like the old Norse Vikings."

Bjorn winced at the mention of his ancestors but didn't say anything.

Porter likened most incidents to a gang mugging in a back alleyway. They wanted easy plunder of cash or cargo, with no use for itinerant seamen who resisted. Only adventurers of value could hope to live.

"Be suspicious of a watercraft under a flat sail coming at us, whether a junk or a Malayan proa with an outrigger. Either one will carry at least thirty desperate men to seize a vessel in a heartbeat. The maximum danger is near the Natuna islands, three days out."

Jones said, "I will harass their ass all the way to Hong Kong, but these southern seas are the worst."

Three watchful days and a brisk wind coupled with following seas sped their navigation through the shoals that dotted the sea lanes until low scudding clouds gave way to a clear night sky and the wind died. *Agilis* drifted to a dead stop.

The starboard watch called to his port counterpart, "Can't see a damned thing with the moon below the horizon, can you?"

Twenty-six pairs of eyes hidden in the darkness could see just fine. Each pair was well-adapted to the black night sky and knew the safe channel. On high alert, their oars made no sound when they slipped to a blind spot under the lifeboat not visible to the helmsman.

"Now!" The nautical bandits erupted over the ends of the lifeboat. One knocked the helmsman away from the tiller, but not before he warned, "Pirates!"

The bandits stormed past the windows of the cabin in two narrow passageways along the belay pins. The watches called for help and hurled the first bricks at the onslaught. Hand-to-hand knives, swords, and bamboo sticks were powerless against the rain of sharp-edged blocks. Confused, the intruders choked the narrow passages in the dark and banged their feet into the sharp edges. Tender toes fractured from the unaccustomed impacts, only to stumble bleeding over the belongings of the Gurkhas. Gaje and Manju didn't mind blood on their weapons, but were outraged at blood on their bedroll.

Porter charged from the cabin with two pistols shooting flames and smoke into the attackers shouting, "All hands on deck!"

Brandishing Gunnlogi, Bjorn yelled, "Action!" and joined the slashing blades of the pair of pissed off Gurkhas.

The head pirate jumped onto the roof of the cabin from behind and demanded, "Where Is It?"

"Where is what?"

"You know what. Gurkhas don't guard cotton. The hold." He motioned more hoodlums over the top of the cabin since bloody bricks and broken limbs blocked the sides.

The Ghurkas screamed their blood-curdling war cry, Ayo Gurkhali. (Gurkhas are coming). "My khukuri thirsts for your worthless blood."

Foes and friends were indistinguishable among the Gurkhas, officers, crew, and rushing pirates, and the defenders could no longer throw bricks. One thief forced open the lock on the hatch and started in. His body was only two-thirds protected when a swish of the mighty Manju blade decapitated him without a sound. Gaje swung the decapitated head into the oncoming pirates by its pigtail. It splashed red on Porter and Bjorn, even as the terrified eyes stayed open just long enough to wince at the impact. The lead pirate collapsed, unconscious in horror.

Bjorn defended one side passage around the cabin, Porter the other. They slowed the oncoming stream with blows and feints, but the screams of the attacking horde unnerved the crew. Porter's pistols eliminated two attackers, but without time to reload, he swung the butts as clubs. Bjorn smashed the face of one fisherman on the deck and threw him overboard.

Gaje flung the dead head to a hungry leaping fish that grabbed it in midair. The loss infuriated the Muslims who buried the intact body of their dead, even with parts retrieved later. Their philosophy was that occupants of targets died, not fellow ladrones.

Jones repeated the alarm, "Pirates!" Seamen poured out of the forecastle with their knives drawn like angry hornets from their nest. It was hard to distinguish the intruders in the dark with their black clothes, except for their screams.

Swords and bamboo sticks were useless in the packed hand-to-hand combat. The crew shoved the Gurkhas into the officers who lurched into the pirates. Nobody could swing a weapon, and friends and foes looked the same in the dark. The melee degenerated into hostile, cramped wrestling matches. Bricks broke arms and smashed skulls, but effective chokeholds removed the recipients from the action.

It was the revived helmsman who jumped to the swivel gun atop the cabin. The head pirate was directing the action from the front edge when the helmsman tackled him from behind. They wrestled but the navigator knocked the pirate unconscious with a cannonball. Over the front of the cabin, headfirst onto the steps, he went.

Thinking ahead, the savvy helmsman had preloaded the swivel gun with lead balls and gunpowder, but could not fire forward for fear of hitting his own men. Turning aft, he blasted the proa. Seawater bubbled through a multitude of one-inch holes and it started sinking. Another falling brick punched a big hole in the hull and finished the job.

The remaining marauders called for retreat as their boat bubbled down. "The lifeboat."

They were experts at untying knots like men of the sea everywhere. The lifeboat splashed while the lascars reloaded the swivel gun. With a mighty yell, the retreating attackers jumped just as the blast from the swivel gun peppered the lifeboat. Or was it a death boat? The ruffians tried to stop the leaking holes, but there were too many of them and they lacked enough fingers to plug everything.

The boat foundered and the Natuna Besar islanders swam amongst the crazed school of carnivorous fish. Flashing knives were unequal to the raw power of the gleaming, triangular teeth.

The Gurkhas to the front and Bjorn and Porter to the rear trapped three pirates in a pincher movement. Between Bjorn and the famously ferocious Nepalese khukuris, the defenders severed arms, legs, body parts, and heads from the black-robed bandits. Jones tossed the parts overboard. They had no time to marvel at the grateful surrounding feeding frenzy.

The attack faded away in a whimper.

Jones' entry in the ship log was precise. "Two chickens died this day." Every Sabbath morning, a chicken disappeared from the pens, to reappear midday as a luscious sea pie, if the cook knew his stuff which Maverick certainly did from his southern roots.

The feeding of the hands was a simple thing. One bell announced the beginning of the afternoon watch and the noon meal. They followed no refinement to eat, but not to say they didn't make their opinions known.

Two lascars stood outside the galley and spoke in elevated voices meant to be heard. "Stay away from that filthy pig cage. The prophet Mohammed forbade us to have any contact. We live on the meat of grazing livestock, fruit, vegetables, nuts, and seeds. This is a quote from the Quran and pleases God."

Maverick heard them shuffle away and continued rendering the pork skins into cracklings. He tasted a sample from time to time to confirm the crispness.

He spent his day whistling a tune and engaging his memory of the woods of home.

A Hindu fellow poked his head into the galley. "That beef better not be a divine sacred cow. It contains all the gods in the universe. Natural food calms the mind and brings peace and contentment."

"Where the hell do you think salt beef comes from? A cow is a cow and I use the dried dung in the stove."

"No wonder it stinks."

His arms ached to think about milking the cow back home. He hated the unfailing morning and evening chores the cow required. Maverick vowed to eat as many cattle as he could, and every meal from his galley had its complement of beef.

According to seafaring custom, the cook and bosun had a duty arrangement to give the cooks more sleep. The unofficial working bosun, who was on watch twenty-four hours a day, lit the fire in the stove so the cook could rise a little later to prepare breakfast over a blazing fire.

In return, the cook shined the bell between meals, traditionally the bosun's responsibility.

Thus, a day in the life of the queen of the dripping pan.

Mr. Maverick Hatfield, Porter was convinced, lacked the tiniest smidgen of quickness of mind, comprehension, or general intelligence. The idiot could not pour a glass of wine. Hell, he couldn't even pick a bottle of St. Regis port wine from the cellarette.

Porter watched Maverick leaning against the capstan with a faraway look in his eyes, oblivious. One of the Gurkhas was sleeping with his head on a bedroll. Bjorn was high on the foremast looking for water secrets, and activity filled the wooden deck planks.

"Dammit, Hatfield, I've had it with you." He grabbed the cook by the greasy shirt and threw him down the four steps into the cabin. He followed and slammed the door.

"I'm giving you a lesson in behavior. I'm sick and tired of whatever junk you are taking." Through an open window, he cried the mate, "Mr. Jones, get in here."

"Aye, aye, sir. What is it?"

Search the galley for opium, cannabis, or anything else this worthless turd is taking and feed it to the sharks." Jones left to execute the search.

Porter in a screaming rage lifted a stout cane from a stand and stood over Maverick. The frustration of a commander with unruly subordinates possessed him and he slammed the cane across the heap on the floor. The whack felt good so he did it again. With a vicious kick, he rolled the prostate form onto the stomach and began blows to the butt, the shoulders, and everything between. The low ceiling and close cabin walls prevented wide swings that could break bones. Instead, he rained follow-ups from every direction, after knocking over a piece of furniture. Another kick rolled the blubbering form onto his back.

"I ought to break your knees and face, but I need you to work. Get out of my sight and let this be a lesson. There will be no dereliction of duty on my ship. Understand?"

Maverick felt no pain, but his body suffered the effects of the blows. He crawled away on his hands and knees but Porter beat him to it. He yanked the door open and dumped the cook onto the deck. No words were necessary because all hands understood the punishment, except for Jones banging around the galley.

Porter said from the cabin as his temper exploded. "Do your duty with no complaint, or I'll pitch your drugged little vagabond body overboard." He emphasized his threat by an oath too vicious for words.

The mess crank could not cook the next meal.

High on the mainmast yardarm, Bjorn thought to himself, What's that funny lump against the binnacle? He descended the ratlines to investigate.

Sitting bloody and leaning against the compass with his arms wrapped tightly around his legs and his head down, Maverick moaned in a low voice.

Bjorn said to the helmsman, "What happened?"

"I didn't see anything, but maybe the captain lost his temper."

Bjorn yelled through the closed window to the cabin, "What is wrong with you, Porter? What did you do to Maverick?"

He carried Maverick to his little room to recover. It was clear the cook felt no pain from the pounding, but his re-injured leg could not support his weight.

Life as a sailor taught Bjorn experience in treating body wounds. "Always learn something new," was his motto in every situation. He wrapped strips of old sails around the bruised limbs to limit the swelling. The only cooling he could muster was to wet them and let evaporation do its job. Rest and sleep were the other measures he knew. Fore 'n Aft sneaked in to lie across Maverick's injured leg. The soft fur soothed the injuries and the licking tongue cleaned off dried blood.

Jones announced from the doorway, it was time to distribute half a pint of rum to the crew. "I didn't find any mind-destroying evidence in the galley. This is an urgent emergency and you're the acting cook. I'll get the rum from under the cabin because you best avoid the captain right now."

The separate cliques among the crew halted their duties and looked forward to the ration of the rum ceremony. Their eyes sparkled to receive their portion of this yellow enemy to humanity and practiced every trick to increase their allowance. If one succeeded, his triumph was complete. But if the same fellow thought he was short, he worked for the rest of the day in ill humor and sulky looks.

Bjorn received numerous comments concerning the pouring of the rum.

"The grog is late, me lad."

"Thankee, but where's the mess?"

"Damn, this sailor-man-jack is one hungry bastard."

Looking straight at Bjorn, a huge, blustery, ordinary sailor named Alan said, "Where's the damn cook?"

Muttering from the lascars sprang from the same attitudes but in muttered words of Hindi and Urdu.

Jones emphasized to the drinking crew their ration of grog was coming, Bjorn was the new cook, and he knew the mess was late but they would have it shortly, "Won't we, Mr. Amundson?"

Bjorn stared at the cookstove, which he called a caboose. There were glowing embers still alive. His stove on dry land stayed flat, except for an occasional earthquake, and the fire burned quietly. So did the pots of boiling beans for dinner. Altogether different was this floating caboose. Pots slid around the stovetop with every rock of the ship, mostly away from the fire. Shifting winds fed variable air that made the heat unreliable.

Picking up the slab of salt beef from the floor where Maverick dropped it, Bjorn wiped it off, threw it in the pot, filled it with water, and stoked the fire with dried cow dung. He ignored the grumbling from above and waited for the pot to boil. Breaking hardtack into man-size pieces occupied his hands while the pot boiled.

Ding, ding, ding rang the dinner bell, "Call the watch for dinner." Bjorn proudly presented his first shipboard cooking effort to the crew. The watch responded with the promptest hustle to the galley hatch they ever showed.

Sailors took their meals on deck in pleasant weather without a table or tablecloth. Who but a wimp needed knives or forks or spoons? Only a slacker looked for plates because eating was simple.

On Jones' signal, Bjorn poured his boiled, desalted beef into a wooden vessel called a kid the size of a peck measure. He set a bag of hardtack alongside, and dinner was served.

Their growling stomachs overcame their desire to complain when they commenced disappearing the tardy mess.

The replacement chef was too busy to sustain his disgust at the leadership of *Agilis*. He marveled at the eating customs when the sailors took their meals on the deck.

Dinner was the same on every ship he had sailed on. One kid, one crew, one choice. Bjorn did not prepare a special separate meal for the midshipmen, officers, or Gurkhas. The mess was democratic in the extreme.

Bjorn mistook the chomping of the starving mouths for approval of his culinary effort.

Bjorn's frontier gourmet touch was not the problem at the officer's mess in the cabin, nor was it the salty salt beef entrée. It was Maverick, somewhat recovered, who still made Porter's blood boil.

"Lose Hatfield. I won't have that addicted monkey endangering my ship. God knows what poison he might feed the crew in that opium-induced stupor. The wine he spilled at our table is a good indication of his deficient mental and physical state."

Mate Jones said, "May I remind the Master a rogue wave contributed a mighty lurch as Mr. Hatfield was serving."

"You may not. I cannot carry an incapacitated person on my ship. We are shorthanded as it is, and he reduces our staffing by one more."

Bjorn said quietly, "I have known Mr. Hatfield as a good man for many years. The crew has never been happier at mealtime. A momentary weakness is not a pang of overriding guilt."

"He's guilty as hell. He can't walk a straight line, his eyes have that faraway stare, and you can't communicate with him. Get him out of my sight. I order you to throw him overboard to the seagoing crocodiles, they're hungry and need to eat too."

Jones, who three years earlier was lashed to a broken spar and jettisoned overboard, said, "You can't mean that, sir. I survived such an experience but it destroyed the morale of the crew and the Master's reputation to boot.

The table fell deathly silent. Diners stared at their plates and quickly finished. Porter fixed his eyes on the fly walking across the ceiling. "How obnoxious to suffer flies so far out to sea. The mother must have deposited eggs in a cranny that hatched to molest us. Now they bedevil me." He swatted at a flying insect but missed. "Damn."

Tapping his fingers on the table and mulling an idea, he said, "It's mandatory to maintain discipline. I hereby order Mr. Jones to chain Mr. Hatfield on bread and water until he flushes that evil corruption from his system. I am distressed because I signed every member of the crew in good faith and expected them to reciprocate by performing good duty. Hatfield is not good duty. Supper is over."

He leaned back, folded his arms over his chest, and stared out the cabin window at the flowing ocean and the calm waves.

As the officers rose to leave, they heard Porter say, "Rogue wave, that was calm a sea as we shall see."

Chapter 9—Lost Cook

A scream of anguish from Maverick shattered the serenity of the wooden community, accompanied by the clank of chains. Unearthly cries poured through the locked hold cover in swirling response to the wild beasts that roared through Maverick's head as they clashed with bared teeth and sharp horns and lashing tails.

"God, that must hurt," said Jones to Bjorn.

Through his bloodshot eyes and skidding in the vomit on the floor, the prisoner lurched for the chest of opium with the loose label. The glorious memory, the ecstasy, the escape from the flying dragon beckoned him, but when he stood to run the chain tripped his ankle at six inches and he fell into the corruption underfoot. Cramps curled his body into a trembling ball covered with goosebumps. Pain, depression, and anxiety provoked another howl.

Anyone would have been uncomfortable shackled in a corner under normal conditions, Maverick too. The iron was cold on his ankles and he could barely reach his chamber pot for use. The hold was dim and the pounding of feet overhead deafened him. But this was not a normal condition, and waves of nausea wracked his insides far beyond the seasickness he suffered when he left San Francisco, his first time on a ship.

"Worst recovery I ever saw," said an ordinary sailor, Alan, "and I've seen some rough ones."

If he had possessed his faculties, which he temporarily did not, he would have heard the inhabitants grumble through the bulkhead of the forecastle, "Our cook turned out a meal we could eat, whatever his faults. That idiot Porter is wrong and we suffer for it. That substitute yellow-haired excuse of a galley servant should vacate the caboose and hide as a lowly idle passenger. I'm starving.

Sober, he might have heard the vertical debate through the ceiling, but he was in a world of agony and paid no attention to the muffled voice of Jones addressing the assembled company, minus Porter hiding in the cabin.

"Our cook is temporarily out of action, so who is prepared to step up for his teammates and prepare our mess?"

None of the crew members twitched so much as a muscle or their little finger or toe. They looked down, observed the birds overhead, two or three studied the waves hoping to see a dolphin, in utter silence.

"Damn your hides, do you want to starve? Somebody has to do it, and I can't, I have to manage the ship."

He glared up and down the unresponsive tars. His eyes fell on Alan sleeping and Gaje watching the deck for strangers. "You soldiers cook your own grub out on campaign in the Himalayas. Either of you could throw a slab of salt beef in a pot. How about it?"

Gaje shook Manju awake and said, "Get up. We have an emergency."

The pair faced Jones with the crew looking on in anticipation.

"Repeat what you just said to me."

"We need one of you to chef for us."

Using words of indignation that were never spoken before by Gaje and Manju, they pulled themselves to their full extended heights and looked over the head of Jones.

"Cooking is not our job. We are paid to guard the chests, nothing more. The answer is no way."

Jones was at his wit's end and slumped without energy. He wished the confined man under the deck was back in Porter's good graces. Hollering through the deck planks, he stomped his foot and said, "Dammit Hatfield, get clean."

Through his stupor, Maverick heard a familiar voice say, "I am only a passenger who learned to cook in the school of food poisoning and starvation, but I volunteer to serve."

"I hate to have a passenger contribute to the well-being of a voyage, but I have no choice." He glared at the cowardly crew.

"I pledge my best but don't know salt beef from hardtack."

Bjorn plugged his ears with his fingers and said, "I'm deaf to your negative comments about my Norwegian galley efforts. Excuse me, I have work to do." He dropped into the galley and stirred the fire to start the marine feast and redeem his first disastrous try.

Bjorn's new duties as executive book and pot washer were not arduous but occupied most of his time.

The most unpleasant duty was simply the cooking. He was not skilled in the mysteries of that art and was disgusted with the drudgery. While on a previous time, he tried cooking after the galley slave was flogged to incapacity. When he bungled the most important activity on board, inhabitants of the forecastle expressed their dissatisfaction in ample profane words and banished him from the stove forever.

Porter was an epicure for a good cup of coffee at breakfast or with a dish for dinner. The big burly man dropped next to Bjorn for a cup amid the rattling of pans and kettles.

"Port, my friend, you're in my way and getting portly shall we say. It's time I put you on a diet, especially if you keep haunting my galley. There's insufficient room for both of us."

"I want my morning coffee."

"You'll get it when it is ready," and he chased the irritable captain up the ladder.

The coffee in the pot boiled dry and left a blackened cake of sludge in the bottom. Bjorn pounded it loose with a fork and dumped the black grounds in his wastebasket. New grounds started a new pot of coffee and a new beginning for a new chef in a new adventure in front of an old rocking caboose. The mess burned before the coffee was ready, and Porter had to wait for his morning cup of java.

He said to the cat, "Here we are near the island of Java where the damn coffee beans are grown. Where's mine? We need a better cook."

Bjorn's response to the rank and file criticisms was, "I'll skin off your hides and make a drum. I'm doing the best I can, you ungrateful bastards. I'll resign and you'll eat worse." He banged the top of an overturned pot with a spoon. "Like this."

A crewman said through the hatch, "I watched my mother in the kitchen. Yes, I had a mother believe it or not. You'd have learned something if your old lady wasn't passed out drunk. We're not as uncivilized as our reputation, even if we act that way, but we need to eat and demand you improve. When do they let out Hatfield?"

Bjorn swung the knife at him because of the insult to his mother, who he barely remembered, but missed.

Jones stepped in, "Beats the hell out of me. I got that dope dragon off my back years ago but suffered through the worst, sickest, hardest weeks in my life to do it. Worse than my fall out of the rigging, worse than the beating on the streets of Tangiers, worse than the cesspit at home. Most agony in my life.

Another crewman piped up, "I hope Porter's not as ornery as you, Mr. Jones. You would drag this lockup out for weeks just to spite us. I know how you are."

"I am not. That sweat of the poppies is more abominably bad than you'd imagine. Once you get through it, you'll abstain the rest of your life or drop into hell."

From the rattling chains underfoot came a muffled, "God, I am thirsty. Anything for a drink of water. I'm draining from top and bottom. Oh Jesus, save me. These vines strangle my breath, and bugs swarm through my head."

To fill a little time between meals, Porter pulled out the chessboard and said, "Let's try a strategic game if you have time."

Glad for a chance to rest a few moments, Bjorn consulted a little red book and said, "Hey Port, listen to this. The *Art of War* discusses how to fend off an enemy. Let's try some unconventional tactics."

"I prefer the strategy I checkmated you with. The glut of pawns trapped your sultan king and left him vulnerable. That's how my regal red queen and my bishop got him. Too many lascar pawns obstructed your fighters. Like in the harbor at Calcutta where international ships hogged the good mooring positions and prevented me from landing in a wharf. Lesser local traffic blocked everything else."

Bjorn said, "My lascar pawns are not fishermen or stevedores, but they obstruct my design. They compensate by being clever, skilled in many arts, and devious.

"Sun-Tsu compares the unorthodox way to the orthodox. The military is unorthodox while the government is orthodox. The ladrones have their own government if my experience is a guide. I call them orthodox, don't you?"

"Orthodoxy is based on years of success."

"Troops conventionally fight one way, but an imaginative, unconventional opponent who avoids frontal assaults wins the engagement. In the competition between conventional and crafty, I am crafty."

"That's for sure, B'horny."

Bjorn read aloud that Sun-Tsu argued for emphasizing flexibility, maneuverability, and swiftness. "Swiftness makes surprise and surprise makes victory. Always follow the five forces of warfare. The first is Tao and the leader that makes his people live with him, die with him, and not fear danger."

"Others?"

"Heaven, Earth, General, and Laws. A leader with the most factors favoring his endeavor will prevail."

"I want examples."

"Compare them to the five forces of the sea."

"What might those be? I've never put them together before."

"The first force of the sea is greed. Why else would we put up with so much agony and danger?"

"I'm not greedy. Just an astute businessman."

"We'll see when the forces of winds and tides strike."

"Let's play chess."

Arguments about the comfortable common strategies versus the unproven tactics of new ideas raged hot and heated, but came to a sudden stop on the cry from the watch above, "Proas and war junks ahoy, all points."

Rushing on deck, their eyes saw a ring facing them on all sides like inward-facing teeth lining the mouth of a sea monster. A closing circle of sharp bows painted with eyes malevolently faced them and prepared to attack. A din of drums and horns designed to terrify them assaulted their ears along with a blast from an ancient blunderbuss.

Porter issued commands from the starboard railing like he was the general in a chess war. He ordered Jones, three lascars, and two able-bodied sailors into defensive action. Around the irregular areas of the main deck instead of regular squares, Bjorn behind Porter's back barked unconventional commands.

From the call on the opposite railing, Gaje and Manju, the wily Liu Fong, and the temporarily-unchained Maverick with a meat cleaver gave their all to protect the line of sailors lobbing spinning bricks, one of which shattered the aged blunderbuss and fractured the arm of the gunman. The Gurkhas slashed every face that rose above the side railings. Together, they repelled their share of bandits.

Maverick waged chemical warfare with boiling hot ghost pepper sauce, "It's my secret recipe." His corruption from wallowing in his waste repelled the intruders even more. "He is a ghost from the dead," a little ladrone screamed.

The attackers moved around the stern to the starboard to the benign defensive for safety, away from Bjorn's unconventional tactics they could not resist.

Ladrones are not all dumb and called off the attack when a second lumbering merchantman with no obvious defenses came into view. It turned out to be dangerous with concealed artillery, and neither side had any losses when the proas retreated to their home base.

The prisoner was enchained in the brig after his loyal defense.

One of the lascars heaved his salty beef overboard along with its container. "I can't eat another bite of this slop. It tastes like the ass-end of a sick cow, and as a Hindu, I'm not allowed to eat meat anyway."

Another sailor's mug of supper followed and triggered a cloud of protested inedibles that mostly landed on the deck, a few flew to the fishes.

"Look at that. Even the fish won't eat it." Several swimming denizens of the sea nuzzled the over-seasoned protein and turned away. The approaching barracuda scattered the fins but turned up his own vicious teeth at the floating morsels as they sank through the water.

"The best cook in the Sea of China is chained up on the other side of this bulkhead. We're being poisoned by this pretender to the galley. Good thing he isn't running the rigging or we'd be on the bottom."

"What can we do?"

"That man is sitting behind me not five feet away. I'll pull off a few timbers and release his ass."

"He's in chains and you ain't got the key." The sailor tugged on the boards of the bulkhead but found they were solid and well attached. Someone else tried his knife but the old, dry oak was too hard for a quick rescue.

"I've got to do something. That mess cook gave me hot coffee on the cold midnight watch."

"Yeah, a bite to eat when I was sent aloft and missed the mess."

Someone pounded on the bulkhead and asked Maverick how he was doing. The reply was weak and delayed.

"How do you think I'm doing? I'm sick and hungry."

"It's a bad sign when the head of the galley is hungry."

The men in the forecastle debated how to get back their favorite cook. There was a fierce argument in progress when Bjorn dropped down the hatch. Bitching stopped dead and they looked at the person of their complaints. The huge, blustery Alan said, "Mate, you're a good man but you fail stove patrol duty. We vote you hell-for-leather quick to desist food preparation."

"I've cooked beans, bears, and biscuits for years. What don't you care for?" he said in a low, ominous tone.

"That salt meat puckers my mouth if not scorches my tongue. They ain't enough grog in the world to cool the heat. Them biscuits is so hard they'd chisel rust off the anchor. My teeth hurts."

"The hell you say. Who's missing a mug? I'm not made of mugs and you'll share or eat with your bare hands. Wash them first."

Despite the unpalatable food, the men were a little intimidated by Bjorn and actually liked him, just not as a man of the mess. They looked away, took a small walk to the other side, a few feigned sleep.

"My mates of *Agilis*, Mr. Hatfield taught me to cook. He is a southerner who whips up the best food in America."

"We ain't in America if you notice."

"He weren't no teacher to you."

Bjorn sat on a ditty box and agreed. "I have an idea since Maverick is getting better. I'll help you write a letter to the Captain requesting to release him. We'll hand it to the Mate to pass to the captain. I would deliver it myself, but I'm not in the chain of command."

The letter sounded like it might work, so several hands offered advice. Bjorn composed a message in his journal and read it back. He promised to deliver it to Jones in the morning.

The crew in the forecastle spent the rest of the night congratulating themselves on their brilliant plan and salivating about the return of Maverick's chow. They offered Bjorn advice on where to stuff his salty spiced beef.

It was not to be.

The Gurkhas, Gaja and Manja, talked quietly for a long time. Manja tilted his head and rubbed his chin when Gaja stood erect and looked directly into his eyes. They nodded together, and Gaja approached Bjorn staring at the white figures lined up on the chessboard waiting for Porter's magic strategy.

Gaja said, "I have been too busy chasing infidels to play games but you, Sahib Bjorn, have learned strategies more powerful than mine."

"This board has shown me secrets for sure."

Bjorn was uncharacteristically silent, planning his next tactical offensive to checkmate Porter's king, when Manja said, "Pardon sahib, would you grant me a moment?" He spoke in a tactful tone with a compelling presence.

Bjorn halted his assault plans and looked at the Gurkha, who he admired.

Manja paused to gain his full attention. "You would be an excellent addition to our brotherhood with your fighting passion. Would you consider becoming an honorary Gurkha-in-training?"

The offer stunned the passenger. He was willing to fight for his own ideas but unsure about defending others he disagreed with."

He looked down at the board to think.

Porter emerged from the cabin door with a stoic expression and saved him. He sat down with authority before Bjorn could answer the Gurkhas.

"I've got you this time, Mr. Porter. What do you say to a little wager?"

"What can you wager? You spent your money in the bazaar."

"I have hidden resources you don't know about, a garnet for instance."

"Show me."

Bjorn retrieved a small red souvenir stone and held it out to Porter."

"I'll wager a hundred dollars to your account."

"How about the release of Hatfield instead. His treatment is working and he is on the mend."

"Okay. You win and I'll remove the chains and restore the cook to all duty. Satisfied?"

Bjorn's and Porter's forces battled for mastery of the sixty-four squares without a clear advantage to either side. Their play was balanced with Porter learning aggressiveness in his deployments and Bjorn employing strategies from The Art of War.

Feelings ran high among the spectators who placed bets on their favorite white or black character and followed the action with rapt attention. Some understood chess but nobody knew chess etiquette. Cheers, jeers, and braggadocios exploded from the gamblers whenever a piece captured another. Only the helmsman, Jones, and the lookout were on duty because somebody had to run the ship when the leader was obsessed elsewhere.

But even the lookout grew fascinated and overlooked a speck on the horizon.

Bjorn frowned at Porter who tensed and studied. Careful consideration marked their movements, and the wager was forgotten. Friendship was forgotten. Their honor was at stake.

The board was nearly empty, the armies had decimated each other, the players and chessmen were exhausted. Bjorn advanced an overlooked pawn that aroused a cheer among the lascar contingent.

"Check."

The lascars bumped their chests and threw each other around. "Yeah for us."

Porter stared in disbelief at the board. His king was directly in the path of the distant opposing Bishop. Bjorn's pawn was poised to take the king if he moved away. The king could eat the pawn but that would expose him to the other bishop. There was no legal move he could make.

"Checkmate."

The match was over.

Porter was angry at himself for allowing a checkmate, pissed at the advice from the bystanders, a thoroughly sore loser. His command was about to get immeasurably worse as he pouted in the cabin.

Bjorn thought over the Gurkha's offer. He liked the idea of the comradeship but was skeptical of submitting to the goals of some distant monarch. After proofreading the letter from the crew to divert his mind, he felt an obligation to prepare the noon meal and turned to the galley hatch.

Waiting on the first rung of the ladder and hoping for Maverick's early release, Bjorn scanned the far horizon from habit and saw a white spec in the clear air that contrasted with the dark blue. He called up the watch in the cross-tree, "Sail, I hope."

Porter came on deck. "Where away?"

"Three points off the port bow."

Lookouts in all directions hastened to their posts on the safe, calm, pleasant, and swift day. Having passed Natuna island with no interference, their next marker was the Spratly Islands. But that worry was in the future under the bright tropical sun. Always, a sail was welcome in this region that carried so much of the world's commerce, and the distant flying sheets caused great excitement. They had every reason to treat the newcomer as a friend that would give *Agilis* the support of numbers.

Porter trained his spyglass on the vessel approaching swiftly under a cloud of sail. Naturally fast with a peculiar color and cut of the canvas, Porter believed they were being hailed by a British man-of-war. High in the rigging, the watch cried out, "Our chance to see a British man-of-war up close."

Hands on the deck did not share his optimism. Porter said, "There are some among us including Mr. Amundson who are not American citizens, although they are under our American protections."

Bjorn said, "What are American protections?"

"An official list of each person on board with the name, status, nationality, and identifying characteristics such as missing appendages or scars like yours. America is a steadfast friend of England but prefers our citizens to sail on our own vessels."

Bjorn had heard stories that the British navy was manned almost exclusively by men who were not volunteers but victims of impressment. The direct description was they had been kidnapped. The victims were treated worse than slaves on land with small pay and severe penalties for misconduct. No wonder the royal navy had problems with manpower.

British warships were especially fond of impressing merchant sailors regardless of their national character. Their method was to fire at American ships and board them for a thorough search. Persons of British, Swedish, Dutch, Russian, Norwegian, or Spaniards, were liable to be invited to serve her Majesty. Despite protests and menaces, they were taken on board and compelled to submit with insults and injustice.

"Ship ahoy to port." The sails looked vaguely familiar. Porter remembered the lines of the vessel from Calcutta and read the name on the bow with relief. It was *Sir Edmund Hughes* flying the British flag. He retrieved his protection list and waited.

Chapter 10—Impressed

The speck materialized into *Sir Edmund Hughes* that Porter had last seen in the Hooghly River. He knew her Captain Hutton from the captain's meeting. The men of *Agilis* could see cannons protruding through the gun ports surrounded by the gleam of muskets, cutlasses, and other weapons of persuasion. Notwithstanding her threat, the sails were so large and neatly fitted, and the lines so symmetrical, and a hull so smooth gliding over the waves, she presented an appearance of charm, elegance, strength, and determination. On closer examination, she was a formidable menace.

Porter pressed ahead under reduced sails with the American flag flying and hoped their status as a merchant ship would protect them. Impressment was on his mind too, and he was already down a hand.

A tongue of flame and smoke belched from a gun port and shattered Porter's hope of neutrality. Chum, whizzed, splash, -ash, -sh, bounce across the water, the well-aimed cannonball across her bow cleared the railings and sank with a fan of foam. The roar startled the deck company and terrified Maverick below who likened it to the attack off Charleston. Fore 'n Aft disappeared into a hidden cranny known only to himself and rolled into the tightest ball he could manage with his front paws over his head and his ears flat.

The message was clear. Porter hollered to the riggers and helmsman, "Heave to." Skilled sailors put certain sails in opposition to others and *Agilis* drifted to a near dead stop. The helmsman lashed the tiller in place and waited against the stern for developments.

Maverick, chained in the brig, was double disturbed by the memory of the ball that fractured his leg. He still limped in pain whenever he was not chained like a dog. His greatest fear was hitting the bottom first when the brig sank, and he cried out, "For God's sake, release my shackles and let me save myself." No ears above heard him in the general chaos.

The armed gunboat HMS *Sir Edmund Hughes*, hove to ten yards from *Agilis*.

Porter said, "What the hell? See what they want, Mr. Jones." The *Agilis* waited only ten yards from the *Hughes*. Captain Frederick Hutton in full uniform crossed in a dinghy accompanied by two massive men. Porter dropped the ladder for them to board.

"Welcome aboard, sir. This is a surprise, but I am glad to see a friendly vessel in these dangerous waters."

The Captain and his two enforcers climbed aboard, one holding a sheaf of papers in a waterproof valise. "Good day, Mr. Pincher, your cooperation is expected and appreciated."

"It's Porter, sir. Why the shot across the bow?"

"Erasing pirates from the Spratly Islands is a serious business and my command is short of hands." He turned to the assistant with the pouch and read from a page. It was an order from the crown of England authorizing him as Captain of her Majesty's gunboat to eliminate threats to the East India Company. It included authorization to board any vessel in British waters and impress any necessary seaman except British commands, American commands, and certain others. Bjorn slid out of sight behind the cabin next to the helmsman.

With an offhand, swaggering air, Hutton demanded to know where they were from, where they were bound, and the nature of the cargo. "Show me your papers." Porter extended the list to Hutton but his assistant grabbed it. "Gather your men for inspection, if you would be so kind."

The Captain ordered Jones to summon the crew who were huddled as apprehensive spectators in the center of the deck. Tall, blond Bjorn was conspicuous at the back, even hunched alongside the helmsman. The sailors muttered speculations about who might be impressed.

"I demand to see these men's protections," Captain Hutton said with authority. "I am required to examine your signing papers for the crew. You may carry only Americans, but I am authorized to confirm the list. You are traversing the British trade routes between Singapore and Canton and I must inspect your vessel."

"You have my list," said Porter, pointing to the hands of the assistant, "The signing papers for every member of my crew are there.

The assistant read each name. Hutton's inspection was as intense as in the slave market of Africans destined for a cotton plantation. *Agilis* had carried one mass of unfortunates before her conversion to a swift merchantman

"Hatfield, Maverick, American, distinguishing feature of an injured leg."

"Indisposed in the hold at the moment. Would you like to see him?"

Hutton, the assistant, and Porter viewed Maverick sprawled in chains and surrounded by filth. The injury to his leg was obvious and the assistant checked off the name.

"Pass."

"Porter, Richard, American and Master, no distinctive marks."

"I am he."

"Pass."

He went down the list to the lascars, many with only one Anglicized name. He stumbled over the pronunciations but they were used to it and respectful.

"I don't want lascars. They're likely pirates already and are protected by the Merchant's Association of India. They are not suitable navy material. Pass the group."

The serang bristled at the insult since he understood English, but his companions clamped his mouth shut before he could say something incriminating.

"Moving along, Gurkhas Gaje Ghale, and Manju Gurung, Nepalese."

"They are assigned under the auspices of the East India Company, and I have no documentation for them."

"I most assuredly doubt they are American, but they are a protected group within the Empire. Pass."

"Who is this? A passenger, Amundson, Bjorn, Norwegian, scars across his arms and back and face."

"Mr. Amundson is a passenger and representative of the kingdom of Norway.

"Bring him forward."

"Mr. Jones, please present Mr. Amundson."

The British Captain looked up at Bjorn. "You are not an American. According to this documentation in the name of her Majesty, Queen Victoria of England, I enlist you to assist the crew of HMS *Sir Edmund Hughes* as an able-bodied seaman and fighter of piracy."

"You can't do that. I represent his Majesty, King Oscar of Norway. I am on my way to San Francisco to assume my official duties. I cannot go."

"You will go. Take him," he said to his two massive accomplices equal to Bjorn in size and robustness.

Porter said, "I protest this outrage. This man is under my command and protection and I cannot allow this." The threat of Porter to lay the matter before the authorities and make an international incident met with total indifference from Captain Hutton.

"Allowed or not, he is coming with us."

Hutton was a short but large man from overindulgence rather than a native constitution. He joined his two enforcers who wrestled Bjorn to the deck, only crushing a chicken cage and smashing a cabin window.

"Dammit, I don't have a replacement windowpane."

Amundson, the fittest of the bunch from his constant climbing the rigging, fought furiously by throwing off one and then the other into hysterical chickens. Only when one of the assistants grabbed his pigtail and slammed his head into unconsciousness did the kidnappers manage to subdue him. The pair pushed the dead weight over the railing and dropped it into a waiting boat. A letter fell into the water while hoisting on *Sir Edmund Hughes*. They hurried to load him before he regained his senses.

Captain Frederick Hutton called over the water to Porter that they were free to hoist sail and continue on their way. Jones ordered the sails reset to resume their course for China minus another valuable hand.

As the ships parted ways, Porter heard Captain Hutton address the crew of *Hughes* in a loud voice. "Our complement is increased by one to support our mission against the ladrones. Mr. Bjorn Amundson has joined us and will prove a handsome addition. I have it on good authority that he is an excellent lookout, and you will welcome him to her Majesty's service with your usual good humor. He will find we maintain close discipline at all times."

He spat into the ocean and pounded the railing for emphasis.

Bjorn, revived, shouted across the water as his new duty station pulled away, "Guard my ditty box. I'll be back."

Monsoonal winds propelled *Agilis* with aplomb up the coast of Vietnam past Hainan island and Cochinchina. Porter missed Bjorn's companionship and honest alternate point of view, even if it was contrary. Solitaire chess did not work and he said out loud, "I really need to treat our friendship better."

Fore 'n Aft had his own concerns. Feline instinct and his supernatural senses picked up suffering from the towns onshore and conveyed that cats were being slaughtered and eaten in Vietnam, especially in the rural villages of Cochinchina.

Porter was distressed and petted his soft black-and-white saying, "What is it? You are a bundle of nerves and tense as a rock."

Morgan Fore 'n Aft made a few little bleeps and crawled into his arms.

Shaking his head and drawing on all his resources, which is to say the navigation of Jones and readings through his trusty sextant, Porter determined they were approaching the Portuguese island of Macau and the Pearl River drainage.

Porter and Jones discussed the protocol of landing on the Chinese mainland. Porter said, "Many ships stop at Macau for refuge, fresh water, and food. The island asserts its own laws and accepts disembarkation from all who pause there. Only a short hop across the bay we find the island and village of Hong Kong, where I have a business."

Liu Fong joined the conversation. "The Chinese Navy patrols the Pearl River upstream from Hong Kong with formidable strength, though less than the English warships. Beijing confines all business with evil devil foreigners to the triangle of Hong Kong, Canton, and Macau island. To violate this law and proceed to Zhaoqing, the ancient capital, is very dangerous but evades taxes, ransom demands, and powerful middlemen."

He cast a warning eye at Fore 'n Aft. "Watch yourself."

Hutton's beefy assistants escorted Bjorn to the forecastle, where they offered a choice of descending the ladder hand and foot or dropping headfirst. He chose the former and wrenched himself free.

After writing his name on a hammock from a neatly stacked pile, he found a pair of unoccupied hooks to hang it on during any rare moment of rest.

The occupants in the forecastle welcomed him with gusto since they were impressed the same way. They shared their stories with enthusiasm, nay competed with tales of times past, old ports, spooky tales, and goings-on in certain cities where things went bump in the night. A compelling experience of one became the shared experience of all, and they welcomed Bjorn into the brotherhood of lost, kidnapped souls.

Bjorn got reacquainted with one older jack tar, a black man, who mentored him on his first voyage from Norway. They slapped each other on the back and punched their chests, after which they caught up on their many adventures. "Garong Wek, is that really you? You have the same tribal marks on your forehead as the master woodcarver from Africa. Weren't you headed up the Nile River to your family in Khartoum the last I saw of you?"

"My people were wonderful but required another trading trip. I was impressed again on a mission to trade carvings for brass goods in Calcutta. My magical Aladdin's lamps are popular back home though they didn't work for me. I rubbed one many times as described by the Syrian storyteller, Diyab, and no genie with gifts came to help me."

Bjorn laughed and said, "You're still one hell of a sailor even without a genie. It's good to see you again."

"Me too."

Bjorn was among the sailors he was comfortable with, except he was the lowest-ranked man in the ill-assorted crew. Impressed men of diverse backgrounds united only by their common goal of survival.

Bjorn's goal was revenge.

Bjorn fit in being the character of the largest, most vocal, angriest person present. Of course, they accepted him as their ringleader. Practicing the profane language he learned from the cussing pilot, he said, "Who's in charge of this half-assed bottom? Experts like us, or the idiots above? I say we find out."

The first mate had shown himself an intelligent man, capable, with decent feelings hiding behind pure granite. After consultation among the old salts, the rebellious crew resolved to test the grit in his composition.

At six bells on the last watch with the wind howling from the southwest, the mate called out in distress, "Forward there. Lay aloft and take up the weather braces."

Bjorn, never to be a candidate for bosun, replied in a loud, distinct tone, "Aye, aye."

The men emptied the forecastle and surrounded him at this signal for the test. The mate rushed into the midst of the group and demanded, "Who said, 'Aye, aye?'"

"Aye, aye, I did"

Bjorn was a fellow of large proportions and good features but could turn belligerent when he was aroused. He developed the attitude from sailing with practitioners of the African slave trade, the nursery of pirates and desperados. At reckless times like now, he showed little restraint.

Listening with interest was the motley crew of foreigners, hardened ruffians who learned their villainy on privateers, deserters, responsible to no government and little better than pirates themselves.

"It was I", replied the newest impressed hand again.

"Do you know the proper reply to an officer?"

"How should I reply?" said Bjorn innocently with his eyebrows raised but invisible in the dark.

"It is 'Aye, aye, sir!' when you reply to me," said the mate in a tone of thunder. He seized the contrary ringleader by the collar, "Don't undertake your monkeyshines on my watch, m'lad. Even twice my stature, you will gladly die the death of a miserable dog, laying aloft in the weather braces."

Bjorn's natural sense of good order prevailed for a short time. "Aye, aye, sir! Aye, aye, sir," was the respectable response from every side including Bjorn.

Notwithstanding the clear outcome, Bjorn stubbornly determined to further infringe the rules of discipline. Captain Hutton was a man of imposing exterior and a countenance that commanded respect. Who knew beneath his gruff features lay a legitimate store of determination to carry him through any difficulty.

The watch was attending his duty when Captain Hutton remarked to the mate, "She blows hard, we may have a regular gale before morning."

Bjorn was passing to windward. He stopped and before the mate could reply said in a tone of insolent familiarity, "She blows hard, and will blow harder yet. Who cares? Let it blow and all be damned."

The Captain was astonished at the impudence, but the mate was equally prompt, divined the test, and instead of a civil reply landed a blow on the left temple that knocked Bjorn against the gunwale. The ringleader leaped on the mate like a cockroach, crushed him in a clinch, and called to his shipmates, "Give a hand."

They were two powerful men and the winner was uncertain if Bjorn fought single-handedly. The men watching didn't care to interfere, but one of the Hutton's assistants did. When Bjorn tried to attack the mate, the man seized a loose belaying pin from the fife rail and gave the new recruit crisscrossing raps over the head. Bjorn fell to the deck with the mate crushing him. Another hand and he dumped the ringleader headfirst down the forecastle hatch.

The matter did not end there. A recovered Bjorn complained loudly about the barbarous treatment. Vowing revenge, he promised to lure the assistant into the forecastle and square accounts. The hand headed to his portside watch did not expect they could entice the enforcer below so approved the suggestion. They did not know Bjorn.

He did not go to his scheduled four o'clock watch. After waiting half an hour, the mate ordered the protester on deck. "Aye, aye, sir, I am coming directly."

"You better do so, if you know when you are well off."

"Aye aye, sir!"

Planted on a ditty box in plain sight, dressed but not moving, Bjorn waited. After a half of a bell period, the mate bellowed out again, "Coming on deck or not?

"Aye, aye, sir, directly."

"If I come down, it will be the worse for you." Bjorn remained seated on the chest and greeted the dawn before the mate ran out of patience. "On deck this instant, you lazy, lounging, worthless, renegade. You refuse to relieve the watch and force fellow sailor into double duty? Show your lovely, battered puss on deck, and let us see how you look after your frolic.

"Aye aye, sir. I'm coming right up."

Bjorn was outraged from his time at sea managing men and said to the intimidated crew, "I'll settle right now whether it's our way or Hutton's on this wreck."

The mate and an enforcement assistant jumped down the forecastle and crashed into Bjorn. Bjorn seldom calculated consequences in this kind of situation and slammed the enforcer down with his brawny fist and a twisting bear hug, but the enforcer refused to back off. The mate bellowed, "Attend your duty now!"

Bjorn held back, expecting his shipmates to help, but not a man stirred. They considered it was unsafe to interfere with the quarrels of others. After a few gentle reminders on the side of his head and punches to his short ribs, the assistant and made towed the big, blonde man up the hatch.

The wind blew heavy, chilling rain fell horizontally. Bjorn in his few remaining clothes, the only ones he had, stood little better than naked on the deck. The mate with Hutton's full approval sent him aloft and kept him there for the greater part of the cold windy day. His battered head, his cut face, his swollen features, and his gory queue faced the weather as his punishment.

"I thought this was the warm tropics, but these raging winds carrying storms off the Himalayas manage to get uncomfortable, and the higher I go the stronger they get. Maybe I need to learn a lesson in here somewhere."

The mate held a grudge, missed no opportunity to indulge his vindictiveness, and schemed for more ways to come because of the affront to his authority.

Bjorn was from Scandinavia and the wet, chilly wind was more comfortable on his body than the winters up north had ever been. He was fine until . . .,

Captain Hutton called Bjorn down to the foredeck and the ship's company to stand at attention in front of the mate. "I do not allow fighting under my command. What happened?"

The three gave their stories, but Hutton could tell Bjorn was not forthcoming. "Did you refuse a direct order, Mr. Amundson?"

"I won't be ordered around, . . . sir" He spoke with a leer and raised eyebrows.

"Mate, you were officer of the deck that day?"

"This ordinary seaman refused his duty position. He endangered the entire ship and forced the watch into double duty."

"Mr. Amundson?"

"I was protecting the integrity of your command, most important at sea, sir."

Hutton looked at Bjorn, "Seven lashes before the mast. We shall have iron discipline at all times in this command."

At ten o'clock, the Captain, to maximize the impact of the ceremony, stepped to the mainmast and addressed the mate. The crew understood the preparations of the officers as they had attended similar disciplines and knew what was coming. "All hands witness the punishment for fighting and resisting an order."

The mate ordered Bjorn to strip off his threadbare shirt, which he modestly accomplished, after which gnarled hands tied him to the mast, ready for the bosun's exertions.

"Well, shit," Bjorn said under his breath to himself. "It's not like you misdeserve this. Less than the cougar attacks, you're a hero to your forecastle mates. They did abandon you when the chips were down, but that is okay."

He gripped the mast with his hands, clamped his teeth, and waited, . . . and waited, . . . and waited some more.

"Maybe Captain Hutton is in charge, after all, he has a heavy responsibility."

"Indeed, sailor, he is," said the mate. "Ready for your discipline?"

"Always."

The whip whistled and the blow connected. The skin on Bjorn's back showed the red mark of the whip from the shoulder across to shoulder. New welts crisscrossed the scars of the cat attacks on top of the bear scars and stung like hell.

The mate said, "With these touches, the new designs over the old will mark you forever as a malcontent, troublemaking, piss-poor excuse to serve in her Majesty's navy. I hope this brings you into line, although I doubt it," and he swung a two-handed lash with such force his feet left the ground. The effort sprained his wrist and the mate behind the whip stumbled to his knees.

The malcontent stood passive at the mainmast with the heart of a tall fir tree. No cry, no word, no sound escaped his lips as blow followed blow and lacerated his scarred skin and the muscles underneath.

Hutton said, "You two, douse the marks of the whip with saltwater to enhance the effect and prevent infection." They splashed buckets of seawater on the quivering back muscles that seized up in protest. Lungs inhaled a full breath of air the diaphragm couldn't exhale.

Bjorn braved through it except for gathering paleness on his cheek and an unconquerable shiver through his frame. Stomach muscles cramped up, back muscles turned to mush under the skin, and involuntary tremors shook his big body.

Hutton, in consideration of blood on the deck rather than the victim's mangled back, declared the punishment complete. "In the future, you will obey orders and protect *Sir Edmund Hughes*. Man your stations, wash the deck of those red stains, I expect to see no trace when you are done."

Nothing about the flogging was personal, just discipline as usual and not nearly as severe as the punishment of deserters, at least on the part of Captain Hutton.

"Help, for God's sake, help!"

Captain Hutton heard a faint call some distance off. Training his spyglass on the sound from somewhere among the islands scattered throughout the Pearl River estuary, he said, "I'll be damned. It is a rough-and-tumble raft loaded with desperate men."

He launched the dinghy and second mate to inspect the makeshift flotsam. Upon approaching the raft, the officer said, "Who are you?"

"We're the survivors from the attack on *Lalla Rooka*, headed for Canton."

He could see the ropes were fraying and ready to break that held the sticks of wood together.

Captain Hutton plied the castaways with rum and biscuits to revive their energy before grilling them. "I see eleven hands. Surely the Rooka carried more crew than you."

"Oh yes, sir. Our captain was slaughtered forthwith, and the officers mercilessly tortured to death. Fifteen of us lowlifes were set adrift with no provisions. We expected to feed the fish but lost only four of us when one of our boards came loose. Your beloved dinghy saved us from the same fate."

The exhausted spokesman leaned against the gunwale to encourage a companion castaway to resume the tale. "Worst off were the hostages they kidnapped.

"Who were they?"

"Don't rightly know, sir, but they looked important. Somebody said they were a trade mission from Norway."

Bjorn, still exiled to the masthead, was horrified at the voice from below. "My countrymen in the clutches of the savages? We have to rescue them."

"Hold on, sailor. Of course, we have to rescue them, but first, we must find them. I don't know where they might be, and I've heard rumors they hustle hostages off to Formosa for safekeeping."

Captain Hutton was a sly old fox. Devious, determined, and dedicated to the destruction of the predators on her Majesty's commerce, he was cunning and bluffing in poker, lethal.

"Nonessential manpower to your quarters. Essential forces make like recaptured deserters. Scrunch your uniforms, ruffle each other's hair, and slouch about your duties."

The fellowship of captains in the ports of Asia made sure deserters received harsh treatment. Skippers were reluctant to sign them and maintained a network to track absconders. Hutton's recruits were not deserters. While the histories of ordinary hands were murky, they followed the examples of the others and did their duties well.

An abundance of men on board *Hughes* meant there was limited make work except for those looking after the ship.

Squalls were an exception. Sudden winds could knock a standing man down when they roared from the sky. All hands stood by the topsail halyards to clew them down in the furious hail storms that lasted ten or fifteen minutes and passed without warning. Moments after, the topsails swelled into great billows, and *Sir Edmund Hughes* sped on like a frightened deer.

The other exception was an external attack. Hutton was always ready to call 'All hands on deck' to repulse danger.

Squalls or not, pirates infested the nearest archipelago in the mouth of the Pearl River. Predators launched junks at night to search for victims that ran ashore or lowered a cautious anchor to wait until dawn.

Experienced ladrone lookouts suspected Hughes was vincible against their hungry raiders. Such a gunboat was a dangerous prey, but their desperate lack of weapons drove their unwise plan to seize an armed vessel. Vessels in those waters, especially gunships, carried stores of muskets, pistols, cutlasses, and boarding spikes to supplement the large guns.

A surprise was their only hope.

They did not reckon on Captain Hutton.

Thieving rascals were reluctant to attack an alert target in daylight, but *Hughes* seemed half asleep. Decades of practice made their hijacking strikes a model of organization. A formidable foe to European crafts caught unawares, the Malays planned to murder resisting sailors, plunder the ship of weapons and blades, and set it afire with superfluous souls locked in the hold.

Their fast-sailing junk almost matched the *Hughes* in size. They were as cruel and bloodthirsty a set of scoundrels as ever scuttled the seas. No mercy came to anyone under their control except for persons who could bring a big ransom.

The marauders slipped their junks to windward and downwind like a fishing vessel, slowly to not excite the rumpled, slouching watch. But that vigilant fellow could see a most unusual item hanging dangling from the masthead of the slithering, approaching junk, an earthen jar that had no conceivable use in fishing. He suspected it contained the most vile-smelling compound only a Chinaman in the barnyard might withstand, and he only briefly.

Having approached, the vessel sent a man up the rigging who tossed the jar down on the *Hughes*. The aim was off and drenched the figurehead of *Ajax the Great* of Greek fame. The fearful stench still drove the forward sailors below deck, and greedy masked pirates tried to swarm on board to begin the work of plunder and murder, but their knives kept slipping out of their masks. The masks had little good effect on the odors, either.

Captain Hutton said, "I always consider it a safe thing to get a gun ready and drop the climbing Chinaman before he gets here. Ninety-nine cases out of a hundred they haul ass and nothing further happens. They got the drop on me last spring and kidnapped two gentlemen from Norway. Not this time. Bjorn! douse Ajax with a bucket of vinegar to purify that god-awful stink on his beard and bandolier before he revolts and sends us to the bottom."

Chapter 11—Gunboat Diplomacy

The hostage from Norway was dejected as he talked to his aide in the steamy, sweaty jungle. Rough short vines tied their ankles to stakes that chafed their skin and attracted ants with the sweet sap mixed with sweat and dried blood. They had to move frequently to stay under the shade of the lone palm tree and slapped away clouds of biting insects. They did not know where they were but surmised they couldn't be far from Hong Kong and the Pearl River because of the sails crisscrossing the distant horizon.

"This is a fine kettle of fish we're in. God willing, we shall be ransomed and rescued.

"In our captivity, we have tolerable health notwithstanding the inconveniences. Our fare is the same as the common captives and savages eat. Red rice with a little salted fish. I'll never eat another bowl of rice. And I miss my big soft bed. Fish I can forget."

The representative and aide sighed together and fell silent.

They faced a compound busy with ladrone life ashore under a thatched canopy, their central gathering place. The gambling casino at Monte Carlo had nothing on the betting action they could see all around. As near as they could understand, the gamblers made bets of stolen loot, fancy uniforms with gold braid, wives, women, slaves, and who could tell what else. Only when two gamblers pointed at the Norwegians and shouted some raucous wager in a loud laden with monetary and physical pantomimes did they get worried.

Less vociferous ones played a game on cardboard marked out in squares. The Norwegian aide said, "That looks like a rough kind of chess. Over there are clear pairs of dice making and taking treasures when their tumbling is done."

One bidder yelled at the hostages, pointed to their throats, and drew an imaginary knife across. His opponent simulated a slashing cutlass move. Only an argument with a flying toss of dies that peppered the board distracted them. They forgot their bets, but the hostages did not.

Traditional healing skills in the hands of the men in the forecastle rapidly returned Bjorn to full function. They had all been flogged as adults and spanked as children, so they welcomed Bjorn with honor into their ranks. A little sweet salve, some stretching to keep the skin supple, and moral support all helped.

Talking up a storm rather than moving his sore back for a few days, Bjorn befriended an outgoing, superstitious Malayan in the group. The fellow was obsessed with ghost stories. He was the lowest class person in the group and nobody knew why he was impressed since his kind were usually rejected.

Not superstitious and open-minded, Bjorn listened with interest. The night was quiet and the other sailors slept in their slowly rocking hammocks. The only sounds were occasional squeaks from the hooks holding the hammocks as the sleepers turned over or rubbed a sore muscle in the dark.

Absentmindedly, Bjorn began whistling the tune of a Viking ballad, Skalder og Legender. The Malayan asked about the words that Bjorn translated,

Grimne flew out from Valhalla.
In the shape of the falcon

"That is nice but don't you know whistling at night attracts rural ghosts?"

"Not really."

"I will tell you. A pocong, the shrouded ghost, is a Malaysian dead person trapped in its shroud. To bury a Muslim requires wrapping the remains in a length of cloth where the dead body is covered in white fabric tied over the head, under the feet, and the neck. The pocong who has been dead for years is a skeleton, but the ghost of a recently died person is partly alive and partly dead. That kind of fresher spirit has a pale face and wide-open eyes, whereas only a dark face and glowing red eyes show in a decayed ghost. Pocongs move by floating above the ground."

Bjorn listened indulgently and wondered how to benefit from the new story.

"The soul of a dead person stays on earth for forty days, but if the ties over the shroud are not released, the body jumps from the grave as a warning. The most feared red Pocong is a person seeking revenge for an unpleasant death."

"Like pirates?"

"Like pirate skeletons seen floating last evening."

"I have seen them at night. They say I have been a bad man and they will punish me for it, but they are wrong. I only torture captives, I do not kill them."

Bjorn's fertile mind swirled around an idea to rescue the Norwegians hostages. His instinct suggested they were on the nearby island of ladrones waiting for ransom money. Ladrone island itself was beautiful and the location was easy to send demands for money from. The seagoing bandits didn't seem organized enough to transport the hostages to Formosa. Bjorn's concern for his countrymen overrode his disgust at Captain Hutton.

Visiting the well-supplied galley, he gathered bags of white ashes and black charcoal. The sailmaker loaned him a section of used, white sail. He had Wek unbraid his hair to spread it into two flat wings, but only after a spiritual protest. His sculptural hands stabilized them with a mixture of flour and water. Bjorn sat upright the rest of the night to let the mixture harden.

The lascar exited the forecastle hatch half asleep the next morning. At the sight of the wings, he screamed and tumbled back even though they were the wings he had seen molded the previous night. He no longer needed to visit the head and avoided Bjorn the rest of the day and night.

Bjorn churned over in his idle mind a plan to engage likely attacks the next day as he polished the endless brass fittings and ship's bell. The watch guard smiled with approval. He had a good idea of the trick being hatched.

Captain Hutton said on his morning rounds, "What the hell are you doing, Amundson? You would scare the piss out of a statue."

"Just wait."

Bjorn spent the day enhancing his makeup. He started by blackening his feet and pants from the knee down with the charcoal. He twirled around and asked the dog watch what he thought. "A real ghost has no feet in the dark."

Using his knife, he fashioned the discarded sail into a shroud with holes for his arms but open in the back. The charcoal marks plastering his chest and torso made a striking background for the white ash skeleton he drew on it. There was no way the shroud could stretch over his wings of hair so he left his head free.

The native peeked from the forecastle and reluctantly climbed onto the deck to start his duties of the day. Bjorn ignored him.

Bjorn completed his disguise in the late afternoon by blackening his arms and coating his face and hands with the ashes. He outlined his eyes with big wide open red circles. Approaching his lascar friend with a grin he said, "Do I make a good pocong ghost?"

The Malay man panting under all his self-control said, "You make a good freak of nature, sahib if you are still a sahib."

The watch nodded, the Malayan ran away.

Bjorn approached Captain Hutton and said, "Ready to rescue the hostages."

"How can you fight in that getup?"

"Leave the fighting to me."

Night fell but the brilliant stars gave enough light to make out forms floating nearby. Anything covered in black like Bjorn was invisible in the night.

A second raiding expedition manned by trained pirates from Ladrone Island did not disappoint *Sir Edmund Hughes*. Their cluster of junks prepared to board in a frenzied search of more valuable hostages and weapons of any kind.

Hoots and hollers meant to terrify the target into surrender stopped in mid-scream at the apparition standing on the railing. The pirates saw a pocong fully prepared to haunt them to their death, as their eyes were well-adjusted in the dark from never using artificial light.

Bjorn's voice was raw from singing ribald sea shanties in the chorus of the forecastle, as well as giving orders in a storm. With every vocalism he knew screamed at top volume, the ghost danced the dead dance on the railing. The final terror was his bloodcurdling Viking berserker shout reinforced by henbane and the seeds of morning glory from Maverick's stash which he secreted in his clothes from his previous ship.

He leaped into the first boat. The white skeleton topped by flying white wings flew through the air like an albino vulture and floated above the boat with no visible legs. Disconnected hands slashed at hysterical pirates as they dove off in all directions to avoid the ghost. The crews of the other two boats saw the floating spook and paddled away faster than they knew they could. Sins committed throughout their life crowded before their eyes and forced apologies to their victims, relatives, gods, compatriots, and unaccountables.

The perpetrators against *Lalla Rooka* were all the more terrified because they had treated the captain with such special viciousness.

Bjorn's natural ability came to the fore learning by quick trial and error mostly error how to single-handedly manage the empty junk which he leaped into. With one hand on the rudder, only his long arms allowed him to adjust the ropes steering the lateen sail. The boat zigzagged through the water and sometimes actually progressed toward Ladrone Island. Bjorn was able to maneuver it five miles to shore, actually eight counting the zigzags. His wings added a tiny extra boost to the sail. He knew the direction from the stolen glance at the chart Hutton spread on the table.

Welcoming cheers onshore reached his ears approaching the inlet but ended in shrieks that faded into the jungle as the apparition pulled the junk onto the beach. He was not the returning, loot-laden victor they hoped for.

A well-worn path marked by torches and seemed important and the ghost took it. Presently, he came upon the pretended ruling raja under a shed surrounded by nineteen of his tribe. They were busy gambling and had the appearance of what they really were, a ferocious set of pirates prepared to plunder day or night. The games were so furious they had no guards posted.

Bjorn burst into the circle of firelight and threw a handful of gravel on the fire causing an explosion of sparks to catch their attention. An earsplitting shout aroused the inhabitants of the encampment and alerted the members of the jungle casino.

Impending damnation convinced the nearest targets they were as good as the dead people they had tortured and slaughtered. The screeching skeleton with no legs and hands minus arms chased after the retreating villagers as they screamed and ran into the jungle to get as far away as they could. A man asleep fled in a sleepwalking panic.

Bjorn reveled in his powers and noted the benefit of surprise, a lesson he would remember.

Bjorn yelled, "Call out, anybody left?"

"Over here." The representative was more startled than the captors. "Now comes the shaman to butcher our bodies and feed the pieces to the warriors, dogs, and animals of the forest. We were better off with the savages."

Bjorn ran to the sound and picked up on the Norwegian words. He said, "Are you from *Lalla Rooka*?"

He saw two men tied to stakes. He could tell his unconventional appearance had stunned if not terrified them because they crawled to the ends of their tethers to escape his curse.

They cringed in their last moments alive and prepared to meet their maker. One said to the other in Norwegian, "What an ignominious end to our trade mission. After we are cannibalized and our bones scattered, the king will never know our fate. These cannibals will not tell."

"Nay, nay," said the apparition. "I ask you again, are you from *Lalla Rooka*?"

"How do you know our ship? Are you going to slaughter us in our native language?"

Bjorn looked into his battered worried face and said, "Don't you recognize a fellow Norseman?"

"No."

Speaking Norwegian, Bjorn tried to calm their nerves by asking their reaction to his disguise, but they would not look at him. He felt like the same person as always and didn't realize he looked like a ghost to others. The closer he tried to approach the captives, the more they moved away, and he could not understand why.

The representative's initial reaction mirrored the indigenous gamblers to the sparks kicked up by the handful of gravel. They were more startled when the blonde, white-haired ghost materialized among the black-haired captors.

Even the sophisticated modern Scandinavians harbored a buried sense of shamanic superstitions from their distant pagan folklore. Bjorn's image summoned horrible visions within their weakened condition.

Watching the ghost cut their tethers gave them a clue the apparition might be a heroic Norseman. His words sounded like an educated real Norwegian from the central region.

Wiping the ashes from around his eyes, Bjorn surprised them again with his light skin. "You are free if we leave before the savages discover my ruse."

They stood up and stretched to awaken their cramped muscles. They conversed in low Norwegian tones, which the ladrones would not understand if they were still around, which they were not.

Without a further word, Bjorn cut their tethers to the stakes and the hostages got a close-up look at him.

"What do you think? Can this thing be real?'

"Hard to tell. I have doubts, but no worse than the others. We can talk to him."

"You are the minister who defended me to the King of Norway."

The representative stared at Bjorn and mentally shaved his beard and wiped away the ashes.

"Not looking like you do now, I didn't. Why are you acting like a pagan witch doctor and traipsing around the jungle half a world away? You look like hell."

"You mean my white wings? They are unconventional, but only for a moment or two. We leave for Sir Edmund Hughes right now."

"They're gone, are they?'

"Not for long. Superstitions and spirits are fleeting."

"Just a minute, I have to visit the bushes."

"No time. Go in your pants and follow me." The three stumbled to the beach and splashed into the rocking pirate boat. "Hurry."

The hostages were out of breath after months of inactivity and barely stayed ahead of a separate group of active natives. But the three gigantic Norwegians made quick work of the hungry, emaciated thieves.

The man they didn't get was a tardy villager. He was in such a deep sleep that the general alarm washed over him, and their retreating screams only interrupted his dreams. He was slow but observant and noticed Bjorn's backside looked like a normal sailor, not a ghost.

Bjorn forgot to disguise his back, and the straggler announced the fraud as he ran down to the shore. He called to the fleeing bandits, "A fake! Capture him and recover our hostages."

Sadistic thoughts of the torture he could perform on a hostage aroused his thrill of molesting a captive. He craved inserting burning needles in the skin, slashing a thousand cuts, hearing screams of pain. A slow death not possible on board, he relished with gusto onshore. The straggler screamed in frustration at losing his fetish.

The natives emerged from the jungle and charged for the beached junk as more attack boats returned offshore. Their leader had regrouped and rescued their swimming companions. Somewhat antsy but drawing on their inherent viciousness, they aimed for Bjorn with his hostages.

Bjorn fumbled with the sail while the representative steered the rudder. He grew up on the North Sea and knew the mysteries of the winds and tides. Propelled by Bjorn's newfound junk skipper skills, the boat slipped out of range of the haunted ghost victims. After a quick redemption from their ancestors, the mob piled into the two proas to retrieve the hostages and the ransoms they represented.

Bjorn and company made for *Hughes* in a zigzag course, with the pirates behind them. The ragged unconventional track under Bjorn's navigation kept the pursuers confused.

Bjorn thought the ship was anchored over there somewhere in the haze since he left mere hours ago. He searched for it and confused the pursuers even more.

The watch on deck, Garang Wek, recognized Bjorn's wings since he sculpted them with his two hands. "Ghost boy ahoy with two Euros."

They reached *Hughes* in a dead heat with the ladrones paddling furiously to catch up. Captain Hutton always mounted capable lookouts who spotted dangers in the moonlight who said, "Hold your fire. Friendly vessel approaching."

The rising moon illuminated their identity and Hutton ordered an overhead attack. "Aim the cannons on the three trailing boats, the lead is ours."

Clouds of billowing gun smoke obscured Bjorn's stolen boat from the chasing junks who were desperate to stop him. Crew of the *Hughes* hoisted Bjorn and hostages aboard post haste.

"Fire at will." The gunner aimed the cannon into the center of the stolen junk's sail. With a chooom and quick whistle the cannon ball blasted a hole through the canvas and the three following vessels. It convinced the disappointed pirates to withdraw and search for a weaker target. They had lost their valuable hostages and the cost of feeding them for a month.

"To hell with hostages," some pirate farmer hollered in Malay. "Kill them all."

Hutton ordered a suitable welcome for the important, disheveled visitors.

"I never expected to see any of you again, Mr. Stang and your aide, I presume. Glad to see the crazy Bjorn, too."

He directed the crew to make an occupied state room suitable for distinguished guests. They aroused the sleeping purser with the message that they needed his room for more important personages."

The disgruntled money man said," I'll go, but I shall be required to examine your accounts very carefully."

The captain apologized to the Norwegians. "You'll have to share quarters until we reach shore. We lack accommodations for passengers."

"Thanks to Mr. Amundson, we are rescued." A tiny joint stateroom is far superior to a jungle village of cutthroat gamblers. We will share with Mr. Amundson. This brave young man saved our souls for which we are eternally grateful. You have a hero in your midst and I compliment you for your sagacity"

Captain Hutton cleared his throat, looked at Bjorn and said "Mr. Amundson has an acceptable hammock to sleep in. He is adequately provided for and does not rate a cabin."

"Only a hammock? Even in shifts, a featherbed is proper for his majesty's personal representative. This gentleman has a glowing future."

"The king's representative? Did I commandeer the representative of Norway? Why didn't you say something?"

Bjorn said, "I told you I was a passenger without protection papers, and you deemed that unimportant halfway around the world. This gentleman," he pointed to string, "presented me to his Majesty in person. King Oscar pointed me his personal representative for California. I am to look out for Scandinavian immigrants in that location if I can get there."

Captain Hutton could see a reprimand in his future and changed his demeanor. He demanded the crew wash off the disguise as befitted a gentleman, even though Bjorn's hammock was the only sleeping accommodation available.

After rest and refreshments, Hutton queried the hostages about their capture a month before. The representative explained they were visiting major countries to organize trading opportunities. "My aide can make a complete report of our capture and rescue. If you would be so kind as to provide him a quill and paper, he will get started while the events are fresh on his mind."

Hutton said the most important information would be the behavior of the attackers, the directions they came from, and thoughts to eliminate their depredations from the South China Sea. "Please use my desk in the cabin."

The aide was skilled at noting information and wrote details from his steel-trap mind.

October 17, 1854

This is a true Journal of the details of our capture by pirates off Guangdong in South China. My objective is to inform the authorities and prevent future outrages.

We were anchored four miles east of Macau when a large junk stood down on us. Captain Krieg said she was a war junk, but whether Mandarin and friendly, ladrone and pirate was not clear. She was the latter.

The captain ordered us to load the guns and bring small arms on deck. We test-fired them to assure they were in good working order. The junk retired to the northwest between two islands. We observed several vessels of different sizes streaming from the north which looked to be fishermen that evening. They were the ladrones.

One appeared to be from Macau. A rowboat was put off full of people instead of the commodore. I was loading a musket when they fired at us and boarded. They stabbed a man in the back and another swung his sword at me. I dove overboard to avoid the blow, but the pirates hauled me into their boat. They robbed everything from me. One who spoke a little English said we were valuable prisoners and they were taking us to their village for our safety. He meant their safety.

I shook my head in bewilderment. This author is a man of books and letters, not arms. They questioned me regarding the armaments on the ship. I answered as best I could, but they were angry at my lack of detail. If they had requested books about armaments or warships I could have satisfied their curiosity in a heartbeat from the royal library.

I thought she carried twenty guns, larger than theirs with a mix of carronades or muskets, or were they blunderbusses? Maybe they carried crossbows for all I know. We were one hundred and fifty men aboard."

Stang said later that, during an argument he overheard their main desire was for six thousand dollars. Our guard claimed they sent letters to Canton referencing *Lalla Rooka* and to Captain Hutton reminding him of our unpleasant situation and the ransom demand. I saw the fishermen entrusted to deliver the envelopes throw them into the ocean.

The next day, a Chinese who spoke English visited our camp. He informed me that without ten thousand dollars for our ransom, they would dispose of us and drown our remains.

They captured a small Mandarin boat with four men. I could see they slammed them on board their junk where their cruelty made an indelible impression on my mind. The leader, they nailed to the deck through his feet with large nails and beat with rattans twisted together until he vomited blood. After remaining for some time in that state, they brought up the bloody remains to our shore and cut them to pieces to dispose of the evil evidence.

End of preliminary journal. Revision soon.

The Norwegian trade minister was an outgoing, savvy, man from a family of staff advisors to the king. He was not particularly wealthy but was highly respected in royal circles. With a rousing sense of humor and an easy smile, he fit the role of an international trade representative. What he did not fit was street smart. He functioned well with the upper half of society but lacked instincts of depravity in the bottom half. Upper half evil was common but better concealed under polished manners.

Bjorn and Wek washed as much of his ghost disguise off as seawater allowed and braided his hair before he visited Stang. "How much did they put on your heads?"

"Thirty thousand for me and ten for my aide. They thought I was the king."

"You are valuable persons about whom I must say, Glad to see you again in better circumstances."

They shook hands.

Bjorn was a good lookout and spotted *Agilis* that night across the harbor at Macau. He decided to visit.

He shook hands firmly with the Norwegian representatives, "Destiny brought us together in Norway and the jungle, and destiny harkens to our future in California."

The modest hero strolled the deck nonchalantly to enjoy the night lights of the Macau harbor. He kicked his shoes off on the foredeck, the hat he hung on a handle of the capstan, a little jump got him out of the borrowed pants at the swivel gun, a dark shadow across the rear deck hid the silk shirt slipping into the lifeboat. No sound came from the rear anchor chain. The recent recruit floated underwater in the Macau Harbor. He thought to himself, Thank you, Mr. Porter, for forcing me to swim.

Underwater breaststrokes got him several boat links away before the watch raised the alarm.

Unlike an ordinary sailor, unique and unconventional, he swam low in the water to evade the pursuing dinghy in the dark. The land-based military men were not whalers and didn't have a chance to catch the deserter. The seawater washed the last traces of flour from his hair, but the charcoal on his torso stuck like glue, making him look like a swimming skeleton.

The strong current and darkness of the night sporadically obscured *Agilis* at wave level. The route took longer than expected, but he was able to look up at the Spirit of Athena an hour after midnight, exhausted. "Shipmates, for God's sake, bear a hand and help. I can hold on no longer."

Bjorn's call for help jolted the watch sleeping on a coil of rope. A second cry from the water convinced the watch someone who had fallen overboard needed help.

"Who goes there?"

Bjorn's replied from below the bowsprit, "Hurry."

Clinging to the cable with his remaining strength, Bjorn looked up, "Help me, mate."

The shipmates hauled him on board.

As Bjorn's chest heaved and he dripped on the deck, they called Captain Porter to explain the situation.

Even in the dark and windy night, by flashes of lightning, he threw his arms around the rescued man and said, "By Jove, it's Bjorn Amundson, a little the worse for wear. Your sorry torso is so welcome." A hand on each shoulder held the dripping, blonde, bedraggled hulk at arms length and read the pattern of marks on his face. "How did you get here? I was afraid we might never see each other again."

No correct charts were available that covered the channel to Hong Kong in those days. Captain Porter relying on incomplete sheets on the polished table said to Jones, "I would have lost her except for the sensitive nose of Mr. Amundson." It happened this way.

"It was about six bells in the middle of the watch. The heavens were clear and unclouded, the stars were brilliant, and there was a pleasant breeze from the southeast to push us swiftly along. The wind was abaft the beam at a rate of five knots.

"Bjorn's nose twitched suddenly, and he stopped singing a tune with the night watches. He sprang from the coil of ropes and sniffed the air with an eager and agitated manner like a hunting hound. He sniffed again and stretched his head over the weather quarter. He asked us officers if we could smell the land. We all sniffed and snuffed but smelled nothing unusual, and told him so.

"I asked the two lascar navigators. One said no, but the other pointed his nose upwind and said of course. It smelled plainly of chicken on a charcoal grill and garlic."

"I couldn't smell anything unusual and disputed his observation. After a long sniff, my mate said people onshore were notoriously fond of spices on a fish over a charcoal fire and you could smell it this far away."

"Upon the strength of this additional testimony, I sniffed again but was nose blind. Daybreak was approaching, so Jones hove to and waited for daylight to test our mutual noses. After two impatient hours, our glances showed a low, hummocky beach, not three leagues distant.

We were no more than two miles from Hong Kong. If Bjorn had not smelled the land we might have foundered on submerged shipwrecks and joined them."

A week later a ship did crash ashore on that very beach and was wrecked. *Agilis* would have been shattered boards except for Bjorn's sensitive nose.

Chapter 12—Glory in Cathay

The village named Hong Kong on Hong Kong Island was up-and-coming after China signed the excessively hot and humid island over to Britain. In both public and private compounds, Britain was constructing solid buildings to support their business of tea and opium from Bengal. Signs of the enterprises of Jardine, Matheson & Company were everywhere, not least the original trading house according to the rumors that Porter had heard.

Engaging a pilot offshore, Porter anticipated their arrival in the city where his dream of becoming a man of the world was to be fulfilled.

Bjorn and Porter accidentally saw a small plaque near the waterfront that read, Trade Representative of Denmark.

Bjorn said, "I have to see what they are up to. Meet you back at the wharf."

"Good day, sir. Can I help you?"

"I should like to meet the Scandinavian representative, Mr. James Matheson."

"He is the busiest gentlemen with the commerce of imports and exports from Canton. If available, I'll request an audience for you. What was your name?"

"I am Bjorn Amundson, the Patriciate Representative to California from Norway."

After traveling fifteen thousand miles from Norway, Bjorn would not be denied an audience with someone important. Pulling himself up to his full height with a shrug to straighten the best suit he owned, he handed the secretary a calling card that read,

Mr. Bjorn Amundson
Chief Trade Representative
Patriciate of California, USA
By order of HM King Oscar I, Norway

The clerk was accustomed to bigwig visitors from around the world and was not impressed. He disappeared through the door, which reopened immediately, "Mr. Matheson will see you.

"I appreciate meeting another person from Scandinavia, especially halfway around the world. I hear you are organizing the patriciate in California for the flood of Norwegians relocating to the United States."

They shook hands, but the only chair in the room was occupied by the head of the company sitting behind the desk. "It is damnably difficult to procure furniture in this remote outpost. I hope to have chairs for my visitors soon."

"I plan to visit again, but I can conduct business with an honorable man waiting for chairs."

"I hear gold rush activities are growing from small personal mines to larger enterprises that require capital. The trading house of Jardine can invest in suitable enterprises because we expand wherever there are profits to be made." He sat back in his chair with an air of immense, confident satisfaction.

Bjorn was not surprised. The pools of gold dust in the river flowing through his New Viking Gold Mine were limited, and the operations had moved several times to newer deposits upstream.

"My duty in California aligns with yours to build the future. The Patriciate of California helps North European immigrants settle in, except that they find our gold rush culture difficult where wolves and land-based pirates lie and wait everywhere."

"I have seen more than my share of these shysters who like to prey on newcomers. We will profit from trading between Hong Kong and San Francisco. Current exports of tea are unpopular in the states, except among peasants and refugees from China, and we are seeking more profitable trading opportunities. The celestial immigrants lack a patriciate and must rely on gangs with whom business for us is difficult. It is a pleasure to meet you, Mr. Amundson."

On the way out, Bjorn made arrangements with the Hong Kong office of the Jardine Empire.

A more imposing but understated sign marked the bank. Its solid and respectable façade belied the money and intrigue inside. Hong Kong was rapidly surpassing in importance the city of Wamponoa on the Pearl River, and the designated money center of China. It was farther from the greedy eyes of the government.

Porter proudly entered the building under the words chiseled over the entrance,

Oriental Bank of Commerce

"I desire to open an account for my trading empire, *Agilis*. Accounts will be in the millions, and I must see a banker immediately."

Captain Porter cleared his throat, shifted in the chair, and presented the letter from the East India Company. The banker scanned the contents in a moment since he was used to handling such amounts or larger ones every day.

The agent was aghast. "Your approvals are not for Canton but Zhaoqing! You will cause me a great deal of trouble and stand to lose your ship in the process."

"Those are my orders, sir."

"I must warn you the mouth of the Pearl River is overrun with waterborne thieves on land and water. Vermin from the rocky shores of the scattered islands prey on honest vessels such as yours and provide hiding places for the worst ladrones of all types."

"I am aware of the menace. How do you manage the movement of money that surely must be well guarded."

"Accounts are handled by paper correspondence. I can move a million pounds with this signature."

"My *Agilis* cannot hope to equal that."

He rang a little bell that summoned a clerk carrying a folder of forms, which he placed on the desk. He leaned forward, "Very well, I am not the one at risk. The Oriental Bank of Commerce expects a deposit of one million two hundred thousand pounds in silver within thirty days. I am authorized to pay your commission of fifteen percent from the proceeds, but no more than one hundred and eighty-five thousand."

The bank agent shoved the stack of elaborately engraved pages in front of Porter to sign, with the explanation that they opened an account and connected Porter as agent for the East India Company. Nowhere did they mention an amount of money. "Sign the signature lines, if you would."

Porter scanned the stack of forms similar to Calcutta at the EIC. He checked the front and back of each page for hidden fine print and was pleased to not find any. Boldly, he signed each with the attitude of a shipping magnate."

The banker said, "Canton or Zhaoqing are unknown spots in the hinterlands and all the same to me. Money is money regardless of the source."

Leaving Hong Kong, Liu Fong gave the dinner guests around the cabin a running history as the ship dodged river traffic.

"Opium, a lucrative replacement for wheat, tea, and silks, is controlled by a Calcutta auction house. British ships come to Lintin Island to offload chests of opium onto floating warehouses beyond the reach of the Qing government ships in the mouth of the Pearl River. They cannot sail in the open ocean. The floating merchants deposit bars of silver in the Hong King bank to cover the losses. Chests removed by trade, trick, or theft by indigenous contrabandists are smuggled inland for distribution.

Porter pounded the table and reiterated, "I've got an account in Hong Kong to receive the *Agilis* millions, and will not pay a bribe to any stinking warehouse ship."

"Our smuggling career is over, don't you think?" Bjorn said to Porter after supper in the closed cabin as they compared their days in Hong Kong.

"I've learned the mysteries of nautical commerce and see great success coming my way."

"There won't be the next time with me, my portly friend. Our adventures are over."

"I don't see why. We're standing on a fortune."

With a knock on the door, Maverick carried in a platter of Tennessee tidbits adapted to oriental ingredients. They dug in for a long argument. Porter asked the cook to open a bottle of St. Regis.

"You once said,' There are good ships and wood ships, but the best ships are friendships.' Still in all, I've got to tell you they can founder on the rocks of greed and stubbornness. We are almost there."

Porter looked out the window, took a sip of wine, shuffled papers, and paced the cabin. He defiantly said in a low voice they had been together for six years from Boston, five from California, and were preparing to visit Zhaoqing after Hong Kong. He pointed out that Bjorn was traveling for free.

"Free like hell. I've stood as many watches as your hands until you let Captain Hutton kidnap me."

"I didn't let anything, and you swam across the bay through the sharks to get back. I had to rescue your sorry dripping body from the muck."

"Thank you for that, but the ship under discussion can still sink."

"Look, Mr. Amundson, a command is a great burden between the cargo entrusted to my care, a community of eighteen souls, two Gurkhas, and now an ex-stowaway. I have to feed them with a crippled cook and a leeching, insubordinate ex-friend."

In a raised voice, Bjorn brought up the damage opium did to the peasants. "We should dump it in the river and make full speed to San Francisco."

"Divers would salvage those chests before we were out of sight."

"You are a hypocrite, Richard Jeremy Porter. You condemn the Chinese to a life of addiction but claim it helps Maverick, at least in paregoric."

Maverick entered with another plate of food, but the delivery was not well received. "Refill, gentlemen?" He sensed the situation was tense and limped out in a hurry.

"It is not my fault the soldiers of the EIC force captured Chinese at gunpoint to eat opium until they are addicted. They call it market development."

"You carry an evil product four thousand miles to Zhaoqing from Ghazipur, and Maverick Hatfield doesn't look all that healed to me."

Porter ate another drumstick and washed it down with a gulp of red wine.

Bjorn saw they were not getting anywhere. He walked outside and stumbled over a few bricks still in the way. "Poor housekeeping."

During his stroll to check the compass reading on the binnacle, he chatted with the helmsman and had a change of heart.

The passenger took a deep breath, smoothed his windblown hair, and stepped back into the cabin to sit opposite the master.

"Richard, your burden is heavier than I realized. I sleep in a warm bunk while you are on call day and night. My only concern is our next chess game and a distant pirate or two."

Porter was braced for another tirade and relaxed when it did not come. The two munched on leftover chicken parts and discussed the cost of feeding twenty-one men.

"Words of wisdom, Mr. Amundson. I almost lost everything including my best friend in the world. Let us agree to not repeat this."

"Us? I had no part in this caper. You had a moment of greed."

"Maybe so."

They shook hands and agreed to forgo future contraband, for the most part. Out came the chessboard that started a knockdown, drag-out match."

Porter won.

Assembled worthies of *Agilis* argued how best to deliver their load into the great land of Cathay, starting from the mouth of the Pearl River between Hong Kong and Macau.

"Where are we? The charts claim we are in China but the land looks like points south," said Porter.

Jones said, "I have been to Canton and can tell you differences are coming. Look around. Over the horizon to port is the island of Portuguese Macau. Starboard is Hong Kong Island where you'll find the muddy settlement we just left that is called Hong Kong. Between lie the ladrone islands where every pirate on God's blue ocean lives and raids. Just ahead, if we make it, lies the confluence of the Pearl River and the Xi rivers.

Bjorn said, "If we make it?"

"The good Captain says we're going to Canton, but carries specific orders to another destination called Zhaoqing, a prefecture-level city."

Porter said under Chinese law that foreign commerce was restricted to Canton, but his specific orders were to proceed directly to the prefect of the Guangdong province.

"That is against the law, sir. Beijing forbids it on penalty of death."

Porter waved his orders to bypass Canton in Jones's face. "It's all right here."

Fong stepped up, cleared his throat, and said, "We approach the junction of the Xi and Pearl rivers. Scattered along the Xi we will pass fortifications from three countries. The pirates are as common as legitimate vessels off Hong Kong."

Bjorn stepped in with his firm knowledgeable voice, "I have an idea that might work. Disguise *Agilis* and sneak up the river at dawn. The lookouts are sleepy after a night of vigilance or crawling from a warm bed next to their companion."

"Never heard of such a thing," said Porter.

"Me neither."

"You are a wise man," said Fong. "*Agilis* come and go before observer spot intruder. I help."

The group discussed Bjorn's idea but could not forge a better one. Porter reluctantly agreed to try it.

Bjorn and the Chinaman inspected junks, proas, sampans, and motley craft in the mouth of the mighty Pearl River, with the Xi entering from the left as they threaded their way among the islands.

Bjorn said, "Look. Our dead giveaway is rectangular canvas sails on a square-rigged brig. You can spot us miles away."

The two disguise masters scoured the area for distinguishing features on international watercraft from vantage points that were high, low, and flat across the water and planned their deception.

Lascars dropped the sails to the decks. Their painter artist added the eyes of the dragon to the bow using a pattern stolen from a passing sampan. Another splashed paint over the names at the fore and sides and drew crude Chinese words on top of them in a contrasting scarlet red. He didn't know the Chinese very well and labeled their vessel as a screaming dragon bitch. He wondered why boatmen in the river burst out laughing when he signed the artwork with his personal signature called a chop.

There was a limit to their efforts to imitate a Chinese war junk. Expecting to be unseen in a fog, but wearing a disguise nonetheless, she was now the Shui Jen, Water Man.

Bjorn with Fong was in charge of the crowning image. The crew spread a mainsail folded diagonally across the deck, over the capstan, over the chicken and pig cages, and roped it outside the railing. Accompanied by grunting and cursing the low intelligence of their leaders, only the lightest spars were sown in parallel strips across the folded sail in a triangle. With a support spar sown across the ends, a crude lateen sail was born.

"Wouldn't fool a grasshopper. I hope there is heavy mist on the river," said Fong.

After a moment of confusion, the confused crew belted out a sea shanty to hoist the crude triangular sail up the diagonal stay lines that guyed upright the foremast and mainmast. "In a dense fog from a distance, it might make a fleeting impression of a lateen sail to a drowsy, hungover lookout, nothing more."

A fire-breathing dragon completed the deception, consisting of loose materials stretched over the golden curls of the Spirit of Athena. A bucket of paint touched up the eye at the bow so their ship could see in the dark. It worked for Chinese ships, why not them?.

Overall, the efforts diminished the image to a lazy observer enough to avoid attracting attention, an alert observer in the guard would give the alarm in an instant.

Bjorn looked on his lateen baby with pride while Porter looked up and complained, "I can't believe you did this to my ship and mascot, Spirit of Athena. She'll retaliate by dropping bad luck on us.

A gust of wind filled the lateen sail and *Agilis* leaped forward like a wounded dolphin.

"Jiminy, that sail really works," said Bjorn. Liu and the lascars smiled because they were used to triangular sails with stiffeners. The helmsman at the tiller struggled as the rudder behaved like an angry beast compared to navigation under square sails. Bjorn chris-crossed the deck helping this hand and that to direct her upstream in the rising light of the next morning.

The Chinese pilot from Macau pointed to an unmarked inlet that appeared identical to numerous others. Buoys marked the way to Canton, but *Agilis* ignored them.

"Are you sure?." My charts do not indicate any buoys or signposts to the channel of the Xi.

The pilot and a confident Liu Fong assured them it was correct since both smuggled countless arms to the Taiping rebels up that same watercourse.

Porter kept up a tug-of-war with the pilot. The pilot wanted to enter the safe, main channel while he wanted to distance the forts from as far away as possible. So did Bjorn.

Porter was on the side of Bjorn, but Jones was with the pilot. *Agilis* under the lateen sail glided upriver more calmly than the argument on deck.

Somehow, they sneaked past fortifications sounding trumpets at reveille, maneuvered among sampans whose thin columns of smoke added to the haze promising breakfast, and faint fading nightlife songs wafted from ending parties on the banks.

The river pilot demanded they reverse course and register with the Ministry of Imports in the exotic and crowded city of Canton. After a high-pitched stream of Chinese Yue words, shaking of heads, and translations peppered with a mix of foul words from many languages, they arrived at a checkmate entering the mouth of the Xi River.

The magic lubricant of money made its ugly appearance to break the deadlock. Porter, at the suggestion of Fong and the encouragement of Bjorn, had the foresight to convert a substantial sum of rupees into local currency in various denominations. They left Macau with a tall stack of bills.

Liu Fong approached the adamant river pilot with several small bills. The body language told Porter and Amundson a low stack did not talk. Porter added larger bills from the middle of the stack. Facing upriver with his back to the transaction after glancing at the bundle of bills, Porter caught the slightest interest in his eyes and added a handful of paper currency from the bottom of the stack.

"Here."

The pilot took the stack and said, "You are serious. I may know a way through the province that evades the guardians of the holiest city of Canton."

"We have an agreement with the prefect in Zhaoqing. You must guide us to that location." Porter added another piece of paper.

"The river is dangerous at this time of year with the winds attacking from the south. I suggest we not ascend the river that far."

Richard put another bill on the stack.

I know a private wharf where you might moor in secrecy. I guide you if the channel permits."

Porter commented to Bjorn, "I have heard of baksheesh, but never have I been subject to such a brazen demand for a bribe. However, it gets the job done and is the local custom. A bit of money is stronger than the sun and tides and powers of us mere mariners.

The pilot issued firm instructions to sail outside the plethora of junks under the guard tower. "We escape the night fishermen returning home." Fong, accustomed to being in charge, disagreed with the pilot in loud terms neither Porter nor Bjorn understood.

The Gurkhas demanded the ship continue up the Pearl River to Canton and pitched the pilot overboard to emphasize their opinion.

Porter and the crew immediately rescued their well-bribed guide to protect their investment.

The wet pilot screamed at the incompetence of the helmsman as they groped among the floating vessels large and small through the cultural heart of southeast China. Their way upstream was enlivened by the dispute with Fong over every little shoal, a ripple in lazy water, floating debris, and possible hazards. The pseudo-fake junk sail approached Zhaoqing looking like some odd beast unknown to man or China.

Wafts of wind brought odors of a populated area to their nostrils, unmistakable and quite different from Calcutta. They could hear the sounds of carts and animals, people talking in the streets. They saw vessels being unloaded to the sound of curses as they disgorged their goods into the hordes of lighter boats that rowed the few yards to shore.

The river was not wide enough to hide in, although the pilot dodged the river traffic. "This is the most active port I have seen. More than London or Bremerhaven or any other. How do these people do it?

The private wharf lay at the edge of a sloping garden that graced an elegant, distant edifice. Guards along the river discouraged disembarkation by undesirable foreigners and unwanted persons. Leading away from the garden area was a road designed to preserve the serenity of the grounds and the palace. The house on the hill was the home of the prefect, Xu Guangjin.

Every clique in the wooden community nourished private thoughts at the end of a long, tumultuous voyage.

The lascars were relieved to be free of experimental food and foresaw a reunion with their compatriots onshore. Finding a return posting from a closed provincial city might be difficult compared to Canton.

A close observer might see softening in Gaje and Manju's stern faces after their mission to escort the chests to the final purchaser. They bumped their khukuri knives and prepared to search for a vessel going to Hong Kong.

Maverick felt a mix of emotions. His body was detoxified and healthy, but his mental images drifted through serene fields of dreams. He hated to think about the chests of ecstasy dispersing into crowds of unknown little people. He hoped they could enjoy the magic trips as much as he because they were more experienced.

Bjorn said, "Time to dump these boxes into the river."

"Not bloody likely,' said Porter.

"I'll heave the first one to start."

"You'll keep your filthy, stinking hands off my cargo, B'Horny."

"You will poison half of China with your smuggled contraband."

"My contraband, as you say, is legal and desired on this end."

"It is not legal here." Angry, Bjorn climbed the ratlines to his lookout post on the foremast.

Porter said, "It is a long way from plowing a muddy field behind a horse to delivering cargo worth millions to China. Today, I achieve my dream of becoming an important man. I shall be the Grand

Master of the parade with marching bands in front and battalions of horsemen in back. I have arrived."

Bjorn had a different point of view from in the air. He dropped to the deck. "You are too big for your britches, Mr. Richard Porter. Standing before me is a stranger. The big payoff makes you greedy, and we are close, but not yet to Cathay. Those phantom dollars are nowhere near the bank of Hong Kong."

The pilot directed them toward a well-maintained wharf with the bottom of the keel skidding over the bottom of the river. Scraping sounds that reverberated through the hull from below terrified Maverick in the galley since he was the lowest man in the ship.

A strange and unfamiliar vessel approaching the wharf caused the well-armed guard to run to the edge and announce that no unauthorized landings were permitted.

Before *Agilis* reached the wharf, crafts loaded with edibles and goods crowded around. They fought for space near the ship in a riot, wedging and pushing. The din of voices sounded recalled the sounds of five hundred canines barking in a dog compound.

The pilot said, "Welcome to Zhaoqing. I am finished and must return home. I wish you good luck." He pulled out a tiny Buddha from his clothes and rubbed his belly with the comment that Buddha gives good luck to virtuous people. "You will need it." He slipped into one riverboat and melted into the mass of humanity.

It was only later the officers learned the pilot cheated them in the amount, but with no alternative, it got the job done. Visions of profit from the sale of cargo overwhelmed regret at any minor loss of funds."

Bjorn climbed higher in the ratlines to get farther away from the commotion. At the very tip of the mast, with the pennant slapping his face, he saw a disturbance from upriver. Echoes of shooting rockets and red exploding fireworks captured his undivided attention.

"Holy mackerel, what on earth is that?" He called out, "Ships ahoy, armed military vessels."

Fong said, "A Chinese New Year celebration at the wrong time of year. Something is happening."

Mount all canvas and show what we can do," shouted Porter. "They do not call us Agilis the Swift for nothing."

Crew members looked at each other with blank faces. They had no canvas aloft to mount. The huge fake lateen sail was it.

Little did they know the prefect of the Guangdong province gathered recruits from across the region and outfitted the Zhaoqing Armada.

But he had.

Chapter 13—Captured

The prefect, Xu Guangjin, was under direct orders from Beijing to halt opium entering his realm. As usual, he required immediate obedience. The government hated that revenues dropped from lazy peasants. Addicts only strived to feed their habit, stole legitimate goods, became criminals, ripped loot from others, and kidnapped local officials for ransom, previously unheard of. Worst was their neglect of their ancestors and family.

Seated next to Guangjin on the observation platform overlooking the Xi River, the admiral was proud of his ability to assemble a military fleet in record time. He was determined to make a favorable impression on the prefect, maybe dazzling enough to impress Beijing. Ships, he did not have, so he commandeered suitable junks from the largest, wealthiest families in the Guangdong province. He drew on the treasury to convert five first-rate junks to war-ship status.

The fleet commodore in charge of the remodeling of the fleet demanded room to mount suitable weapons and accommodate ten crew members plus thirty-eight fighting soldiers on each vessel. Wings decorated with dragons to symbolize power flanked a raised forward observation platform. It was useful to fight from them when necessary. Ferocious hawk eyes glowered from the base of the wings to guide the vessel to the enemy, and a high poop deck resisted rear attacks.

To assure good luck and attract women to the sailors and soldiers, the mobilization crew hoisted red flags with gold Chinese writing up the masts. The soldiers boarded after the sailors and hung their brass shields on the gunwales, making an impressive show of shining metallic reflections in the water.

The admiral and commodore were impatient to polish their reputations. They organized a rapid strike demonstration in front of the assembled dignitaries of the region. An expert in New Year celebrations spent his unlimited fireworks budget on the launch of the fleet.

War-junks five abreast spanned the wide Xi river, guided by a line of menacing yellow hawk eyes under bows that glared up to the reviewing stand. The convoy planned to demonstrate their strength to subdue any enemy. Strings of hanging firecrackers deafened the awed spectators. Shooting rockets and exploding fireworks lit the skies and signaled for lesser traffic to get out of their way.

The admiral at the top of the reviewing stand leaned in his chair toward the dignitaries. "This strike force can surely halt smuggling into the Guangdong Province that evades paying taxes. The emperor will be pleased, don't you agree?"

"Well done. You can never know about the Emperor."

"Your skills are obvious, admiral. I am surprised you accomplished so much."

"Honored to serve you." He bowed. "I credit my loyal Commodore standing on the platform of the center flagship." He pointed to the elaborately dressed figure.

Through the morning atmosphere, they could see the commander who appeared to be distracted from the ceremonies. They followed his gaze to an odd-looking shape maneuvering erratically. Despite the eyes of a dragon on the bow, the figurehead was crude. Intuition from battles ignited the fleet leader's suspicions when the strange craft grounded itself with a severe jolt. Boatmen based in Zhaoqing knew it was poor navigation.

"How could her skipper miss the warning signs? They are strangers on our river." The commodore and his individual skippers watched with disgust as the grounded crewmen scrambled to free the vessel. They laughed at their efforts to free the nondescript hulk that accomplished nothing useful.

Chests pushed out in pride, Xu Guangjin and the admiral watched the aquatic hornet's nest swarm of dinghies from the convoy paddle to surround the helpless, invading vessel. The commodore nodded approval of hordes of well-trained soldiers leaped to the gunwales unopposed. The Sino forces immobilized the illegal foreign devils in a spectacular show of military skill.

Caught by surprise, the first campaign prize of the glorious Zhaoqing Armada was to the misfortune of *Agilis*.

A pair of intense hawk eyes on the bows of the junks guided the attack straight on the contraband carrier that was bobbing in the midst of the busy river traffic.

Porter heard the angry commodore shout through a megaphone to identify himself but did not understand the words. Spoken in the Yue dialect of Canton, only Liu Fong responded with massive obscenities but did not think to translate for Porter.

Actions followed the words and a trigger-happy skipper lobbed a warning shot at the uncooperative wooden vessel. The cannonball missed with a whistle and sank a fishing sampan.

Porter thought to himself, What now? They've seen my ruse so what should I do?. The officers, Fong, and Bjorn clustered on deck.

Fong wanted to fire back. Bjorn was of a mind to swarm their flagship, confident in his hand-to-hand skills. Jones' attitude was to let the confrontation develop before responding.

Porter weighed these opinions but knew that Anglo-Sino relations were tense and wanted to avoid provoking an international incident.

Clearing his throat, Porter threw caution overboard and ordered the swivel guns to return fire. Their little pops were laughable compared to the deep booms of the warship cannons.

"Choom, whiz, crash." A well-aimed ball struck the mainmast which knocked the entire jury-rigged lateen construction overboard. The valiant helmsman could not maneuver *Agilis* and ran the keel aground.

Forward progress stopped with a crash and men, animal cages, Gurkha bedrolls, and cargo slid forward into the first obstruction in the way. *Agilis* lodged on a submerged hazard.

Before they could wiggle free, multiple boats from the armada converged on the anguished brig. Grappling hooks clamped around the railing as though she were in the grip of massive octopi. Streams of yellow faces in uniforms mounted the gunwales and overpowered the outnumbered mariners. High-pitched screams and flashes of scimitars struck terror into the sailors confronting the Chinese hoards.

Lascars and lazy sailors were experts at evading capture and did. Gaje and Manju simply didn't go.

Rude, rough, short soldiers looped the last five confused culprits to each other by a rope around their necks and pushed them to shore. The shipboard lieutenant signed the captured crew over to the prefect's land-based army.

The Agilis Five found themselves lost in the alleys of Zhaoqing. They looked through the dark, tortuous passages, snaking down rows of gloomy shops. Little daylight filtered to the pavement. Not only was the sun blocked by close buildings but overhead advertising placards colored in blue, red, white, or green filled the remaining sky. Strange characters covered their surfaces.

A musician squawked to attract attention to the noisy parade of roped smugglers trudging through Zhaoqing.

Bjorn and Porter were the last two of Agilis Five to emphasize the power of the Chinese military over the hated foreign devils. Porter said, "What a hell of a change of status from the seat of authority to criminals facing the unknown."

Fong said, "We can expect a court date in a day or year."

Their belligerent captors harassed the soon-to-be convicts through narrow lanes, forcing the residents against the walls to let them pass. The noise of the crowd competed with the orders of the guards shouting to clear the way, and everybody wanted to see the strange-looking foreign criminals.

Mothers brought their children and passersby stopped to stare at the unfortunate Five as though they were animals in a zoo. "This is a lesson of what happens when you are a naughty child."

It was almost a relief for the stumbling five to enter an open gate in the fence around the criminal holding compound.

Back on the flagship, the commodore assigned a skeleton crew to assist the army to free the *Agilis*. In full view of the reviewing stand, the substitute Sino-officer of the deck screamed out high-pitched orders for the oriental sailors to jettison the remnants of the failed disguise and restore the normal sails. Individual seamen learned their sailsmanship on trips to India and Madagascar and knew how to manage a square-rigged brig such as their captured vessel.

Unfamiliar with the behavior of the brig, the new crew of soldiers scraped a few watercraft maneuvering the captured brig off the rock and to a stop in front of the armada in full view of the reviewing stand. Used to water duty, they hated serving under a land commander.

"What an amazing demonstration of the Zhaoqing Armada in action, admiral."

"My pleasure, your eminence. Perhaps the emperor would be interested in our capabilities as well." He made a hand signal to the flagship behind the bedraggled *Agilis*.

"I shall prepare an appropriate message promptly. His Eminence will approve of our quick action to stop the flood of Indian poison into the region."

Understanding the signal and prepared for a grand finale, the commodore gave an order. A wall of rockets made a red, orange, yellow, and green background to silhouette *Agilis*. War junks on each side shot rockets skyward in front of their sails. Two vessels at the ends of the convoy added their displays and the whole celebration inaugurated the Zhaoqing Armada in an overwhelming display. The climax was the ceremonial dumping of a carved opium chest into the roiled waters of the Xi. The prefect, the admiral, the assembled ministers nodded and clapped enthusiastically. "Ah so. Most good outcome."

In the crowd of spectators under the reviewing stand, a plump merchant awaited his shipment of carved chests and hurried to the waterfront to greet the captain. What he saw was the master being kicked up the path to town by the ferocious Chinese military. Soldiers who had never sailed overran the transport ship. "Incompetent clods."

The merchant despaired to lose his shipment from India of the highest quality product that commanded a high price. He had greased the palms of the distribution channels all the way to the interior of southern China, and that money was gone forever.

He wept to see the stevedores pitch the box into the Xi. It carried a street value greater than the entire operation. Enough to pay the wages of the crew for a year, enough to buy Agilis, enough to pay bribes all the way to Nanchang and points beyond.

Crowds lined the fence outside the criminal compound shouting insults at Agilis Five and other inmates. At the sound of an enormous gong, the villagers surged into the public arena. They expectantly faced a grim wall. Amid screaming and wailing and anticipation, guards brought a prisoner through a far door, bent him into a kneel in the center. Only Bjorn and Porter were tall enough to see over the crowd. What they saw was the prosecutor delivering a lengthy dissertation from a scroll.

Total silence fell over the crowd when he stopped, and everyone gawked with attention. Rolling up his scroll, he bowed to the guards and pointed to the captive kneeling with his hands drawn behind him. The condemned man appeared dazed and submissive, motionless.

The hooded executioner practiced a swing with a heavy sword, swishing a breath of foul air. A second stroke passed through the man's neck, and his head rolled across the ground. Cheers erupted as the torso pumped a brief fountain of blood and toppled in a heap. The executioner raised the head by the pigtail to show the crowd it was clearly separated from the body. The overpopulation was reduced by a criminal for some crime or another.

Porter and Bjorn were horrified yet fascinated at the spectacle, and Bjorn said to Porter, "I can't be comfortable in this place."

"What can you do?"

"Let me think on it."

Chapter 14—Sino Justice

A disturbed night filled with groans of detained criminals and the wails of death row inmates lasted until dawn. Rude guards burst into the yard and jerked Agilis Five to their feet. Pointing to the entrance, they unlocked the gate and dragged the five into the narrow early morning streets of Zhaoqing.

Curious citizens poured from their residences, shops, or looked up from street businesses. It was impossible to overlook the parade led by a drummer playing the gong to call attention to the stumbling foreign barbarians. A clerk tied a red banner on the sides of culprits' heads to make them conspicuous. Their hands tied behind their backs emphasized their status, lowest of the low. Two men brought up the rear, one with a bundle of cleft canes. He used it from time to time to hurry the prisoners to their fate.

The public humiliation ended at the entrance to four elegant buildings clustered around a courtyard. Enclosed by a six-foot stone wall, the compound included an especially ornate structure. "The home of the Mandarin of Justice," said Fong. The roof was impressive and stood above the others.

Beats on the gong and a shout from the guard alerted the gatekeeper. He opened the red gate with a humble bow.

The hostile hustle of the streets gave way to serene grounds of flowers, pet peacocks, trilling birds in gilded cages, a waterfall into a pond of Koi fish, along the path of raked stones to the front portico. Six arches crowned seven columns on the front edge of the porch under a tile roof.

The prisoners were anything but serene as their captors beat crisscross blows of the canes on their lagging, sweating backs to force them up the steps and through a large doorway. Liu Fong said, "We shall be accused before the Mandarin of Justice. It is the conventional procedure."

In an unconventional move, they encouraged public visitors to enter as witnesses to the gravity of the charges, as well as the evil of the product they smuggled. The caravan of five entered the great hall, followed by throngs of angry spectators.

Looking at the room, Bjorn said, "More beautiful than the city streets." The walls of the room were decorated with gold paneling, the floor tiles were polished but without furniture forcing spectators to stand. The hall of justice was dominated by a table at the far end.

"This isn't like any court I've heard of," said Maverick.

"Me neither."

A resounding gong announced the start of the trial. The crowd in the room became deathly quiet and bowed when the scarlet curtains behind the dais opened and three personages entered.

The Mandarin wore a long robe, embroidered. A gold neck chain held a large square emblazoned with a red-headed crane. It designated his status as the first rank. A man stood on his right with a scroll. A haughty gentleman entered left.

Fong said, "We are honored by the presence of the personal emissary of Xu Guangjin, the prefect, to observe and assure our sentence is death."

The three seated themselves before the table in the only three chairs in the hall. Implements of writing were laid on the table for the secretary to record dispositions and defense. Their combined countenances were as frosty as a glacier.

Porter said, "My instinct tells me there is trouble coming."

"Many times over, my friend. We may be headed into the sunset."

Liu Fong understood the proceedings and whispered the progress to the anxious ears of Bjorn Amundson, Richard Porter, Oscar Jones, Maverick Hatfield, and to reassure himself.

Fully prepared and ready, the Mandarin pointed to the bailiff. In a loud voice, he announced, "The court of his Imperial Highness, Prefect Xu Guangjin of Guangdong, will now hear the charges against these filthy, unworthy, and clearly guilty foreign devils." The bailiff shuddered and looked away from the prisoners.

"Prosecutor," said the Mandarin.

The persons on either side glared stoically. "I call the commander of the navy."

The naval gentleman stepped forward, bowed, and said in loud words, "This undesirable trash has disturbed your serenity and endangered the foundation of the government, as well as your high personage, your ancestors, even to the Palace in Beijing."

"What are their crimes?"

"Your Highness has designated the heavenly city of Canton as the center of commerce. It is prohibited for barbarian ships from Hong Kong to travel into the heartland of the universe. The presence of this ship in Zhaoqing is illegal, but worse are the chests of opium in the hold, far more than their needs of the entire crew to feed their filthy weakness of character.

A dark shadow passed over the Mandarin's face and the speaker realized he hit a sore point. Was it possible the prefect liked opium for himself but hated the effect on the inhabitants of the realm?

He cleared his throat. "Your order to halt the importation of opium is clear. Effects on working people are beyond doubt. Rice is unplanted, chickens starve, and sweet smoke fills the air."

The Mandarin pointed at the Agilis Five. "Show respect to your accuser." Soldiers knocked the mariners and translator to the floor and pushed their heads down.

The translator said, "We must lick the floor to the tribunal table." As they crawled the length of the hallway, the rabble of spectators raised a great cry and shook their fists. By the time they reached the table, their mouths were dry as cotton.

"Rise and explain yourselves." He pointed to Porter.

Porter said in a dry, cracked voice since he had not eaten or drunk water for two days, "Your beautiful country . . . is most . . . remarkable, eminence. I bring to you. . . great luck."

With a dismissive wave, the Mandarin said, "Not valuable. You bring distress to my subjects."

The naval commander pushed Jones to the front of the table. "I bring you the scum mate who ran the daily operations."

"Speak up."

Jones was a man of action, not words, and was acutely uncomfortable in the elegant court. "Err . . ., don't know what to say. . . ., followed orders of Captain."

"Guilty." He gestured to the scribe, who noted the verdict with an ink brush on a scroll.

"Who are you?'

Bjorn said, "I am a passenger. I didn't know about the cargo that was loaded in the hold.

"Liar, liar, liar. The law of Confucius says an associate of a criminal is also criminal. I accuse you of being on the ship. Also guilty."

"What does the fourth criminal outlaw say?'

Maverick said, "I am the lowly cook. I boil rice to make porridge for the sailors, no more."

"See how he trembles and shakes," said the prosecutor. "Your eminence might observe that he suffers from a lack of opium. This sorry derelict piece of human shit shows the danger such a vile product inflicts on our population."

"Add him to the list of guilty persons."

"Speak, traitor,' he said to Liu Fong.

"Mercy, mercy. I served the Royal Navy for many years. Barbarians of the south kidnapped me from a ship and sent me to the gem mines of Burma."

With interest, the Mandarin said, "Go on."

"Guards beat me daily and nightly because the Burmese hate us Chinese. My quota of rubies was double for everyone else."

"Reserve the verdict for this one until later."

Consulting a long scroll, the scribe said, "You are guilty of plotting to violate the sacred rites of Confucius. You bring disorder into our midst. I don't know your tricks to escape our Canton forts, but you will find our skilled guards in Zhaoqing are more vigilant."

Xu Guangjin said, "I am merciful and just. The penalty for smuggling into China is beheading with a sword, but I grant you time to confess wrong behavior. Your ship is smaller than others and brings goods of value."

The Agilis Five relaxed to keep their heads attached to their bodies, at least for a time. Liu said, "Bow to the honor of his mercy." The five bowed.

The Mandarin requested the status of their confessions, but none existed.

"Our punishment cages will help you confess your evil nature. We will sentence you to death for wrong behavior when you have confessed."

With orders now written in black ink, the magistrate signed and sealed them with a chop, a jade stamp carved with his impression and dipped in red ink.

They bowed as jailors roughly escorted them from the courtroom to the criminal yard, their final destination.

The townspeople's faces jammed the streets to get a view of the captives destined for death. Their favorite exclamation, straight eyes foreign devils, was frequent although unintelligible to the prisoners. In the midst of the great unwashed, Liu Fong said this class was deliberately taught to hate, despise, and distrust foreigners.

A glimpse into the shops revealed a contrast to the narrow streets. Many were eighty feet deep, the center open to the roof. Interiors might have been comfortably organized, but they couldn't look.

An itinerant barber offered to trim their hair to make a noble impression at their beheading. His outfit was a bamboo pole balanced on his shoulder, the badge of his profession. One end held a small brass basin with a charcoal stove for heating water and a shared towel for every customer. A wooden cabinet that served the client as a seat held razors, lancets, tweezers, files, and other surgical instruments to balance the other end.

The Agilis Five could not understand the offer, but guards said foreign devils were beyond redemption and deserved to die in squalor. One kicked the barber away.

Bjorn said to Maverick, "You were always a rebel. I rescued you from the police department in Bremerhaven because you chased beer and from the den where you smoked opium. They sentenced us to be criminals. And you didn't stop in Calcutta. No, you broke into a chest and stole from the merchant of madness. You should have known it would enrage him to lose his blessed product. A dealer here demands a full shipment."

Maverick stumbled along in pain and ignored Bjorn's accusation.

"You are a marvelous cook, but your behavior slurred when you delivered the mess. That time you poured the terrine of soup over Mr. Porter, it took everything my comradeship had to stop him from locking you in chains. You would still be in chains if anyone else could cook. He was prepared to throw you overboard. Our friendship hasn't been the same, and it's your fault."

Close from the canes of reeds harassed the Five back through the streets of Zhaoqing to the jail. The residents came out of doorways and around buildings to scream and throw filth on them, including human waste.

Shadowing the doomed gang, the merchant watched the unfolding drama when the guards hounded the five through the alleys to jeers from both sides.

The gigantic foreign Bjorn received more than his share. His massive size and golden hair struck terror into the population, as they had never seen such an apparition. In their superstition, they considered him an evil spirit from their ancestors. A few stepped forward with clubs to beat him before the escorts intervened. "Be careful. He will haunt you as an angry ghost and cause your family great harm.

The local dialect was unfamiliar to the mariners. Waves of hatred from the public and perils of bodily harm came on all sides.

Relative peace welcomed them back to the criminal yard, peaceful for the moment. The prison guard said in broken English as they stumbled past square bamboo cages with inert bodies hanging from distressed heads, "You are the same in three days."

The Chinese stowaway said it was considered very bad to behead foreigners.

"Not as dishonorable as for a Chinese who loses the soul without the head. He is damned forever. Foreign devils are lost already because no ancestors to worship."

"We are sentenced to enter the punishment cages," said Fong.

"What is a punishment cage?" asked Bjorn as they were towed, pushed, kicked, beaten, and deluged with filth from the onlookers and otherwise exposed through Zhaoqing to the criminal yard.

The Chinese stowaway described a punishment cage as somewhat taller than the prisoner restrained inside. It was about a yard square and as tall as the prisoner, plus a foot. A stack of flat stones lined the bottom and held the cage upright. The sides were open wooden bars. Across the top is a divided board with a hole in the center the size of a man's neck.

That doesn't sound all that bad," said Maverick.

"They lash your hands outward through the sides. You stand on the stones and they lock your head outside. You eat or drink by the kindness of strangers if you can open your mouth, but only in the criminal yard are vicious guards and other criminals who hate you, no strangers permitted."

"We are not criminals,' said Porter.

"Yes, we are," said the ex-stowaway. "We were delivering illegal chests to a location banned by the laws of China."

"But opium is legal in the world trade. It lubricates and protects the sensibilities of users around the world,' said Bjorn.

Retching in awful condition, Maverick said, "Master opium is heaven on earth when you have it, when you need it. I am most sorry, Mr. Porter, to visit that spice shop in Calcutta. It is not my fault a sneaky man showed me the array of spices in India, and then, 'A special spice that is so valuable, we only show it in a special room. Like to try it?' My excuse is the experience was highest adventure of my life. My leg pain melted and I roamed the hills of home a healthy young man."

Beatings and shouting forced the prisoners to a cluster of cages at the far edge of the yard. A confined prisoner in the compound hollered out, "You all did, and me too. China loves opium, no likes devils."

Bjorn looked around but could not determine which dejected prisoner cursed them. He noticed cages sized to hold a man standing upright at the far side. Within one was a man with his arms lashed to the outside bars and standing on a stone. His head protruded through a hole in a board on top. Another confined a man whose head stretched above his neck could not move anything but his eyes.

It looked decidedly unpleasant and his tongue stuck out in thirst. The cramped muscles of his calves looked like the stones he stood on.

Someone roughly hustled the five through the crowd of spectators to cages that baked in full sun all day. Coolies stacked flat stones in the bottom of each cage according to the height of the incoming inhabitant.

Liu Fong was first with six stones. Guards rudely tied his arms to the outside bars and clamped the boards on top around his neck. He stood defiantly on tiptoe on the stones and spit on the guards. Two large cages were reserved for criminals from the north of China, who were taller than southern criminals. Something about the climate of Mongolia made the natives grow as tall as Bjorn and Porter, though not as heavy.

Deputy guards thrust the two into bamboo cages with two layers of stone at the bottom, their hands and heads in the sun to get instantly sunburned. Bjorn got special treatment by having ropes deliberately tightened across his scars and scabs from the galley knives. Maverick was shorter, and they adjusted his cage with another stone.

The prisoners faced each other in a ten-foot circle. The jailer deliberately picked the spot in direct sunlight all day and also received a glare from the tile roofs at certain times of the day.

"Well, hell," said Porter."So this is how it ends?'

"They pull a stone each day from the bottom of our cage to stretch our necks', said Liu. It makes a contest how many they can remove before we are gone from the flies and the sun. The first day your calves cramp to stone. On the second day, hands tire from standing up. The third day overwhelms by a stretch of the neck."

"I am sorry I got you into this."

Fong explained in short little gasps from his confined throat the workings of the courts they faced.

"The Tang code ignores law and punishment to maintain order. Confucian code of rights is the philosophy for civilized behavior. The rule of law applies to those outside civilized behavior. People observe proper rights, and only social outcasts have their actions restrained by law.

Bjorn looked disgusted with the Chinese courts. He disagreed.

"Any of ten abominations that disturb serenity must be punished, justice does not enter. Persons guilty of the ten abominations destroy human bonds, rebel against heaven, go against reason, and violate justice. Punishment can be minor flogging, caning, imprisonment, exile, and in the final disgrace, death. But they will not convict a person without a confession. Torture gains a confession.

"Ten abominations?'

"Worst is plotting rebellion. Perpetrators must die. A father puts a rebellious child to death."

The mariners shuddered at the thought of murdering their own children, although they had none of their own as far as they knew.

"Most bad is sedition to damage royal temples. To break feng shui is to curse the sovereign. Contrary to virtue.

"Seven more are . . .,'

"We hear you. Enough and shut up."

Fong continued anyway. "Against the ten abominations are eight deliberations for justice.

"Deliberations? The abominations are not enough."

"To lessen punishment on the upper class. High status is virtuous in all things. Relatives of the sovereign, individuals of virtue, individuals of ability, and descendants of imperial families."

Bjorn spat at the strange concepts of the Chinese legal system. "Stupid."

"Heavenly kingdom, observe proper rights. Laws and punishment are only necessary for those beyond civilized behavior, like us."

"We are civilized," said Bjorn. Porter looked doubtful, and Maverick suffered from a lack of paregoric.

"The Confucian code is stability and tradition.

"Explain in words from English," said Porter

"Goal of the court is deserved punishment, not guilt or innocence like in England."

"I am civilized society," said Bjorn. "Let them have their damn Emperor and government."

"You just broke the sedition abomination by cursing the Emperor."

Punishment cages indeed. In a foggy mental moment at the end of day one, before their calves were cramped to stone and their necks tight but not stretched, the lives of *Agilis* Five passed before their eyes.

"What a muddle we are in," said Richard in halting bursts through his constricted throat.

"Well dammit to hell, you did it by loading that poison and dragging me with it."

"But what of the sea's many complicated, humanlike, awe-inspiring, and terrifying moods?"

"The sea is like a woman, loving, warm, tender, comforting, exciting, but fickle too. Unpredictable, uncontrollable, jealous, wrathful, and vindictive."

"The blue brine is all or none of these. Who knows what whim may engulf our wee being?"

"Aren't we a bit of each?

"With faith that tomorrow, the sun will rise."

Maverick said, "I shined our bell to impress the Chinks before we were captured. Wasted my time."

Thoughts turned to the gleaming bronze bell, the heart of the ship, engraved,

Agilis
1841, Johann Lange Shipyard
Bremerhaven

As a friend of years standing, Bjorn whispered, "My New Viking Gold Mine improved both of us when you left and the Hatfield twins blew in. We sucked gold out of the American River like nobody's business . . .." he looked at Maverick Hatfield, listening from the next cage."

"Yeah, man."

". . . until that damned Brannan stole my mine. After the riot, Maverick served the best barbecued wild boar in California. Good thing, or we'd have burned down Sacramento."

"It was my special sauce."

Porter bemoaned the difficulties of a command, Bjorn bemoaned no respect as Patriciate of California. Jones and Fong remained silent in misery.

Insects buzzed, flowers bloomed through cracks in the packed dirt,

"It's your fault I'm a smuggler," said Bjorn.

"Trading cannot be smuggling. Opium is legal."

"I had to move my moonshine still to stay ahead of the revenuers," said Maverick.

Porter ignored their comments, "Chinese peasants can't get enough, even when the government executes smugglers, British treaties be damned."

"My shipmates may visit smoking dens on leave but recover back at sea."

"Weakness, I can tolerate, but not opium. Too easy to get, unwise to use."

Maverick said, "A man needs self-control. Take me, I can handle anything but the ship's mess and boiled beef. Know a spice vendor in Zhaoqing?'

"Another reason against dumping opium in China."

"What's that?'

"Remember the time you broke me out of La Grange prison barge floating in the Sacramento River?'

I remember an oriental family who chopped an escape hole with their wicked sharp battle axes. I smuggled you out of town."

"You're a born smuggler, Richard Porter esquire, you are." The head of that family ran a ditch to my mine. Back in China, he was the project manager for the Hangzhou Grand Canal until he joined the Taiping rebellion and ran British guns to the fighters."

Porter looked at Bjorn, "I didn't know celestial orientals in San Francisco came from such a war-filled province as Zhaoqing."

"Burmese troops kidnapped their cousin on the way to Calcutta to pick up snuff and umbrellas according to vague rumors floating among the Sino communities. His family in Zhaoqing has not heard from him and fear he is dead. The younger members of the family emigrated to California as miners. The rest of the family stayed behind in danger without funds for a passage but reluctant to sell themselves into California slavery."

A family from this cesspool made it to Sacramento and started the Lucky Ducky Mine upstream from me. Their leader brought water to my workings and I let them borrow from my ditch."

"Running a mining operation is as complicated as commanding a brig."

"What can we do?'

Liu said, "My cousin escaped to the east. He was a wizard with water."

Gasped comments proved the family running the Lucky Ducky Placer Mine in California was from the extended family of Liu Fong.

Bjorn said, "They helped me when I was down and almost out. I will find your family."

"Is hard in cage."

"I'll find a way."

"My family is hiding here in Zhaoqing of the Jiangxi province. They were Hakka and treated with hostility by the Han population. They had to rebel."

"Hard to search when hanging from punishment cage, Hard more without the head."

"I like my head attached better."

They sank into the gloom to suffer through the night.

Xu Guangjin, Prefect, was supreme in his position but knew the seriousness of executing foreigners, especially from the East India Company. His advisors recommended he keep a close watch on the prisoners and extract their confessions at the earliest possible moment. He selected his highest minister to hasten the progress of the punishment cages.

Announced by drums and horns, the minister entered the criminal yard and faced the circle of criminals, just in time for the ceremony of lowering the stones.

The weight of the occupants required a stout man to pull a flat rock from each cage. Bjorn and Porter had one left. When gone, if the last flat rock did not stretch their necks to force a confession, they were destined for beatings. The last resort was to break their legs and render them unable to stand and support their heads. The other three were ready to confess soon.

Walking outside the circle of cages, the minister spoke in elegant Mandarin Chinese that only the superbly well-educated class could understand, in contrast to the ordinary Yue dialect of old Guangdong.

He gave each inmate a reading of the abomination he violated, and the desirability of an early confession to end their agony. A translator repeated the words in pidgin English and added a description of the agonies to come.

The prefect needed those confessions to justify the closure of the incident. The court scribe had written the proclamation to instruct the Guangdong province. "Smuggling opium is prohibited."

Starting with the captain and progressing through the others, the minister confronted Liu Fong last. "You are the lowest worm in creation and Confucius is ashamed that you committed the abomination of defiling the name of the ruler. Your associates are guilty of blasphemies. You, I accuse of violating the abomination of perdition by poisoning the citizens of this province. It is necessary to add treason, a failure to correct by your death."

He thought it unlikely a common low-class peasant would understand his Mandarin. Fong's answer in perfect, years-educated, Mandarin verse with perfect inflection shocked the minister. Their culture respected mandarins above all other classes.

"Most honorable, wise, scholar of Confucius, you are acquainted with the traditional rights of correct behavior."

"I have devoted many years in study and learned the abominations beyond question. I immortalized my words for all to learn."

Fong said he studied those very writings. As proof, he quoted obscure passages that only a dedicated scholar would recognize.

The minister questioned the stretched-out man on fine points and convinced himself that Fong really was a master in the traditions of Confucius and interpretations of the abominations.

Fong nodded his forehead through the cage top, all he could do. "I am humbled by your expert knowledge, Excellency, master of the writings of Sun Bin, descendant of Sun-Tsu, author of the Art of War."

"My guiding light is his wisdom, the most famous son of King Wei of Qi."

"It is my greatest pride and honor that Aisin Gioro Yongyan was the fifth Emperor of the Qing China and my honored ancestor."

The astounded minister questioned Liu with the zeal he administered the examinations for a scribe in the royal court. Satisfactory and brilliant answers to his impromptu questions convinced the minister he was truly addressing a descendant of the Emperor.

Fong continued well aware of his success at convincing the minister of his royal lineage. "Your honor certainly knows how Confucius balanced ten abominations by eight deliberations. Balance is life is everything." The minister paused.

"I claim the deliberations for the relatives of the emperor, the achievement, and the guests of state by virtue of descended from a previous dynasty."

The minister exploded at the lowly guards, doing their job. He beat them with his staff and demanded they release Fong and his associates with profound apologies.

As he stretched his cramped legs and worked his shoulder, Liu Fong stood upright and said, "I request approval to appear before the prefect."

With a bribe of small rubies to the guard, the Chinaman left followed by the minister's retinue.

Chapter 15—Redemption Inspiration

Fong was resplendent in borrowed robes, suitable for a Mandarin. He straightened his shoulders under the heavy robe. Mandarins always defended each other, and he fortified his thoughts to excel as a credible witness. The feeling of the cool, silken surface of the carved jade box concealed in his robe soothed his hand and strengthened his resolve.

Xu Guangjin required his testimony in the secret disciplinary action against the Mandarin minister, accused of misidentification of an esteemed scholar.

The minister and Fong together entered the waiting room of the regional ruler.

"Why do you waste my time?"

"Please permit a humble petition for your Honorable consideration."

"I am ashamed of my minister, who misidentifies an educated Mandarin. There is no time for you."

His eminence realized the status of the punishment cages and wanted the confessions.

Fong summoned every bit of courage he had to address the highest personage he had met in his lifetime and bowed.

"Esteemed heir of a thousand generations of wisdom, I request permission to speak."

The head of the regional government frowned and looked at Fong with indifference and raised eyebrows.

The room froze for a moment.

"This Honorable man perceived at my first breath that I have pursued the writings of Sun Bin, the son of King Wei of Qi. My guiding light and honor is that Aisin Gioro Yongyan, fifth Emperor of the Qing China, was my honored ancestor."

"Can this be true?"

"Low-level clerks erred in the administration of justice, I am afraid. Yes, I perceived the injustice and present to you a Mandarin for your consideration."

Prefect Guangjin weighed this information before saying to Fong, "It is my honor you live in my province."

"To be in your presence is the greatest moment of my life. For you, may this offer of a small token show my gratitude." Liu Fong presented the carved jade box by laying it on the table. "A token of my loyalty to your regime, may I say." The precious carved jade box was breathtaking. The minister opened it and handed it to the prefect.

People in the room could see that the box contained a red gem, but only the prefect could see the shimmering star glowing within. All conversation ceased to watch Guangjing tremble at the beauty of the largest star pigeon's blood ruby in the world. After fondling the stone and kissing it, he raised the medallion around his neck to compare the center ruby to the gift. The medallion failed the comparison, as did the ring on his finger.

"Your gift is from the heavens. I will grant a wish that you may have. What will it be?'

The emperor's descendant bowed and asked permission to speak the truth. After a wary nodded approval, he continued.

"Officers of Agilis give honor to your emissaries from the Celestial Kingdom and promote your interests in California. I petition under the deliberations of ability and diligence for the release of the four from the punishment cages."

The words of Confucius were unequivocal, and he commutated three deliberations without hesitation.

Emboldened by his success, Fong further petitioned for the officers to help oversee the unloading of *Agilis*. Fong seized the moment and requested that the prefect allow Porter and Jones to assist the imperial stevedores. He pointed out retrieving the silks, cotton, and trade goods, not to mention the Chinese chests, was slow and difficult. Destined for the provincial warehouse in repayment for his mercy, faster was better. Leave the Chinese workers free to dump the chests in the river.

Responding to the ring of a little bell, several ministers assembled for a conference."

"We never negotiate with criminals."

"True, but a Mandarin cannot be criminal."

The debate continued for several hours before the august group reached an uneasy decision.

"I grant release of the four and permission to oversee the retrieval of goods, nothing more."

With great respect and ultimate humility, the Fong pressed for the release of *Agilis.*

The second debate ended quickly. Fong knew the fleet had little use for a square-rigged brig because *Agilis* was unwieldy in the river, and their junks did not sail in the open ocean beyond Hong Kong.

"We humbly request your esteemed eminence to grant a modest payment to cover disposal of the chests."

The prefect hesitated before judging this as a beneficial idea but agreed on the condition his minister supervised the plundering of the hold. "One chest I want to be delivered to me personally. This is the identifying mark." His scribe brushed a Chinese character with an extra dot

The descendant of the emperor recognized the mark of the special chest.

As they were leaving, Fong asked to see the ruby one last time before the guards safeguarded it in the vault of the royal treasury. He turned to a window with his back to the guards to study the shimmering star.

He whispered to the guards, "I must leave quickly because you have royal work to do."

Bjorn and associates prepared for the worst when jailors creaked the open doors to their captivity boxes. They wondered at the leg massages and welcomed healing ointments on sunburned skin.

"I never expected the last dinner before I lost my head,' said Bjorn, facing a rich feast with unlimited heated wine. They were confused but happy to eat after three days of forced fasting.

Maverick stumbled from his companions to a private room. Premonitions of dismemberment, nausea, withdrawal, and despondence overwhelmed him. A tray of metal tools and rattling needles, carried by a young woman, worsened his attitude, but his breakdown was absolute when she pulled down his pants to expose his tortured leg. Death by a thousand cuts starting with an amputation?

Her manner became so calming when she served a cup of tea that Maverick felt comforted from the effects of the herb concoction and faced death with calm despair. "I hope it doesn't hurt too bad."

She stroked his forehead to prepare for his fate. A master entered and the young woman bowed deeply and left. With a touch as light as the air, the master felt, observed, and studied Maverick's leg from hip to toe. Reactions to the view of the ill-healed fracture told him everything he needed to know.

The acupuncturist selected five needles and inserted them along the earth meridian of Maverick's Qi. Painful inflammation faded to a healthy pink, and within moments the leg relaxed.

Outside enjoying the feast, Porter thought to himself. If I survive this predicament, I'll never smuggle again, but he said nothing to no one.

A mean-looking guard with watchful eyes shepherded the Agilis Four and Liu Fong to the prefect's private wharf. Their wooden home rocked in the breeze and tugged at the mooring lines with all sails furled. The stevedores, supervised by the navy, prepared to heave the chests overboard.

Cheers from the spectators greeted a wooden box fourteen inches square by thirty inches rising from the hold. It seemed heavy. The label had an extra dot that none of the stevedores understood since they were illiterate.

Willing hands lowered the special box into a waiting boat that a boatman paddled to the private wharf. A relay passed the container to a cart pulled by coolies up the garden path to the prefect's home.

Members of the crew Calcutta huddled in a dejected group onshore and watched their home of months overrun with exotic stevedores.

The ex-captain stood with a friend, both showing intense interest in the operations. "I understand your desire to own a ship for freedom. My gold mine was hope for me."

What most animated observers onshore was the ruckus when a bundle of silk erupted from the hatch followed by a bag of wheat. The items of useful cargo filled a stream of lighterboats to the wharf. Carts carried the unloaded contents along a side path to the provincial warehouse.

A second chest balanced on the gunwale before two sailors rudely tipped it over the railing. A third and fourth made splashes that distressed the Captain and passenger.

They discussed the splash of each chest that was equal in value to the entire endeavor. "Captain McIntyre bought Agilis for six thousand dollars. My share of the profit was to be a hundred and eighty thousand dollars that would support retirement. What a sad ending."

Splash, splash.

A little apart stood a portly Chinese man dressed in a brilliant robe. His steady stream of invective and waving hands attracted no response from the active hands on deck. The merchant was sad as he counted the splashes of his precious opium. "What a loss of heavenly profit. Seven, eight . . ., no . . ., no . . ., no!'

The value of each splash equaled the expenses of the ship for a tour of duty and back. Funds left over would buy Porter's wines in any port in the world and the sailors' grog.

Representatives of the minister and a tax collector counted the chests to prevent shrinkage.

"Seventeen, eighteen . . .,'

"I suspect the EIC will be angry at my loss of their shipment, but we delivered it to Guangdong without paying the Beijing taxes. I'll be far away over the Pacific when that message gets back to Calcutta. The EIC still makes a three thousand percent profit with no risk on other deliveries.

"I would not call this a delivery, but the chests are here. I may have difficulty getting another cargo, but must try."

"Why?'

"To uphold my honor."

"Honor among thieves is overrated."

"I'm not a thief."

"Next best thing."

They mused about the ethics of theft and the analogy of stealing health as opposed to stealing wealth.

Among the Chinese and Indian words on the chests, they read the exact weight in Arabic numerals. Fanatic record-keeping by the tax collector drove him to record each one before he allowed the stevedores to dump it.

The gigantic balance beam sat between the capstan and the mainmast. Assistants added weights opposite the box. Ten-pounders started as the balance needle approached the center point. They added five and one-pounds, minute weights, and bits of foil placed with tweezers. After an eternity, the needle stopped at the center of the marks. With a click, click, click, click on an abacus, the clerk added the weights and compared the total with the inscription. When they agreed, the official stamped his chop symbol and pointed to the gunwale. His final report to the supervisor, up the chain of command to the emperor, would credit the weight intercepted by the prefect.

"Twenty-six, twenty-seven, . . ., thirty-four and we call our work complete. Thirty-five if you count the special delivery to the prefect himself. They loaded the last chest on the balance beam, added the weights, and halted the proceeding. The supervisor called a local official to the measuring station as a witness to the accuracy of the gauging. He and the tax collector checked the weights one by one and watched the clerk click the abacus to sum the total. "Repeat the measurement." Starting over from the beads at zero, he arrived at the same total.

"There is a theft of contents. The measurement is short."

A fishing sampan on the other side of *Agilis* held a skipper counting splashes in the river. He knew the chests had an initial tendency to float, but sank within a few breaths. Three divers lined up on deck marked the sinking interval with a trained breathing technique. Six cycles of inhalation and pause followed by long exhalation and longer pauses judged when the box would submerge. The end man dove without a sound under *Agilis* as a dripping man propelled a chest over the stern. Eager hands pulled the rescued chest aboard before the label or wood soaked up water. Dry in no time, they would be ready by next morning for clandestine smuggling to the interior.

Even from a distance, the crew members could see the final chest did not balance the weights. A tiny corner of the label looked bent up. With a scream from the mouth of the tax collector, guards arrested the obnoxious, noisy merchant. The guards took him away.

An alert Gurkha onshore said to the group, "What is going on? Things were so smoothly."

"A tragedy. The weight of the last chest is lower than the weight on the label. The police have arrested the merchant for the punishment of theft," someone said.

"Imprisoned or executed. Justice is heavy on a man who steals opium."

"They have raped and looted our vessel, and we are helpless to resist," Bjorn said to the dejected crew.

Gaje and Manju patted each other's shoulders. "We are not responsible for shrinkage after we deliver the opium. We fulfilled our mission. Home to Nepal."

The richly-dressed supervisor sent an aide down the hold to confirm it was empty, even while the last diver pushed the last chest aboard the sampan.

"What do you mean done? I counted thirty-five."

The comment passed through several before coming back to Porter.

"It is unfortunate that seven chests were empty and the eighth contains a problem." The official confirmed a credit of twenty-seven boxes. "A deposit for losses will be made to the Oriental Bank of Commerce in Hong Kong, less a reduction to cover money changing fees and handling costs."

The *Agilis* carried sixty-three thousand dollars in her strongbox that no one mentioned.

Turning to Bjorn, "What is your count?"

"Thirty-five."

Liu Fong said, "Thirty-five but there are certain costs of business to account for."

"Eight chests! That's the value of a fleet with cargo."

Liu Fong said it was customary and the value of twenty-seven chests would appear in Hong Kong."

"How?" said Porter.

"Silver moves in mysterious channels and I cannot say exactly. Unknown parties now have your carved chests, but the prefect also knows that a loss of a shipment without compensation could lead to war. You can be certain that the account of *Agilis* in Hong Kong will be fat and happy by the end of the month."

Porter jumped on board to inspect the hold. His footfalls echoed in the empty space.

The Sino Army released the empty vessel to the custody of Captain Richard Jeremy Porter with barely enough stores to reach Hong Kong. And those only if they hurried, but night closed in and they had to wait for the dawn to break the eastern sky.

Released from the private wharf at dusk, Fong, acting as an illegal pilot on an illegal visit, suggested they anchor near a cluster of sampans. Porter disagreed and paced the deck because they were sailing on illegal waters in a forbidden area of southeast China.

Liu Fong pleaded, "My people are hiding somewhere along the shore."

Porter said, "Why so sure? The sampans all look the same to me."

"I know my kin. We smuggled arms to the Taiping rebels together with the boats of the Tanka water people and are good friends. Unfortunately, slave traders captured and sold me to the ruby mine at Magok, Burma. I escaped and joined your ship."

"You mean stowed onboard the way a thief does?"

"That is an ugly accusation. I say accompanied."

"I say hid under a bag of rice, ate a little."

Despite Porter's objection, the crew dropped anchor near a cluster of sampans in front of Zhaoqing, only to be surrounded by a sea of small watercraft. Each was manned by a standing oarsman crying, "Taker me boat!" "Takee me boat!" to transport cargo and people to shore.

Go away. Nothing left to unload. All gone."

Liu hailed a rowboat whose owner looked especially diligent and explained his mission to search the tied-up Tanka sampans.

"Fong! Is there someone named Fong?" he called to every boat, whether a dinghy, sampan, junk, or simple rowboat. The only responses were from river people disciplining a lazy son, chopping chickens for dinner, gossiping, throwing a fishing net, a soft rattling from a departing sail. Rising columns of smoke from charcoal fires were the only movement.

Dejected but not defeated, Fong returned to the home on the water.

"How goes it?" said Bjorn.

"The boats ignored me. I hope for better luck tomorrow." He rubbed the belly of his laughing Buddha.

"My mistake was asking the wrong question. The boat people are Tanka kinship and speak their own language. It grew in sampans through generations of life on the river, rejected by those on land. Tanka is the bottom class of barbarians. My family is Hakka and despised by the ruling Han, but the Tanka smuggled guns to the revolutionaries as friends."

The same rowboat returned for the second day. Fong tried another approach. "Can you spare the waste tail of a left-over fish? I ask little to feed my hunger."

Time after time, he was ignored until help came from the busiest person on the smallest craft, a mother holding an infant and managing the sail, oars, and rudder better than a fisherman.

The vessel was as long as five people with rounded cover reeds protecting the center. Using an oar, she maneuvered the shallow dinghy over to Liu Fong.

His plea greeted the busiest boater on the river. "Please, a bite of fishtail for food."

"If you help me with this dinghy."

Fong jumped in and grabbed an oar. "Where to?"

"My husband is fishing around the bend."

It surprised the fisherman to see a stranger with his wife and accused her from a distance. Only when they approached did he recognize her companion. "Cousin Lou Fong, is that really you? Do you bring weapons?"

"Yes and no."

"Our heroic fighters need arms. These are hard times since your last visit."

They hugged and pounded each other's shoulders as they wept. "Your companion sailors said the Burmese kidnappers took you. What happened?"

"They sold me to the ruby mines as a slave. I escaped and have searched for my family ever since."

The catch of fish loaded, both crafts returned to the home sampan.

"Who is that voice?" The hidden family recognized the sound and called out, "Please to come in. We cannot show ourselves or the Han soldiers will murder us."

They had a joyful reunion because they never expected to again see each other.

Liu waved for the passenger and captain to join them on the sampan. Maverick sniffed and said, "What's that cooking? I'm coming too."

Fong could not translate the flood of emotion between the family and himself. Unstated was their relief to have a son back who could provide for their old age.

After the group became emotionally united, questions arose about the emigrants. Hearts ached for those who left for San Francisco.

"Father, any news from San Francisco?"

"Messages never reached us refugees, hiding among the Tanka. No money either. I asked visiting mariners in the harbor, but no one had news." He looked at Bjorn and Porter with questions on his wet, wrinkled face.

A wave of joy swept the little boat when Bjorn said he worked alongside a family of their name in California.

"You know them?"

"Know? We worked our claims together. The engineer brought water to my mine and dug a ditch to the Lucky Ducky they operated."

The father reacted at the mention of water. Fong translated. "My brother was a famous master of water engineer and built canals throughout China."

Fong said, "We were important until we joined the Taiping rebellion and the Han called us enemies of the state."

Stepping onto the sampan and packing the foredeck, Bjorn said to Porter, "Here is someone you should meet."

"Who's that?"

"Remember the Chinese family who broke me out of the prison barge in Sacramento?"

"How could I forget? They had the sharpest battle axes I've seen. You're lucky they didn't cut your foot off when they chopped a hole through the floor of your cell with their insanely sharp battle axes."

"The head of that family was a renowned water engineer in China. He dug the canal that connected the Pearl River to the Yangtze. In California, he brought water to my mine."

Without room to bow in the cramped space, they smiled at each other.

Maverick, hoisted up by Bjorn, limped to the entrance said, "Can I see the food I smell?"

An ancient, revered mother passed hot tea and bowls of steaming Chinese food. She handed Maverick a pair of chopsticks and gave him a quick lesson in eating her stir-fried dinner.

"Amazing."

She pointed to Liu Fong's scar and lit an incense burner to make a spell before examining the vicious mark on his thigh. "My son, you are wounded."

He repeated the story of how he concealed a ruby in his thigh. Without a word, she pushed the Chinaman down on a bed and applied an acupuncture treatment to the scar.

After a meal of the finest fish yanked from the river, accompanied by the hottest wine and the freshest stir-fried vegetables, the family caught up on several years of lost history of funny and tragic stories in Yue, that neither Porter nor Bjorn understood.

Followed by Fong's translations, the elder explained how his family remained undercover in the sampan for years, only able to venture out in darkest night. Refugees like they had to flee in their second riverboat, used for fishing, to evade roving Han death squads. These escapes made them skilled mariners, especially in the emergency department.

Bjorn said to Porter, "Can you imagine their skills in the water? Brine is their natural brother."

Never one to overlook an opening, Fong said, "I miss the Gurkhas, who returned to India. They are a tropical man used to the Asian changes of wind, mood, and imagination, but no cold winters like Nepal.

"They were not among the lascars, either," said Porter.

"Lascars have gone. They want to work with their warm-weather companions."

Porter sighed and mumbled. It was too true.

Two young brothers in the sampan asked Bjorn about serving under Porter. He assured them the captain was no worse than others and better than most.

Fong's eyes sparkled as he made a suggestion. "My brothers, uncles, cousins, and father in early years traveled to Madagascar and India on every kind of vessel you could imagine. They were fine sailors before the war forced them into hunted fugitives."

He stopped to let Bjorn's thinking catch up. "You must be undermanned."

"That is true. Your suggestion?"

He repeated the proposal that able-bodied men of his family join the crew in exchange for passage to California. They know water, weather, ropes, boats, and work hard.

Porter asked Bjorn, "What do you think?" With an affirmative reply, Porter said, "I do not have a full crew."

Porter accepted the proposal.

Onboard *Agilis*, Jones added them to the roster of the designated criminal crew, released by the ruby pardon.

Porter gave each person a brief explanation and accepted the able-bodied members and added the rest of the family to the passenger list. "Hope we don't meet *Edmund Hughes*, or Hutton would steal them all." The remaining shorthanded crew welcomed their help.

Fong offered to pay his way and became the official shipboard translator for his help during the court proceedings. Not to be outdone, the mother insisted on a position as assistant cook in charge of Chinese stir-fry and the resident acupuncturist.

Bowing deeply to Captain Porter, Liu said, "I am most grateful for travel to America. I will never again be a slave, not in Burma, not in China, not in smuggling. I offer a small gift." He pulled a carved jade box from his robes and presented it to Porter.

Porter lifted the lid to see a priceless star ruby, possibly the largest in the world. "How did you get this? The prefect kissed it the last I saw." He rubbed the glowing stone on his shirt.

"The art of the baksheesh is my specialty. Remember when I examined the gift before we left the prefect's chambers?"

Porter allowed as he remembered because he had been desperate to leave the mandarin's guesthouse, but wondered why Fong was so panic-stricken to exit.

"I switched a common stone for the ruby. We had to rush out, and should leave here quickly as well."

The arrangement satisfied everyone, at least until they could leave Hong Kong far behind, and the prefect called for his jewels.

Bjorn was the best master of disguise, but a surprise spook image would not work down the Xi River among the cluttered watercraft. Pardoned or not, they were still outlaws where they were not supposed to be, and the celestial Chinese navy outranked the Zhaoqing Armada. Even with the Xu Guangjin pardon, they feared his double-cross. and were out of ideas.

The Chinaman barged into the tight group planning their escape to the confluence with the Pearl River, Hong Kong, and into the wide Pacific. "Most important, leave soon, river level drop, boat stranded, many dangers on way."

Porter said, "What would you do?"

"Last disguise unlucky and we make capture. Must do better."

The bow still had painted eyes on the bow, the shroud over the figurehead, and Shui Jen, the Chinese name on the side. The urgency of the ruby did not come up but lurked in the back of his mind.

"Must look Chinese, sound Chinese, smell Chinese, act Chinese, be Chinese. Slither like dolphin downriver. River-dogs must know channel of Xi river. My family can do. Leave Zhaoqing and enter Pearl River District. Much different, much dangerous."

Captain Porter knew the riverboats were the lifetime homes of the Fong family. He could see they were obviously fishermen who understood the mood and current of the flow like old friends, and certainly new Taiping enemies. They lived close to the storms in the atmosphere.

Bjorn communicated back and forth in the Yue dialect, pidgin English, Chinese body language, and Norse body language. Understanding one-tenth of the words was enough to design a replacement lateen sail for the one they jettisoned during the capture. This one was larger and much more unwieldy, given the nature of the beast.

Porter said, "I shouldn't have trashed my first one."

Jones said, "Fault of the heathen navy."

Bjorn agreed. "Haste without foresight makes trouble."

The family got to work, mainly at night, transforming the ship into a relatively-fake Sino warship. The highly respected grandmother cleared a cooking spot on the crowded deck to make the strongest smelling Chinese cuisine she could manage, issuing odors the epitome of seven families cooking dinner. They loaded an extra bag of garlic to assure a supply. Family musicians gathered gongs, a silk-stringed zither, a wooden drum in the shape of a tiger, a gourd with bamboo flutes attached, Han-style dance costumes, and enough appurtenances to mount a theater production. They were the essence of a Han family celebrating a wedding.

The cousin brought out a counterfeit military uniform to appear like a military guard at the railing. A few even had ancient firearms along with modern smuggled firearms. Ever the essence of peace, many of them were participants in the Taiping rebellion and could fight equally with their weapons or hands using Kung Fu from the Shaolin Temple of martial arts, nine hundred miles to the north.

Bjorn leaned on the Chinaman as interpreter to meld the old crew, new family crew, and hungover seamen into a cohesive unit. He alternated between translations for Bjorn and screaming at the new crew in a mixture of languages as they converted *Agilis* to a semblance of a Chinese warship.

Porter commented after one exercise on deck, "My God, we could fight our way out of a naval battle."

Bjorn assumed control from Jones of the disguised deck. "Sailor there, pull a British and Portuguese flag from our stack of foreign flags. Fly the Portuguese rag from the starboard. Hoist the British Jolly Roger opposite so the sail hides one from the other. Two-faced identification is our unconventional new rule."

An able-bodied sailor objected saying you always fly your pennants from the top of the mast. "You cannot see them from the other side."

"That's the idea," said Bjorn with satisfaction.

As a final element, Bjorn draped a large American flag off the stern.

"Hey Port, see our creation."

"What have you done to my poor ship?."

"If we head downriver in the mists of early morning with a jumble of river traffic, I hope to confuse the sleepy fortifications and patrol boats just long enough to reach the open ocean."

"Hope is not a plan but it's all we've got to go on."

Cool, calm air surrounded the departing ship the next morning, between scattered squalls of rain and early scudding fog. Porter's morning stroll made him impatient, waiting for a breeze.

The chaotic weather included sporadic gusts of wind as they embarked slowly down the Xi River. Smoke from early morning breakfast fires aided their disguise, especially when they added their own smokescreen from the Chinese woman's breakfast bar. They only scraped the bottom a few times.

Luck left them when the Xi River emptied into the Pearl River off Macau. The wind moved the fog back and forth and confused the observers as to who the disguised vessel was. Fortifications on the north regarded the British flag above the low-lying mist as an odd-man-out vessel. Shore patrol boats on the southwest looked at the Portuguese flag from the other side and let her pass according to the customs of Macau.

The suspicious war junks at water level could barely make out the eyes and Shui Jen, Water Man on the bow. They conferred with the commander on their next step.

Bjorn in the rigging and Porter on deck also debated their best course, but cut it off when a strong southwest wind hit. Porter issued an order to mount all sails. His second command was, "Full speed ahead and damn the traffic, light the smoke pots to hide our wake." An American ship glimpsed the stars and stripes hanging from the stern before smoke and mist hid the brig. The confused cloud of canvas fought for air and hanging space between the lateen sail, the mainsails, the topgallants, and the topsails.

"What did I just see? It looked American but I'm not sure," said the American skipper. "Too small to be consequential. Do not waste our time or ammunition."

The *Agilis* slipped through the intermittent mist before the waking pirates from Lintin Island could mobilize. Their morning fires fouled the thick air. Glimpses through the swirling clouds convinced the lookout of a lost itinerant, evasive fishing junk. A trigger-happy gunner lobbed a volley of cannonballs just for fun, the signal for an armed multinational riot. Competition broke out among the British, Chinese, American, and ladrones for the fastest turnaround of their cannon fire.

Maverick tried to pull his head in like a turtle, but he lacked a shell. Fong's new riverboat crew was prepared for mayhem, but their civilian families huddled below in fear.

Bjorn grinned at Porter. "This is an oriental sendoff for the books. I did this?'

Gunsmoke billowing from the competing weaponry obscured the lower delta of the mighty Pearl River.

Bjorn savored his power to precipitate an international incident. The balls bounced on the sea, hit foreign bottoms, and one or two even clipped the rigging lines. She raced past Hong Kong under full sail and pointed the helm east toward Formosa. More speed encouraged the overworked crew to unleash the lateen sail and pitch it overboard. The behavior of the helm returned to normal, and the beleaguered helmsman relaxed into usual duty.

Porter knew relations were tense in the Hong Kong area and felt a slight regret at contributing, but only until they cleared the river. Despite too few provisions to make it to Hong Kong, the brave rig raced past and hoped to catch a fish or two. Nothing interrupted their escape from the Celestial Kingdom in their rush to the South China Sea.

Porter broke into a broad grin. They shed the elements of the escape like a stripper in a bar. Distant booms of a naval engagement faded behind them. Free at last, the Spirit of Athena took charge of their spiritual life, and shared it with Morgan Fore 'n Aft. She looked on with satisfaction with new paint covering the dragon's eyes on the bow and shed the nameplate of Shui Jen.

She was the new *Agilis* again. "Goodbye, Cathay. Don't think I won't miss you because I will not."

Her return to a proud tall ship sped her southeast. Fong hailed a merchantman returning from Manila and arranged a trade of the two swivel guns for food and water for all.

The golden hair on the *Spirit of Athena* matched the gilt trim on Porter's hat and Bjorn's blowing blond glory. Gentle waves caressed the bow as they faced the widest expanse of water *Agilis* had sailed, the north Pacific. Their resolute optimism swept above mere waves and winds to the promise of San Francisco.

Captain Porter broke into their reverie. "The heart of man, my heart, echoes the sea. It has its storms, it has its tides, and in its depths pearls too. Dance with the waves, move with the sea, let the rhythm of the water set your soul free."

"I don't dance, but the swells of the deep grant to each man new hope and sleep to bring dreams of home. To every man there opens a high way and a low. And every mind decides the way his soul shall go. One ship sails east, and another west, on the self-same winds that blow."

"What are you saying?' said Porter.

Bjorn thought for a long time. To break the silence, Maverick said his grandfather told him the heavens open and a rainbow falls to earth after a spring shower.

"The hymns of the hills call me to green and brown, to stone and streams. You and the blue waters will always be my friend, Port, but my destiny lies on the shore."

"You cannot be serious after our lives together, can you?'

"I leave you Mr. Maverick Hatfield, a superlative nautical mess cook, and Oscar Jones, the most loyal mate a skipper may have. I give to you a fine Captain over a soon-to-be-yours ship, a wave floater of the first degree."

"That is true, but a voyage will be lacking without you to harass me from time to time."

The two friends stood with their right hands on their left shoulders, heads tilted, to discern their profound souls. Shared humanity and proven courage united their kinship, while their innate spirits aspired to futures on land or water.

The passenger and the captain shook hands and meditated on the arriving horizon during which time a tropical rainstorm crossed their path. Glimmering in the shower was an arch arrayed in the colors of heaven.

"That rainbow is an omen our voyage will be blessed," said Jones as he deliberated how to manage his new crew for several months. "A smooth sea never made a skilled sailor. I hope my crew will be skilled when we enter the Golden Gate."

"I hope you're right," said the captain.

"'Tis the set of the sails, and not the gales, that tells the way we go."

Porter stepped away into his private spiritual world. We seafarers are without a lord, without wine or the company of women, only the waves surrounding us. No man undertaking such a life could fail to fear, at least a little, what the Lord Jesus might have in store for him at the end, what his fate might be.

Crossing the wide Pacific, religious duties on the Sabbath were rare in the forecastle. Distinctions between sects and creeds were unknown, and yet simple common piety was implanted in the sailor's heart. Without the fuss of a wise creator, they anticipated rewards and punishment in a nautical theme, not deserts and mountains.

Whether from the Bible or Koran or Sanskrit, those who could read gained comfort from the wisdom. People who did not listened to guidance from those who did.

Though their sins were many, the sailors down inside believed temptations would balance their spiritual account. With little fear of death, he gained insight from the five forces of the sea.

The ship's company was treated with kindness by Captain Porter and assisted in return with many of the duties of a mate minus titles or payment.

Occasionally, the captain exhibited symptoms of piety and read a chapter in the Bible with gravity and discoursed on some topic, but half an hour afterward might resume his profane and lordly habits, sometimes by getting drunk.

"Aren't we the philosophers?" said Bjorn.

All onboard were inspired, each in his own manner.

The disguised brig rocked becalmed in the dead, still air with warm waves extending to the circle of the horizon.

The grandmother made herself useful. Quicker than a cat, she captured rats and drowned them with glee before feeding them to Morgan or faithful, following fishes. Naturally reticent, she held back from approaching the cook until one day when she presented him with a pair of chopsticks carved from firewood. Speaking Yue, she murmured, "Most grateful for plentiful food with no effort."

The woman picked them out of Maverick's hand, climbed down the galley, and prepared a chicken stir-fry. A new food fare, it overjoyed the crew and Porter. Bjorn loved it because he did not have to prepare it.

Returned from delivering the stir-fry, Maverick's leg crumpled on the ladder, and he collapsed in a heap at the feet of the oriental. He moaned and could not move until the stir-fry expert helped him to his unsteady feet.

"Are you hurt?"

"I'm fine, a little wobbly."

"Acupuncture will help you."

"What is that?" he did not know the name of the treatment that rejuvenated him from the punishment cage.

Fong overheard the conversation and joined with a boast of his grandmother's studies at the Chengdu School of Chinese medicine.

The *Agilis* group knew the grandmother was a woman of many talents, even less than half the size of Maverick.

A call for help brought Bjorn into the tiny galley, where there was hardly room to breathe. Bjorn pulled Maverick up the hatch and said to Liu, "Take him to my bunk."

Maverick groaned and sucked in shallow breaths that exhaled in low whimpers.

It was when the Chinese woman opened her box of needles that the injured man exploded. One glimpse through his pain-squinted eyes and the eyes slammed open in sheer terror.

"No! I'll jump in a pit of vipers first."

Maverick leaped out of the bunk, knocked himself unconscious on the low ceiling, and crashed half in and half out the door. Bjorn returned Maverick to the bunk and pulled up the pant leg to reveal the angry, inflamed injury.

With a speed that fascinated Bjorn, the acupuncturist inserted five very fine needles around the injury and more along the earth meridian of Maverick's Qi, or life force. It took only a few moments for the unconscious leg to relax and the inflammation fade to a healthy pink. The final needle was emplaced to enhance drowsiness. The practitioner lit a time candle and explained that part of her philosophy was to offer healing to pain. "I am ready to treat anyone who hurts for my passage."

After the candle burned down two sections, Maverick fluttered awake to a leg that looked like a porcupine. He smiled, "That feels good,' and drifted back to sleep. Two more candle sections burned before Maverick walked upright out of Bjorn's cabin like a new man. He looked away from the tray of needles.

Bjorn passed the information to Mate Jones and Captain Porter with recommendations to try it. His example encouraged several sailors to try the needles. Others demanded an extra portion of grog and ignored the acupuncture instruments.

Bjorn took his own advice on the spot and found the procedure soothed the discomfort of his many scars.

"I can't believe how much better I feel. I can turn to higher things."

"We're an empty bottom in ballast and iron weapons on deck combined that makes the wooden kingdom liable to capsize," Porter said to Bjorn.

"I feel it too and the weather is still calm. A typhoon would founder us for sure and Maverick is already terrified since he hits the seafloor before the rest of us.

"The winds, the tides, and contrary currents make a stop at Honolulu difficult from the Western Pacific. I won't go near China although Shanghai is logical. We have a choice of Tainan city on Formosa (Taiwan) or Manila in the Philippines. Barons of the sea in the captain's meeting emphasized that San Francisco is in dire need of foodstuffs with the growth of the population, but what the shipbuilders especially need is hemp for rope making.

Jones said, "The port of Manila is open and sells agricultural products to all comers."

"I agree," said Liu Fong, "but business there is different than in China."

It was Bjorn who claimed more time in San Francisco than everyone else combined. "Times have to be worse than when I left. Decent food was short and expensive then, especially in Sacramento. I once bought a single egg for a dollar in gold dust."

"Enough said. We'll have to fill our hold to pay for our voyage across the northern Pacific. What and where to get it."

As the one with the widest experience, Jones said, "Major sources of trade for us are Shanghai, Formosa, and the Philippines. We should avoid China which eliminates Shanghai due to the recent unpleasantness. We could reach Tainan on Formosa in a week and a half but the port is engulfed by fighting tribes and their banking system is rudimentary. That leaves Manila, the farthest destination at two weeks. The Spanish government supports trade and the islands offer many foodstuffs. Also, Chinese merchants import treasures from the mainland and as far away as Japan, spices from Sumatra and other places for sale. Our widest range of choices is Manila."

"Are you finished?" "Two weeks in ballast in these waters is a great risk because we are dangerously unstable. Typhoon season is upon us.

The best decision still seemed to be Manila, because they had workable charts.

"Be prepared to discard the iron weapons overboard in the event of storms. God be with us. What goods are most desired in San Francisco?" Porter looked at Bjorn and Maverick but focused on Bjorn.

"Wants and needs, there are aplenty. The dens under the laundries want the fruit of the poppy, but the population needs fruits, food, and furniture to sit on. The ladies of the boudoir want silks to seduce customers and positions want camphor to treat the lungs. Infants of the immigrants want carpets to crawl on. Not to mention hemp for rope to rig ships."

The cook had different priorities. "The cooking clans need pepper, cloves, nutmeg, curry, and cinnamon from Indonesia. Maybe you throw in wax to seal bottles of wine."

"You are forgetting samurai swords, bronze items, hammocks, and coconuts from Japan," said Bjorn,

The China connection added jade and incense.

"Whoa! We can't have everything. Let's check the markets of Manila. I want unconventional trade items you don't get in Canton and yield a better profit."

Rolling out the chart for the South China Sea to the Philippines, the party studied the southeast route from Hong Kong to the Philippines.

"Here's a note by a previous captain. The entrance to the Manila harbor is twelve miles wide with good soundings and is protected by fortifications on the island of Corregidor. Look for a new lighthouse on a point at six hundred forty feet high. Who has been there?"

Fong said, "I have. My extended family runs the commerce to Manila while the Spaniards manage the international trade. We can enter the harbor only in daylight because local boats called bangkas fish the harbor in droves. They are lax in marking their fishing nets, long lines, and traps. Dragging their gear will make you a fight. No Bjorn, you cannot disguise us again. A bangka they make starts with religious rituals to choose the timber from the woods. The new boat gets a bonito (guardian spirit) through blood sacrifices, and is decorated with a carved face."

Jones said, "This area receives many typhoons, so we must watch the weather. The sailing part of the Fong clan should be skilled from their trips across the Bay of Bengal. We cannot trust the charts as the bottom changes in each storm."

The wooden community with expert canvas control and savvy navigation reached the white mouth of Manila Bay in eight days. They watched but outran any pursuing junks that might want a ruby back.

As usual, Captain Porter approached the new area cautiously. The fortifications on the island of Corregidor guarded the entrance to Manila Bay. It was from there they boarded a harbor pilot to guide them the thirty miles to the market for Manila. "I hope the commander is friendly. We are flying our Stars & Stripes flag as high as we can raise it."

Jones said, "We shouldn't appear a menace to the Spanish trade to the port thirty miles in. We'll moor in the town of Cavite because the water is shallow closer to Manila. The bay is vast, being thirty by forty miles."

They soon encountered busy fishermen in their bangkas. Opposite outriggers on the local fishing craft made them wider than first appeared.

Bjorn gave directions to the helmsman from the foremast and they missed everyone. But the area received at least one major storm a month in the rainy season and a dark cloud hovered on the horizon. They hurried to complete their mission.

A forest of tall masts made a beacon to the shipping port of Cavite City. Jones knew it from previous visits.

Swarms of boat owners were disappointed when Jones said they were empty. "Come back in a few days."

Porter, Jones, Bjorn, and Maverick went ashore to check in with the harbor officials. Mounds of paperwork followed but they survived and registered to enter the bustling warehouse district of the island.

Porter went alone to the bank of *El Banco Español Filipino de Isabel 2*. He presented his bill of exchange from the *Oriental Bank of Commerce* for one hundred thousand dollars. With their blessing, both financial and religious, he arranged for purchases to fill the hold and credit to the bank in San Francisco for any extra charges and to cover insurance.

Back in the market, Porter said, "We try again. The agent said their largest export is rice, but not the most profitable."

Bjorn said, "Most Chinese in California ate rice but lacked the resources to pay the high prices. The ladies of the Barbary Coast are rolling in dollars and will pay anything for silk to make their dresses and seduce the gold-laden miners. And don't forget the knives and samurai swords from Japan which are always popular with armed gangs."

"Silk is on the list."

"My family traders brought jade, coconuts, wax, and gunpowder to sell in Manila. Camphor from Formosa is especially in demand by the captains of the ships who also wanted porcelain, vases, lacquer ware, rugs, and furniture."

"You are missing the boat. Rich people eat three times a day. We should buy as much pepper, cloves, nutmeg, and cinnamon as we can find for the San Francisco kitchens." Maverick salivated at the prospect.

Wondering through the vast area of warehouses, Porter found the Philippine-Chinese mestizos were eager to engage in commerce. The sellers, he discovered, were intelligent, active, and well dressed. It took everything in Jones' power of persuasion to prevent Porter from overloading the *Agilis* across the wide Pacific. The one missing item was opium in any form.

Crowds in the vast warehouse aisles were from everywhere. Diverse dialects of Castilian Spanish mixed with similar conversations in Portuguese, Italian, and with Dutch, Greek, Canary Islanders, Javanese from Java, Japanese, Bengali, and the polyglot group including slaves from Africa. Enterprising merchants always had an interpreter available who could make a deal with any purchaser in any money, but silver was the best.

Jones could not caution everyone fast enough and said, "It would take five vessels to convey everything you want. Something has to go."

"Look at these swords. Their Damascus pattern is amazing and you can appreciate the sharp edge." Bjorn tossed the edge of a piece of silk skein at the next booth into the air and neatly cut it in two as it floated down over the knife."

"You have bought the rest of the silk roll, sir," said the merchant in the next display.

Add to his account," Bjorn said pointing at Porter.

"Make that sixteen bundles of your finest silk."

Holding a gorgeous vase, Liu Fong said "This is from the imperial court of the last Ming emperor."

Porter thought about Captain McIntyre, the owner of *Agilis* who had promoted him to master. It was from him Porter planned to buy the ship in San Francisco. "That will make a fine gift for my mentor who raised me from a starstruck indentured farmboy to a master by the title of Captain.

Fong selected the finest table the merchant had to display the priceless Ming vase.

Porter and Jones added up the costs of all the purchases, their expected volume in the hold, the expected profit in San Francisco, and arranged for their delivery to the wharf for loading.

The Fong family prevented the customary pilferage by the stevedores and Lou had a severe confrontation with the spies asserting there was no gold, silver, or opium on board and to leave them alone or they would be sorry.

Porter exchanged the bulk of their weapons for useful products and made room."

Chapter 16—California Ruby

With *Agilis* loaded and ready for embarkation, Bjorn raised his glass of St. Regis port. "To Captain Richard Porter, my compliments. A toast. We vanquished the five forces of the sea."

They held up their glasses for Maverick to pour a libation of wine.

"I haven't thought about it. What are they?"

"Ships are the nearest things to dreams ever made by the hands of man, but they can turn to nightmares from the forces of the sea. The first force is greed. Smuggling, piracy, and business drive money everywhere to encourage it. It entices men to evil."

Maverick said, "Even moonshiners in Tennessee are represented, except that's what we do."

"We live and die on the forces of winds and tides. North and south they go, and east to San Francisco."

Jones said, "Friends and foes they are. Winds batter one way and tides another. Between them, they destroy us in their fighting jaws. Only the skills of the complement move us forward."

"That's three forces."

They drank another toast.

"I saw a unicorn and angel yesterday riding on a storm bank, an unconventional pair for sure."

"Now that is imaginative my friend."

"Fourth is the mood that encompasses all. The faces of the sea shine before us with benevolence and hostility. Poets write about her mood, but we seamen know her face to face. She is volatile. Captain Richard Porter brought us through. A toast to our leader."

Maverick opened the third bottle to supply the toast.

"Expand your imagination, my friends. Imagine swimmers under the surface and flying creatures. Envision the messages in the clouds that whisper or shout to you. Look to the visions yet unseen."

Porter said, "Your mood is enthusiastic because of a rendezvous with a woman. Doesn't she live in the Petaluma Adobe Rancho, where I own a vineyard?"

"Maria, I'm coming," breathed Bjorn.

"You saved my life and are my truest friend. Best wishes to you and Maria."

They drank a toast and puffed clouds of visions on cigar smoke. The sea greased them with the mood of harmony.

"We have our heads, and I can just purchase Agilis, but no more of smuggling. Neither souls nor sin. Once was too much."

Maverick placed a platter of barbecued chicken wings on the captain's table and served each circumnavigator a glass of their favorite red port wine. Captain Porter invited him to raise a glass with them.

Bjorn said, "The prefect was insanely greedy for rubies, but you may not have a world-class gemstone next time. The world of major smugglers is too big for you and me."

"Here's to a jolly good crew and my loyal friend, Bjorn Amundson."

They toasted friendship.

Bjorn said, "My ally in adventures far and wide."

They drank another round to cement future adventures

"Here's to our chief cook, Maverick Hatfield, best chef above the fishes."

"It's my secret sauce." He refilled their glasses and didn't spill a drop.

"That's only four forces. What's the fifth?'

"Inspiration my friends, inspiration. These noble wooden planks under our feet are taking us to our futures, diverse, unknown, exciting, and our destinies. We are inspired to reach for the peaks and grasp the future with everything we have. We begin in San Francisco."

Crossing the North Pacific from Manila was uneventful. *Agilis* skirted the doldrums and entered the Strait of the Golden Gate in triumph.

How had the gold rush changed the village on the rocky peninsula, San Francisco, since July 4, 1849? Bjorn said, "I stamped the vision of the forest of abandoned masts in my memory five years ago? I can't believe it is that long."

The Fong family lined the railings while Jones struggled to counter the variable winds and strong currents past Alcatraz Island. He jumped in surprise at a sudden explosion. A series of bangs, actually.

Fong hung strings of firecrackers from the bowsprit. Their deafening pops echoed from Alcatraz to Points Diablo and Fort Point on alternate shores of the Strait of San Francisco. Rounding North Point, the staid inhabitants of San Francisco crowded the wharves to welcome a fire-breathing spectacle none had seen.

Hello Frisco," Bjorn said, waving his hands at spectators standing on a host of new construction along the waterfront. "Our return completes a circumnavigation of the globe. After escapades to curl your ears, I am looking forward to representing my countrymen from Norway. They are pouring into the northwest. No more international incidents."

Morgan Fore 'n Aft watched from the top of the cabin as far from the fireworks as he could get and still see the golden hair of the Spirit of Athena.

Porter approached Bjorn with one hand behind his back and placed the other firmly on his shoulder. "I have something for you."

He held forward a carved light green jade box.

Bjorn opened it to show the largest, deepest pigeon-blood star ruby ever. "Where did you get this?"

Liu Fong grinned, his eyes sparkled, his mouth said, "I am an expert in baksheesh."

Porter said, "It was good for Fong, it was good for the captain, and I pass the luck to you. May it bring fortune to your future on land, Mr. Amundson."

Bjorn said, "I know the person for this."

"I am home, Maria."

# # #

Request for Reviews

Thank you for reading my book. If you enjoyed Bjorn Amundson's adventures, other readers would appreciate your honest review at the bookseller where you bought the book. You can contact me directly or visit the website.

cliffordfarris@Desertcoyotepress.com

www.Desertcoyotepress.com

Don't miss out!

Visit the website below and you can sign up to receive emails whenever Clifford Farris publishes a new book. There's no charge and no obligation.

https://books2read.com/r/B-A-YYKI-SLJDC

BOOKS 2 READ

Connecting independent readers to independent writers.

About the Author

From his life as a cowboy, farmer, engineer, and author, Clifford Farris brings gripping stories about real folks to his novels—always with a touch of humor. He has penned and published writings on woodworking, gardening, and meat smokers. Other credits include short stories, a musical melodrama, and a hundred and fifty technical writings. He and his wife, Ann, live in the Denver Metro area of Littleton, Colorado.

Read more at https://desertcoyotepress.com/.

Homeland of
Desert Coyote Press

About the Publisher

Your book is a portable piece of magic. Immerse your adventurous and independent spirit in historical fiction from the **Desert Coyote Press** DCP. Novels are filled with adventure stories of heroes and villains, escape and companionship, and lives, and travel set in historical times. One reader said it is a vacation with interesting people to intriguing places.

Our motto is, ***Sit down and have a drink, read something.***

Invest in the books that you love. Live with complex characters and everyday people facing extraordinary challenges in vivid locations. You will have a thrill, a laugh, shed a tear or two, and live moments of sheer terror. Enjoy the ride.

Clifford Farris founded DCP in 2019 on the premise that you should live with passion. Come join our community and journey with us.

"Fair winds and following seas," to you the reader.